HEART
OF GOLD

HEART
OF GOLD

By
BUD CAMPBELL
With
GLEN ONLEY

SANTA FE

Cover art by Kristina Tripp

Sunstone books may be purchased for educational, business, or sales promotional use. For information please write: Special Markets Department, Sunstone Press, P.O. Box 2321, Santa Fe, New Mexico 87504-2321.

Library of Congress Cataloging-in-Publication Data:

Campbell, Bud, 1930-
    Heart of gold / by Bud Campbell with Glen Onley.
        p. cm.
    ISBN 0-86534-476-0 (pbk. : alk. paper)
    1. Basketball coaches—Fiction. 2. Lottery winners—Fiction. 3. Texas—Fiction.
    I. Onley, Glen, 1943- II. Title.

PS3603.A466H43 2005
813'.6—dc22

                                      2005010484

WWW.SUNSTONEPRESS.COM
SUNSTONE PRESS / POST OFFICE BOX 2321 / SANTA FE, NM 87504-2321 /USA
(505) 988-4418 / *ORDERS ONLY* (800) 243-5644 / FAX (505) 988-1025

TO

My wife Nay, who has for several years encouraged me to write this book, before I die again.

ACKNOWLEDGEMENTS

I want to extend a hearty thanks to all my friends and family members who have been so instrumental in the completion of this book. Though I can not list everyone who has helped, I must express my sincere appreciation to Loraine Campbell, Floyd Moody, Jack Hicks, Sid and Patsy Hudson, H. P. Munn, Dr. Ralph Poteet, Henry Suche, Phyllis Onley, John and Debbie Boose, Gerald Skidmore, Dr. James Terry, and Dr. Don Woolley, all of whom contributed of their time and offered their expert suggestions and evaluations regarding the story.

PREFACE

"... For unto whomsoever much is given, of him shall be much required ..."
Luke 12:48 (King James Version)

Rather than another story of a heroic character's continual struggle against adversity, this one focuses on how one man responds to his blessings. As suggested above, good fortune, when viewed as a blessing, brings with it accountability. For those who gladly share of their abundance with others, life can be an especially rewarding venture.

This story is fictional, and any similarity to known people and events is purely coincidental.

Early Years

This glimpse of Dale Rory's formative years prepares the reader to better understand the focal character's adult life, which fills the following chapters.

Though young Dale appeared much like the other boys in his neighborhood in Bloomington, Pennsylvania, those who knew him best recognized his unique personality. Even prior to his school years, he insisted on doing things for himself.

As a toddler he preferred to crawl or walk, rather than be carried. Each successive birthday marked additional examples of his independent behavior, such as lacing his own shoes, buttoning his shirt, and climbing into the car without help. His mother purchased a stepstool for him so he could reach the lavatory to wash his hands and brush his teeth without climbing to the counter top, using drawer handles as ladder rungs. Fortunately, even as a child, he was observant and learned quickly, which enabled his ballooning self-sufficiency.

At eleven years of age, Dale was mowing the family lawn. Previously, he had repeatedly watched his father crank the mower and had attentively walked alongside him as he cut the grass. Knowing his energetic son's penchant for taking control, Dale's father dedicated a couple of Saturday mornings to explaining and demonstrating proper techniques for cranking and handling of the family lawnmower. Satisfied with Dale's grasp of the essentials of mowing, the father soon turned the job over to his eager young son. After a couple of months, during which neighbors often commented on the Rory's well-manicured lawn, Dale added customer after customer until he soon had a lawn-care business that reached the length of the block and spilled onto an adjacent one.

An early riser, Dale noticed an older boy riding his bike through the neighborhood during the gray dawn of each morning, throwing the local newspaper in each driveway. With the mowing season over, he soon had his own paper route. His father offered to get up a little earlier each morning and help his son prior to heading to work at the steel mill, but with the exception of Sundays, Dale always managed on his own. Due to the size of the Sunday paper, he could not carry a complete route's supply on his bike, so his father delivered the leftovers.

During these early years, Dale's parents focused a predominance of their attention on their only child. Their love and support would have a lifelong impact on their son. Dale's father stressed the importance of serving his newspaper and lawn customers in a courteous and responsible manner and treating all people fairly. "The world is like a mirror," his dad would say. "It will reflect only the image you present to it." To be viewed as a positive, hardworking, and cheerful person, his father stressed, Dale must consistently exhibit those traits in daily life. Another adage that stuck with young Dale was, "It makes no difference how high your grand-pappy has flown, son, when you are grown, you're happiness and success will depend upon how well you do your own flying."

Like the Rory family, most everyone in Bloomington lived in modest homes, which consisted of two bedrooms, a bath or bath and a half, a living room, and a kitchen combined with a dining area. In the typical home, the father worked while the mother looked after the children and cared for the house, thus a simple one-car garage was standard.

As a steel-mill worker, his father received an adequate salary, but from such pay only a miser could save more than enough to take care of an occasional emergency. It was the same throughout the neighborhoods of Bloomington, so class distinction based on money and property had about as much chance there as a snowman in a Sahara summer.

As Dale reached the middle grades, he spent his Saturday afternoons playing basketball with neighborhood boys at a community center only two blocks from his house. Encouraged by his playmates, he joined the school team and immediately took a liking to the coach who saw basketball as more than a physical activity. For many of his boys, the coach knew that financial assistance was necessary for a college education, something he believed every boy with adequate scholastic ability should seek. A basketball scholarship was one path to that goal, and the coach planted and nourished that seed to motivate his players. The idea took root with Dale and bloomed into a plan from which he never wavered.

Living in a one-school town, Bloomington parents and students focused with pride on their educational system and its many extracurricular activities. So prominent and frequent were school events, that the local movie theatre was forced to cater to the older folks whose children were beyond school age.

Competitive events took center stage in town, while both academic and sports achievements were prominently celebrated in the local newspaper, by civic organizations, and by the school administration. Bloomington youth were not slow to recognize the link between their successes and community praise and were steered by caring adults to apply their time and energy in activities that best fit their skills and talents.

Though Dale was one of the town's most purpose-driven youngsters, he indulged himself in one relaxation: watching western movies on television. The open spaces of the West, the energetic life of the Texas cowboy, and the massive herds of cattle and horses fascinated his young mind. Friends who learned about his enthrallment with the West began calling him "Tex," a nickname he relished.

During his freshman year in high school, Dale was one of the few underclassmen on the basketball team who garnered appreciable playing time. Each year produced a taller and more talented Dale Rory until, upon reaching his senior year, he stood six-foot-two and exhibited basketball skills that attracted college coaches to Bloomington games.

By this time Dale's sights were firmly fixed on the future he wanted for himself, which included coaching basketball while owning a ranch with a few cattle somewhere in West Texas. Dedicated to that end, he arrived promptly and stayed late at every basketball practice, using the time to develop a regimen of drills designed to produce shooting accuracy, agility, and ambidextrous ball-handling skills.

Upon high school graduation, Dale had saved enough money to purchase an old car, which he then needed for transportation to western Ohio where a university had awarded him a basketball scholarship. A young man with a fiercely independent spirit, Dale was ready to step out into the world on his own, but he would carry with him some invisible treasures.

His parents had not given him an abundance of material things, but they had molded his character and rooted him in a value system that he cherished. While driving west, mile after mile along Interstate 70, many of Dale's parents' sayings came to mind so clearly that he could have quoted them verbatim. "First thing in the morning, spend five minutes dwelling on life's blessings. Identify at least five." They had stressed that developing this habit would make it impossible for him to start the day on a negative note. A favorite of his father was, "An individual's thoughts have a gravitational effect on his or her life. Think positively and positive things will gravitate to you. Think negatively, and negative things will dominate your life." However, the parental truism that would ultimately test his character came from his mother: "It's not what you have that counts, but what you do with what you have."

Reflecting on these thoughts, this unusual young man arrived on the university campus, determined to spend the next four years preparing to realize the solitary and unwavering dream of his life.

Dale quickly adjusted to campus life, devoting the vast majority of his time to study and basketball. Through the fall he established himself as a solid student and a promising basketball talent, while becoming a close friend of a fellow freshman player named Thomas Newberry.

Near the end of the spring semester, the university's upperclassmen athletes practiced an initiation process for all freshmen players who had earned a letter and applied for entry in the "L" Association, a lettermen fraternity. This annual ritual included both physical and emotional challenges designed to test each applicant's worthiness, often belittling the pledges to the point of abuse. Throughout the year Dale and his friend Thomas had performed all the demeaning tasks assigned by the older players. They had cleaned rooms, shined shoes, and made midnight runs for pizza. Then initiation day came, the day every pledge dreaded.

Due to the physical abuse involved, the first-year lettermen were advised to prepare themselves beforehand by consuming enough alcohol to numb their bodies to the pain to be inflicted, typically by means of belts and sticks. Dale balked at the idea and took his case to Woody Woodson, the association leader in charge of the initiation. After listening to Dale explain that he and his friend Thomas did not drink and that they refused to intoxicate themselves to endure the beatings, Woody became alarmed. A hard-line position with these two promising athletes could explode into a news story sure to reach the coaches and school administrators who had already expressed concerns about the fraternity and campus gossip regarding its unauthorized cruelties. New evidence could lead to an investigation and possibly a suspension, if not destruction, of the lettermen association. Accordingly, Woody promised Dale that he and Thomas would not be subjected to physical punishment; however, he warned that other "tests" would likely be more severe for them.

Dale and Thomas agreed to Woody's conditions and showed up for the initiation. While these two drank a concoction that induced repeated vomiting, Frank, a junior college transfer, endured the physical punishment. Later, while taking showers, Dale and Thomas witnessed the resulting welts, cuts, and bleeding wounds that would permanently scar Frank's backside. Right then they agreed that they would make sure that any freshman players assigned to them in the following seasons would not have to endure such abuse. In time, they hoped to permanently eliminate the cruel practice.

At the end of the spring semester, Dale and Thomas secured jobs at a local packing plant, while other players and students went home for the summer. As compensation to the school for retaining their dorm rooms, they followed eight hours of work at the cold storage plant with three more hours on campus.

When July 4 arrived, the holiday brought a welcomed break from their labors, so that morning Dale and Thomas walked to a nearby drugstore to have a late breakfast. From their corner booth, they noticed their basketball coach walk in and order a fountain drink. Seeing his two players, Coach Morrison stepped over to chat. In the ensuing conversation, the coach mentioned that Frank had left the team and gone home. "Says he doesn't fit in here," the coach explained, shaking his head at the loss of this talented player.

Dale and Thomas pounced on this opportunity to try to save future players from the abusive process that they believed had driven off Frank. They explained how upperclassmen required so much time of the new players that the recruits often performed poorly both in the classroom and on the court, adding that athletes from other sports took particular pleasure in abusing new basketball players. Dale and Thomas suggested that two new players be assigned to them each year, with the understanding that the only demands they would make of the recruits would be good study and practice habits. Dale believed this would help the new players to adjust to college life, while avoiding driving a wedge between the rookies and the veterans.

The coach asked if the "L" Association's rumored harsh initiation process had driven Frank away. Neither Dale nor Thomas could positively confirm his suspicion, but they explained that they would have left the team rather than endure what their teammate had suffered. Whatever the coach concluded, he agreed to assign two new players to Dale and Thomas, and to get other basketball recruits assigned to their upperclassmen teammates. Before leaving, the coach expressed his appreciation to Dale and Thomas. Thus, the first step had been taken in breaking the cycle of abuse so long administered by the lettermen association at the university.

At six-foot-two, Dale was shorter than most of his teammates, and yet with hard work, well-honed skills, and intelligent play, he became the starting point-guard his sophomore year. Teammates with greater physical ability recognized Dale's leadership skills, his dedication to his teammates, and his focus on team success, which earned him their respect and admiration.

As the key ball-handler on the team, Dale capitalized on every opportunity to showcase his teammates' strengths, even at the risk of masking his own. When they saw the results, they mimicked his example, thus creating a cohesiveness that made each of them a more effective player. Additionally, Dale and Thomas focused their attention on the freshmen members of the team, helping them in their transition to college life and pursuit of a higher level of competitiveness.

Throughout his sophomore and junior seasons, Dale managed to see his parents only a few times. During the school year, basketball and classwork consumed his time, and throughout the summer months he labored eleven to twelve hours a day to earn enough money to pay for the things his scholarship did not cover. His family offered what financial support they could, and they encouraged him in his pursuit of a career as a basketball coach and Texas rancher. Throughout the long months and hard work, Dale's love for his father and mother never wavered, and he continued to feel that he owed his best effort to them in whatever he did.

Then near the end of his junior season, Dale's parents made arrangements to travel to Ohio and see him play basketball, but what should have been a joyous occasion turned into the most devastating event in his young life. Yet, in this tragedy, Dale found a springboard to his future

1 —

Sitting in a second period calculus class, Dale scribbled hurriedly in his notebook as Professor Watson stood at the front chalkboard developing the proof for computing the volume of a sphere. Then the professor hesitated, distracted by a knock at the door. While the teacher dealt with the interruption, Dale scanned back over his notes. Then he heard his name called.

"Yes, sir," he replied as the professor made his way toward Dale's desk, holding out a folded note.

Hurrying forward, Dale took the note and returned to his seat where he waited for his classmates to refocus their attention on the instructor. He then slowly unfolded the small yellow paper, taking care to minimize the crinkling noise.

The brief message said, "Please report to Coach Morrison's office at once."

Reluctantly, Dale stuffed the note in his shirt pocket, gathered his books and papers, slipped into his coat, and headed for the door, puzzled and a little irritated.

The basketball season had ended the previous night, and the coach had told his boys they need not check back with him until Thursday of the following week, when he would hand out instructions for their after-season routine. Also, due to extensive travel, basketball players necessarily missed classes during the season, so in the off-season, Dale made sure he never skipped a class. And Coach Morrison had been very considerate of his players' academic schedule and study time. Through the past three years, he had never summoned Dale from a classroom. So, something unusual must have come up.

Frustrated and apprehensive, Dale stepped into the outer room of the coach's office complex. Becky, the receptionist, glanced up and then jumped to her feet.

"Dale, come in," she said, slipping around the corner of her desk, taking him by the elbow, and ushering him toward the coach's doorway.

Normally, Becky would have had him take a seat while commenting on his play at a recent game, and then would have casually notified Coach Morrison that he had a guest waiting.

"What's wrong?" Dale asked.

"Oh, uh, Coach Morrison will explain."

The coach turned from the window where he had been staring out into a cold, overcast Ohio morning, and stepped haltingly toward Dale.

"Have a seat, son," he said as Becky pulled the door shut on her way out.

Something was not right, not normal. And now the coach's uncertain manner and strained appearance set off an alarm. Within seconds Dale's heartbeat spiked to a chest-thumping level.

"Son, there's no easy way to tell you this," the coach said, easing over beside Dale's chair. "The plane carrying your parents back to Bloomington crashed early this morning. There are no survivors."

Stunned, Dale felt numb, lightheaded, and unable to comprehend. Fleeting thoughts and images swirled through his mind like debris in a tornado. As if in an earthquake, everything seemed unsteady.

"Are you sure?" the young man finally muttered.

"Dale, I'm sorry," Coach Morrison said, laying his hand lightly on the youngster's shoulder. "The authorities seem certain. Do you have family, anyone you would like to contact?"

Dropping his gaze to his shoe tops, Dale shook his head.

"There must be an uncle, an aunt, or a cousin," the coach said. "Dale, you need to be in touch with someone, a relative or a close friend. You're welcome to use my phone."

Slowly, Dale stood up and eased toward the door.

"What'll you do, son?" the coach asked, his hand at Dale's elbow.

"I'll make arrangements with my teachers, and then pack my things and go home," Dale said.

"Can I do anything to help, anything at all?"

"Thanks, Coach, but I prefer to take care of this myself," Dale said, then hesitated at the doorway. "But when this is all over, I'll be back for basketball and to finish my education. That's all I have left."

The words sounded firm, the thought resolute, but they belied the turmoil inside. Dale's entire life had been tightly interwoven with his parents, and with no one else. Now, the sudden void created by their deaths sent him tumbling helplessly down through a dark, seemingly bottomless, emptiness.

Outside, he hesitated, struggling to get a grip on his emotions. Though he felt like running as fast and as far as he could from this nightmarish evil that was gripping his insides, he began a brisk walk across campus to the solitude of his dorm room. There he tried to drown the overwhelming hurt with tears.

After a time of unrestrained anguish, Dale knew he had to regain control and take action. He contacted each of his professors and made arrangements for a ten-day absence, and then he discussed his plans with Thomas, his roommate.

"Dale," his friend said, "let me know if I can do anything to help. And no matter how long you're gone, I'll be here waiting for you when you get back."

Meanwhile, Coach Morrison had called and explained the circumstances to James Knox, an alumnus as well as an ardent supporter of the university and its basketball program. As owner of Beavercreek Real Estate and Mortgage Company of Ohio, Knox had both the means and the inclination to lend a helping hand whenever called upon.

"Jim," the coach said, "Dale has little, if any, family support, so I'd like his teammates and this university to play the role of a surrogate family. I expect the funeral to be in Bloomington, and if you could arrange a private plane, I'll get the boys together and we'll be there for him."

"Just give me a day's notice, and I'll have one ready for you."

In Bloomington, Dale contacted family members of his parents' traveling companions, and together they made arrangements for the local Underwood Funeral Home to transport and make final disposition of the deceased. Due to the already charred state of their bodies, Dale chose cremation for his parents' remains, to be followed by a memorial service.

At the ceremony Dale was astonished at the outpouring of friends, former lawn and newspaper customers, old high school classmates, and of course his coaches and teammates from the university. Even more surprising was the attendance of two of his professors. Initially overwhelmed by all the love, concern, and support, Dale soon realized that it had helped to fill the void that had so nearly consumed him earlier.

Following the burial, Dale spent three days arranging for the Clayton & Son law firm, in coordination with a local real estate office, to handle the legal process required to settle and sell the estate. A thoughtful neighbor volunteered to look after the house and mow the lawn until the sale was complete. Before heading back to school, Dale packed up and stored family keepsakes, while delivering excess items to the Salvation Army.

Back at the university, Dale quickly caught up on missed classwork and completed the semester without his grades suffering appreciably. Then, to complete the settlement of the estate, he headed back to Bloomington after notifying the personnel department at the cold storage company that he would not be available for his usual summer job.

Driving home, Dale worried that his family's bank account might not be adequate to pay the law firm and for funeral arrangements, but upon meeting with Mr. Clayton, he was surprised to learn that Marcum Motors had purchased his parents' car at a fair price, providing the needed funds. Further, a neighbor's son had signed a contract to purchase the house. The lawyer estimated that after all expenses, taxes, and debts were paid off, the estate account would consist of about twenty-five thousand dollars. Also, Clayton explained that in a safe-deposit box his parents kept at the bank, he had found a deed to forty acres that his paternal grandparents had willed to his father. The land was located on the edge of Youngstown, Ohio, and had sixteen months remaining on a ten-year lease to a horse training and stable business. The agreement provided for the lease payments to be deposited into an account from which the property taxes were paid, and the current balance was a little over ten thousand dollars. Dale chose to leave the money in the account to pay yearend property taxes.

When everything was settled, Dale placed twenty thousand dollars in a savings account and the remaining five grand in his checking account to get him through his last year of school.

In spite of relief from his financial concerns, Dale found himself despondent. All the reminders back home amplified the loss of his parents, while friends and former classmates, who had been so helpful and thoughtful immediately after the tragedy, were now busy with their own lives. Without a job or school to occupy his time, he felt lost, so he packed up his few things and headed back to school, hoping to find a job to finish out the summer.

Though his old job at the packing company was not available, Dale made arrangements to move back into the dorm room with Thomas, and the university put him to work with a team who maintained the various lawns and landscapes on campus until classes resumed in September.

As his schedule became more demanding and contacts with his teammates and college friends increased, Dale regained focus on his education and basketball goals, both of which were essential to his post-graduation plans. He even found time to order and study various maps of West Texas, along with Chamber of Commerce brochures from several towns. Specifically, he focused on a geographical box bounded by an east side that ran from Wichita Falls south to Abilene and a west boundary from Amarillo to Midland. Ideally, he preferred a small town located within reasonable driving distance of one of the larger cities, because he thought a small school would more likely afford him the opportunity to pursue his dream of owning a ranch.

First, Dale had two more semesters of study and a final basketball season to complete, both of which he pursued with his usual dedication and vigor. The basketball season proved to be his best, not only in terms of his contribution to a conference championship, but as a senior and team captain, he filled the role of a player-coach, something encouraged by Coach Morrison.

A couple of days before the graduation ceremony, Dale dropped by his coach's office and asked for a letter of recommendation.

"I'll be heading to Texas as soon as I get that diploma in my hands," he explained. "I hope to get a coaching job, and I believe a recommendation from you will help more than anything I can put in a résumé."

Morrison gladly documented Dale's basketball career, listing both individual achievements and team accomplishments. The last paragraph especially pleased the young aspiring coach.

"I've never coached a more team-oriented young man, and in twelve years of working with college basketball players, Dale Rory stands above all the rest in his knowledge of the game and leadership qualities. If not for his dream of going to Texas, I would hire him as my assistant in a heartbeat," the coach wrote.

With the letter of recommendation and his college diploma in the car seat beside him, and all his belongings stuffed in every available square inch of his old car, Dale headed south on Interstate 75, destined for West Texas and hopefully the realization of a long-held dream.

2 ——

Having turned west on Interstate 40 in Nashville, Tennessee, Dale continued to Oklahoma City where he headed south, crossing Red River into Texas just north of Wichita Falls. After two long days of driving, Dale was finally standing at the northeast corner of the geographical box within which he would begin his search.

In his room that evening he reviewed all the information he had collected regarding the area, with excitement building to the point that he had trouble sleeping. After a fitful night, he rose at five o'clock, packed, checked out of the motel, and drove to a twenty-four-hour restaurant for breakfast. Then he climbed back into his car and headed west on Highway 287.

With each mile traveled, green vegetation gave way to a sparse scattering of scrubby, dried up clusters of weeds and mesquite bushes on the increasingly desert-like landscape. Where there had been groves of trees earlier, Dale saw a forest of oil wells, with their teeter-totter-looking pumps, and the small towns became dustier and countryside houses fewer. Noticing more pastureland to the south side of the highway, Dale turned southwest at Vernon, and twenty-three miles later he pulled into the small town of Crowell. Needing to fill up with gas, he turned into a station already occupied by a dual-wheel pickup pulling a cattle trailer. While pumping gasoline, he struck up a conversation with the driver, in which Dale mentioned his hopes of coaching and starting a ranch.

"If you want to see a real ranch," the cowboy said, "drive yourself down to Guthrie. Just out of town you'll find the Four Sixes Ranch."

"That seems like an odd name," Dale said, after the man had given a fuller description of the huge ranch.

"Quite a story," the cattleman said with a laugh. "Legend says Old Cap'n Burk Burnett won it in a poker game back about 1870. The previous owner, the story goes, had dealt himself a hand as strong as cowboy coffee, but being fresh out of cash, he put up his ranch. He had a high-stakes hand, alright, but it didn't beat four sixes."

"Wasn't this land still roamed by Indians back then?"

"Sure was, but Cap'n Burk had an arrangement with Comanche Chief Quanah Parker. Don't know the details, but the Cap'n's cattle grazed Indian lands all the way to the Wichita Mountains up in Oklahoma."

Tempted to head south and see the famous ranch, Dale resisted and continued westward where a roadside sign indicated the next town, Paddock, was only fifteen miles farther. Mile after mile, the highway was bordered by endless barbed-wire fences which hemmed in vast open spaces, dotted here and there with a corral, a barn, or a cluster of grazing cattle and horses. Thinking back over the brochures he had read, Dale knew the land about him was richly steeped in the history of Texas cattlemen. Besides the Four Sixes Ranch, the home of the Pitchfork Land and Cattle Company was near Guthrie, having its beginnings in 1883 with over fifty-two thousand acres and nearly ten thousand head of Hereford cattle. The brochures said the ranch had since tripled in size.

Two miles east of Paddock, a sign indicated that the junction with Highway 83 lay ahead. Dale surmised that most of the town's businesses would likely be bunched around that traffic crossing.

It was eleven o'clock when he reached the junction. Pulling in at a convenience store, he asked directions to the most popular eatery in town.

"Martha's serves sandwiches, hamburgers, and the best plate lunch in town," a local volunteered, pointing west along Highway 70. "If you've got your heart set on something fancier, I recommend the Steakhouse just to the south on Highway 83."

Dale's primary objective was to learn about the school and coaching opportunities, so he chose Martha's where he expected to find a representative sample of the town's citizens, those with school children and those most likely to be friendly to a stranger.

Since it was only a few minutes after eleven, Dale decided to take a look at the town prior to having lunch. He noticed Tolbert's Pharmacy, Corner Grocery, Washburn's Seed & Feed, and Melba's Variety Shop, all interspersed with vacant buildings. Soon he located the small but stately courthouse and then the public school complex. Labels on the buildings identified each as belonging to the elementary, the intermediate, or the high school. Dale needed no sign to point out the cracker-box-shaped gymnasium.

He saw no evidence of recent construction, the landscape and shrubs appeared neglected, and the parking lot needed repaving. Everything pointed to an educational system forced to limp along on limited funds. Even if Paddock had an opening for a math teacher and coach, and should make him a job offer, he expected the salary would be minimal. Under such circumstances, how could he hope to acquire land and cattle? Though he had anticipated a somewhat depressed economy, the reality of Paddock struck a blow to his hopes. But he had over twenty thousand dollars in savings, and for the right situation, he reasoned, he would be willing to invest liberally.

With his watch showing straight up twelve o'clock, he headed back toward Martha's Cafe. The pockmarked parking lot had collected a few dusty cars and three times as many faded and dented pickups, most with baling wire and strings dangling here and there.

Stepping inside, Dale grabbed a local paper from the entranceway newsstand, dropped a quarter through the rusty slot in the metal collection cylinder, and entered the dining room. His first impression was of an old western saloon: noisy, a soiled floor, cattle and horse pictures covering cedar walls, heavy wooden tables and chairs, a serving bar fitted with swiveling barstools covered with bare cowhide, and two apron-wearing waitresses hustling about, delivering food and collecting dishes while chatting with familiar customers. In one corner, on a miniature stage, elevated about six inches, sat a dark-stained piano with its ivory keys dancing of themselves, pounding out an old western ballad that had little chance of being heard over the din of the crowd.

Spotting a vacant two-person table jammed into a corner, Dale made his way over, knocking askew a fellow's wide-brim straw hat as he slipped between two seated patrons. Blue jeans, frayed western cut shirts, and stained boots made up the predominant costume, contrasting sharply with Dale's polo shirt, dress slacks, and loafers.

Settling in at his table, Dale perused the five-page newspaper until one of the waitresses hesitated beside his table, a small tablet with carbon inserts protruding from a slot in her apron and a stubby pencil jutting out from above her ear.

"Want the special?" she asked. "Comes with ice tea and a dish of peach cobbler."

Fortunately, Dale had noticed a chalkboard tacked onto the entrance wall on which the special was spelled out in detail: chicken fried steak, mashed potatoes, fried okra, and a choice of vegetable soup or garden salad.

"I'll take it with the salad," Dale responded.

"Cornbread or roll?" the woman asked.

"Roll."

No sooner had Dale turned back to the newspaper than he noticed a middle-aged man making his way over.

"Welcome to Paddock," the man said, smiling and extending his hand. "Have friends or relatives here, or just passing through?"

"If I can find a job, I just might settle down here," Dale said.

"Arthur Johnson, mayor of Paddock," the man said as Dale rose and shook his hand.

"Dale Rory."

"What kind of job?"

"I just graduated from college up in Ohio, and I'm looking for a coaching job."

"What sport?"

"Basketball. I played on the university team."

"Mr. Rory, I can't speak for the school administration, but there's a fellow right over there who can. I'll see if he has a minute to talk to you."

Soon the mayor returned, introduced Principal Charles Kennemer, and wished Dale luck before heading back to his table.

"The mayor says you're interested in a position with the school," the predominantly bald, sixty-three-year-old principal said.

"Yes, sir. I'd like to coach basketball and teach, and have a little ranch nearby."

"What a coincidence," Kennemer said with a laugh. "I'm the high school principal, as well as the boy's basketball coach."

"Sir," Dale said, awkwardly, "I'm not here to take your job. I was just hoping there might be a vacancy."

"Don't worry yourself, young man," Kennemer said, easing his six-foot, two-hundred-pound frame into the spare chair. "You just might be a godsend. My plans were to retire from coaching after one more season, but if you happen to have the right qualifications, I could be persuaded to step down a year early."

"I wouldn't want you to do that on my account," Dale said, shifting in his chair.

"You mentioned teaching," the principal said. "What classroom subjects can you handle?"

"Mathematics was my major, but I'm qualified to teach health science and physical education, also."

"Mathematics," Kennemer repeated, nodding. "Could you teach high school courses?"

"Yes, sir. I'm qualified to teach algebra one and two, geometry, both plane and analytical, trigonometry, and calculus."

"How do you feel about students who just cannot seem to grasp algebra, considering they must have three math credits to graduate?"

"First, success in the classroom depends upon the teacher as much as, if not more than, the student. Second, I know there are exceptions, but I believe the vast majority of students can grasp the essential elements of algebra and geometry. Third, I won't ask students in basic courses to memorize a bunch of formulas and rules that they can easily look up in a book. I'll stress using logic and reasoning to analyze everyday problems and applying basic mathematical principles to find practical solutions. Finally, if I see a student failing to comprehend the basics, I'll seek new ways to motivate him, and I'm willing to change techniques to best meet the needs of students."

"And you played college ball up in Ohio?"

"Yes, sir," Dale said. "I have a letter of recommendation from my college coach that summarizes my experience and qualifications. Also, I'd be glad for you to contact him."

"What position did you play in high school?"

"My freshman season, I played guard, but as I grew taller, the coach moved me to forward the next year, and I actually played the post position some my senior year."

"Not many players get experience at all positions. That should serve you well as a coach."

The principal quickly realized the advantage of having a coach who could teach mathematics, an area where he currently had a hard-to-fill vacancy. Also, he knew that Dale could, with his unique qualifications, land a job with most any school district in the area. And, if this young man could develop a winning team, he would be the find of the decade.

"Do you have a copy of your transcript and a teacher's certificate?"

"I have a transcript with me, but I'd have to request the teaching certificate from the Ohio Education Agency. Of course, it's specific to Ohio's requirements."

"Is there anything in your official records, school or otherwise, that might influence our decision regarding employing you? If you apply, we'll have to do a background check, you know."

"Sir, I think you'll find my record to be spotless."

"Dale, this is a small town, a tight-knit community. Parents get to know the teachers and coaches, both officially and unofficially. They'll know where you buy your groceries, what church you attend, where you gas up your car, and what you do with your spare time. I'm afraid they scrutinize the people who work with their kids rather severely. Can you handle that?"

"I grew up in a small town, Mr. Kennemer. I think I understand parents' concerns, and I welcome their scrutiny, particularly from those who are actively involved in their child's activities."

"Some of our boys have begun getting tattoos. I don't see any on you. Will their tattoos bother you?"

"Some of my teammates in Ohio had them, so I'm used to it. However, it's not something I've done or would encourage. I've known men who got tattoos while in the Navy or Marines and, later in life, wore long-sleeved shirts or patches to cover them up. And I've known others who displayed theirs proudly. I suppose our views on such things are personal."

"Dale, are you married?"

"No, sir. I want to get a job and get a start in life before I take that step."

"Tell me about your parents."

"Both deceased, killed in a plane crash over a year ago."

"I'm sorry to hear that," Kennemer said. "What's the origin of the name Rory?"

"My grandparents lived in Germany during World War I. Then in the 1930s they believed that country was headed for another major conflict, so Granddad Rorschach brought his family to the United States, and wanting to disassociate himself with the homeland, he Americanized the name to Rory."

"I don't see a lot of German characteristics in your physical features."

"My father and grandfather were my height, with blue eyes and blond hair, but some say I took after my mother, who was a black-haired, dark-eyed Italian beauty. Obviously, I got her dark features, but not her looks."

"I know you must miss them," the principal said quietly, then hesitated before continuing. "Now, I'd like you to meet my wife."

Dale followed the principal over to where a graying woman with a winning smile waited at a window table.

"Dale, this is my wife, Melba. Honey, this young man is Dale Rory, and he's interested in teaching and coaching basketball here in Paddock."

"It's a pleasure meeting you," the woman said, extending her hand. She glanced at her husband and smiled as she continued. "I'm sure our boys and girls would be happy to have a teacher a little closer to their age, and I know we'd all like to see a younger man leading our basketball team."

"I suppose that settles the question of whether or not we have a coaching vacancy," Kennemer said, with a laugh. "So, the next step is for you to meet our superintendent, W. C. Phillips. I'll contact him and try to arrange an interview for tomorrow morning, if that's okay with you."

When Dale agreed, Melba invited Dale to dinner at the Kennemer home at six o'clock that evening, with her husband providing directions to their house, which was just off campus and right behind the gymnasium. Without hesitation, Dale accepted the invitation.

The principal then suggested that Dale might get a room at the home of Sam and Pamela Everett on Tumbleweed Street, explaining that the school district would cover the cost since he was staying for an interview.

"And Dale, please bring along the letter of recommendation and a copy of your transcript," the principal said.

After arranging for the room, a tiny garage apartment, Dale arrived at the Kennemers's a couple of minutes early, and while Melba completed setting the table, Dale handed over his college transcript and the letter from Coach Morrison.

First, the principal scanned the transcript, finding it dominated by a letter grade of A, especially in math and science. The lowest grade was a C in a general studies course surveying art and music.

"Impressive," Kennemer said. "Too many college athletes barely get by in the classroom, but I see that you took your studies seriously."

"Yes, sir. I played basketball so I could go to college, rather than the other way around, and I always expected to coach after my college days, rather than continue playing."

Kennemer then read the letter of recommendation that listed Dale's athletic achievements, which included four letters in high school basketball with all-state honors his senior year when his team won the state championship, four letters in college where he made the all-conference team his last two seasons, selection by his teammates as team captain as a senior, and two conference championships. The coach had also listed a few statistics, such as his eighteen-point scoring average with nine-point-five assists per contest during his final season. Then the principal read the last paragraph.

"Wow!" he said. "With these qualifications, you'll have no trouble landing a coaching job."

"Thank you, sir."

"And you mentioned wanting some acreage and a few head of cattle. Do you think you can handle that along with teaching and coaching?"

"Mr. Kennemer, establishing a ranch is an essential part of why I'm here. Also, I've always kept busy, always had lots of energy. I firmly believe I can handle all these responsibilities, and do so with enthusiasm and skill. Now, I don't mean to sound boastful, but I am confident in my abilities."

"Oh, to be young," Kennemer said, smiling. "Especially a young man with an education and a ton of talent."

Dinner was simple but delicious and the Kennemers made their guest feel especially welcome, so much so that Dale's growing interest in the Paddock job pushed aside his earlier concerns, as well as any thoughts of surveying the area before settling on a specific offer.

"Dale," the principal said as they settled into the family room, "Mr. Phillips can meet with you at eight o'clock tomorrow morning. I hope that's not too early."

Dale assured the principal that he would be there. Then after another hour of visiting and discussing the town and surrounding area, Dale thanked his hosts for dinner and an enjoyable evening, and then headed back to his room.

After breakfast at Martha's, Dale drove to the school administration building where Mr. Kennemer was already briefing the superintendent.

"Come in," the principal called to Dale, and then made the introductions.

Phillips appeared to be in his early forties and carried a lithe one hundred fifty-five pounds on a five-foot-nine frame. His brown hair was well on its way to gray, and his dark eyes were lively and steady. Clearly, he was energetic and enjoyed being in charge.

"Young man," the superintendent said, "you have a remarkable transcript and impeccable qualifications. We believe your lack of on-the-job experience is more than offset by your record, athletic and academic, and your positive attitude. We want to offer you the job of high school math teacher and boys' basketball coach, but we have little flexibility when it comes to the salary we can pay. The most we can offer is twenty-seven thousand a year, but the cost of living out here is considerably less than in the Northeast. And, assuming you meet expectations, I'm committed to improving your pay at the first opportunity."

"I'm interested," Dale responded. "But, before I accept, I need to mention that I want to have summer basketball camps. I believe they'll increase enthusiasm for the team, elevate skill levels, and the fees will add a little to my income. Will you and the school support this?"

The superintendent agreed to mention this to the school board when he met with them to recommend Dale's employment, and to encourage them to provide the facilities, supplies, and whatever financial help could be found.

"Without a doubt they'll approve hiring you," Phillips said, glancing at the recommendation letter. "Also, I'm confident they'll also support your basketball camps to the limit of our means."

"With approval of the camps, I'll accept the job," Dale said.

The superintendent rose and shook Dale's hand vigorously.

"Dale," Kennemer said, "have you looked around for a place to live?"

When Dale explained that he had not, the principal suggested that he might talk to the Everetts about renting the small garage apartment.

"It'll be affordable, and they're fine people," the superintendent said.

When Dale asked the Everetts about the apartment, he found that Kennemer had called ahead and urged them to take on the boarder.

"The principal says you'll be our new basketball coach," Pamela said.

"Yes, ma'am, assuming the board approves of me."

"We'll be pleased to have you rent the apartment," she said.

"I want you to know that I'll be looking for some ranch land, and might not be renting very long," Dale explained.

Since the apartment had been vacant for months and the Everetts had no other prospects, they voiced no concern. In fact, they suggested he might check on the Estes Ranch seven miles west of town, indicating it needed work but was probably the best deal available.

"It's about four hundred acres, I hear," Sam Everett explained. "And I think Claude is running about fifty head of cattle on it. With more water tanks, a man could graze about sixty-five cows and heifers, I'd say."

Dale scribbled down directions to the ranch, unloaded his few belongings into the apartment, and then headed west on Matador Road, agreeing for the Everetts to alert Claude Estes of the impending visit.

On the way, Dale remembered that James Knox, owner of the Ohio real estate and mortgage company and a rabid basketball fan, had told him to call if he ever needed real estate advice or a related loan. "I'll give you free advice and guarantee you the best possible interest rate and payment plan," Knox had said. Still, Dale wondered if he was financially ready to become a landowner and rancher.

As forewarned, Dale spotted a road sign pointing left to the turnoff to the Estes ranch house, a stucco bungalow consisting of a living room, two small bedrooms, a bath, and a kitchen-dining room combination. A hundred yards back of the house, on the side of a hill, stood a barn that would swallow three of the bungalow. The west side of the barn was open for the storage of hay while the east consisted of eight stalls adjacent to an enclosure with a long hay manger against the wall. A storage building, a couple of cattle pens, and a corral with a loading chute completed the complex. A sprinkling of white-faced Hereford cattle grazed the hillside while a few frisky calves romped among them, kicking their heels high in play, and inside a lot surrounding a couple of covered feeders stood several steers being fattened for sale.

Claude Estes, an elderly man whose hawkish face bore ample evidence of his years and an outdoor life in the brutal West Texas sun, met Dale at the front door. The white-haired old rancher's timid but gracious wife reminded Dale of his now-deceased grandmother. The amiable couple invited Dale inside and immediately put him at ease. The rancher's price was one hundred dollars an acre, plus two thousand for mineral rights, and an additional ten thousand for the simple, stucco ranch house, a total of fifty-two thousand dollars. Having just sold his parents' house, Dale knew that a comparable house in Bloomington would have cost quadruple that price.

When Dale asked about market value and operating costs, Estes produced a file with tax appraisal records which showed a value in excess of sixty thousand dollars, and a ledger that itemized all monies spent on the ranch for the past three years, including taxes. After studying these for a few minutes, Dale copied down the crucial numbers before returning the file to the rancher, convinced the price was fair and the ranch had been profitable.

With the basics covered, Dale asked if there was a way he could see the place more thoroughly. Ten minutes later, he and Mr. Estes were in an old pickup that, though once blue, had taken on the rusty color of the land, bumping and bouncing along a two-rutted trail with a swirling dust cloud constantly on their heels.

The ranch consisted primarily of open pastures spread over rolling hills, cut by red-walled ravines that ran like roughly chiseled fingers to the shallow end of an ever-narrowing canyon. The chasm deepened as it continued southward beyond the Estes property, carving a severe gash through the elevated north side of the Thompson Ranch and finally exiting the canyon's mouth, where it became a shallow arroyo that crossed fertile lowland until it intersected the Pease River on its north bank. The Estes land was randomly splotched with clusters of mesquite trees, scrub oaks, and patches of cedars. The dominant feature of the landscape was an east-west ridge that ran the width of the four hundred acres. The water supply came from a windmill atop the ridge, pumping from a deep well into a twenty-foot-wide zinc tub that overflowed into a nearby pond. All of this was enclosed by a little over three miles of barbed wire strung on native cedar posts, interrupted by five sagging gates, the bottom edge of each plowing a shallow furrow when swung open.

With the survey completed, Dale and Mr. Estes retired to a swing hanging from two chains on the west end of the front porch. If Dale had initially harbored any doubts about the ranch, they were dissolved after five minutes of swaying back and forth in the cool of the afternoon, looking out over a landscape bounded only by a distant horizon, beyond which a mellowed sun was settling. He knew he had to own that ranch.

"Mr. Estes," Dale said, "I'm going to try to get a loan to buy your ranch, but it might take me six weeks to get it finalized. Do I need to put down some good-faith money for you to hold it for me?"

"No," Estes said. "Young man, you get your loan approved before any money changes hands; however, I think we should get a contract drawn up to fix the terms of the deal. How about if I round up the necessary papers and meet you at the title company in town tomorrow morning?"

Dale nodded, and then he asked about adjoining land, about any neighbors.

"The nearest folks would be the Stone girls, Sybil and her daughter Marilyn," Estes explained, pointing northeast to the Stone Place Ranch. "Mighty fine neighbors. If you buy this place, you'll come to treasure their friendship, and I hope you'll be right neighborly to them in return."

"Do you think I should drop by and meet them?"

"Off out here, it's mighty important to know what neighbors you've got," the old rancher said. "It's not like city folks who don't know or care who lives next door. Out here your neighbor is your policeman, your fireman, and even your nurse at times, and you've got to be the same to him."

The wily old rancher had just opened Dale's eyes to one of many lessons he had to learn, one way or another.

On his way back to town, Dale turned through the entranceway to the Stone Place Ranch, and followed the long, winding drive that circled around a large birdbath. Off to the right of the house, parked in front of a weathered one-car garage, was an old dusty, dented Ford pickup, blotched like a leopard with rust spots. Following the red brick walkway, he climbed onto the wide, wooden porch. Where he expected to see a doorbell, he found a doorknocker made from a hinged horseshoe and a rusty bell. Dale gave it a couple of clangs.

The greeting he had planned somehow stuck in his throat when the door opened and there stood a woman who looked strikingly like his mother.

"You lost, young man?" Sybil Stone asked, a smile creasing her tanned, wishbone-shaped face.

"Ma'am, I'm Dale Rory," he managed to say. "I've been looking at the property next door, the Estes Ranch, and thought I'd stop by and meet you. I hope we'll soon be neighbors."

"If you're gonna be a neighbor the likes of Claude and Hazel, I hope you buy the place. If not, then there's lots of other land for sale around here."

"Ma'am, I hope to be, but in any case I'm the new basketball coach and math teacher at Paddock High School. Possibly your daughter attends there."

"No, she got her diploma in May," Sybil said, profiling her work-trimmed body as she called into the house. "Marilyn, come meet the new basketball coach."

"Didn't mean to be a problem, ma'am," Dale said, shuffling his feet.

"No bother," Sybil said, stepping out onto the porch where a breeze played with her dark, gray-streaked hair. "Marilyn will want to meet you. She was the best player on her team the last two seasons, and she's interested in anything to do with basketball around here."

While Sybil introduced Dale and explained the circumstances of his visit, he stood admiring Marilyn's thick black hair, hazel eyes, and olive skin, whether natural or tanned, he was not sure.

"What're you doing now that you've graduated?" Dale asked while reaching through the doorway to shake Marilyn's hand.

"I'm taking a few courses at Texas Tech," the shapely eighteen-year-old replied

"Mr. Rory is a math teacher, too," Sybil said to her daughter.

"Mother's pointing out that I'm taking a math class, and that's never been my strong suit," the girl explained.

"Well, whether or not I buy the Estes ranch," Dale said, "I'll be glad to help, if the need should arise."

"I hope you're a patient teacher," Marilyn said, stepping her five-foot-seven frame onto the porch.

"I might not have the patience of Job, but then I can't imagine that you'd ever test me to that extent."

"Once basketball season starts, I doubt that you'll have much spare time," Marilyn said. "I'm afraid you've taken on quite a challenge."

"The boys haven't had much of a coach," Sybil said. "With proper training, they might not be all that bad."

"Mr. Kennemer seems like a fine man," Dale said, a little uncomfortable with the criticism of the former coach.

"I agree," Sybil replied, smiling. "And I'm a fine woman, but that doesn't make either of us a basketball coach."

"Well, I'll be getting back to town," Dale said, amused at the woman's directness. "I've enjoyed the visit, and hope to see you again soon."

"If you move in next door, I'm sure there'll be plenty more visits," Sybil said. "If not, we don't miss many basketball games, so we'll see you plenty, once the season starts."

"By the way," Marilyn said as Dale headed for the porch steps, "what'll you name your ranch?"

"I'm not sure," Dale responded, turning at the top step. "Maybe the Roryian."

"The Roarin' Ranch?" Marilyn asked, laughing as she joined him on the steps.

"That might be more appropriate," Dale replied, noticing how her figure filled out her threadbare denim shirt and worn jeans. "But it certainly won't be the Borin' Ranch."

"Regardless what you call it, let us know if you buy it," Sybil said. "We'll come over and help you get set up. I've never known a man who could put a house in proper order."

Driving back to his apartment, Dale reviewed the day, and what a day it had been. He was feeling great about being in Paddock, Texas.

Back in town, Dale looked up the toll-free number for James Knox, owner of Beavercreek Real Estate and Mortgage Company, and borrowing his landlord's phone, placed a call. Fortunately, Knox was in his office late that afternoon. Glad to hear from Dale, he repeated his earlier promise to help, asking for the documented particulars of the transaction, Dale's financial status and expected income, and that he package and mail all pertinent information to him the following morning.

"Mr. Knox," Dale said at the end of their conversation, "I inherited forty acres of land in Ohio that I'd like to sell to pay off as much of this loan as possible. It's currently under lease, but that'll expire soon. Can you make arrangements to get it on the market and find a buyer?"

Knox agreed to contact Dale's lawyer in Bloomington and get copies of related legal documents and handle the land transaction for him.

Before going to bed, Dale did as Knox requested, providing details regarding acreage, appraisal value, water and grazing capacities, condition of buildings and fences, three years of taxes and maintenance records, and the asking price, indicating he would pay down about two thousand dollars of that amount from his savings.

First thing the next morning after Dale mailed the letter to Knox, he leased a post office box. Then he opened an account at the local First National Bank. With the aid of Chet Williams, bank president, he transferred his meager checking account to Paddock, along with the twenty thousand dollars in savings.

An hour later, Dale met Claude Estes at the Wichita Title Company. After updating the rancher regarding his conversation with James Knox, the two finalized a contract that documented the conditions the two men had agreed upon the prior day, all contingent upon approval of Dale's loan.

After purchasing a few items for his apartment and getting it arranged, Dale made a more thorough tour of the school system. Absent many of the fineries of schools back East, the facilities were clean and serviceable. The gymnasium was small but quaint, with a sparkling floor and big fans installed high on both ends of the building to vent the West Texas heat. These would especially come in handy for summer camps, he thought.

When Dale's head hit his pillow that night, he lay quietly, thinking of his parents. How he wished they could be there and share in the excitement. He missed them terribly, but somehow he knew they would approve. He whispered a prayer, thanking God for blessing him beyond measure, and for loving parents who had planted within him a moral and ethical compass that had brought him to Paddock, Texas. Then he recalled his father's words: "Regardless how high your granddad might have flown, son, the day you become a man, you'll have to do your own flying."

Now that day had come.

3 ___

On Sunday, Dale visited the First United Methodist Church, which he had located the day he arrived in town. Slipping into the sanctuary just prior to the start of the service, Dale sat near the back and spotted Sybil and Marilyn Stone sitting several rows ahead of him. Afterwards, as Dale eased toward the exit, Marilyn caught up with him.

"I hope you enjoyed the service," she said. "We don't have many visitors, so when we do, we try to be friendly."

"Thanks. I'm glad to find you and your mom here," he said, thinking how grown up Marilyn looked in her summer dress and high heels.

By then, others had noticed Dale, and began coming by to offer their welcome.

"Who is he?" one of Marilyn's former basketball teammates asked as she surrendered Dale to other church members.

"Our new boys' basketball coach," she explained.

"He sure is young," another said. "Is he married?"

"No," Marilyn replied. "But he just might be our neighbor soon. He's looking at the Estes Ranch."

"Lucky you," her friend said. "I'd like to have a young single guy living next door, especially a cute one like him."

"Next door in the country is not quite the same as in town," Marilyn said.

"Maybe you could introduce us to him," the friend said.

"I don't know him that well," Marilyn replied. "Besides, it looks like he's going to be occupied for a while."

Dale finally managed to slip out the door and drive to Martha's for lunch, where he met several more of Paddock's friendly citizens. A newcomer certainly doesn't go unnoticed in this town, he thought.

The next day James Knox called Dale to report the approval of his ranch loan. West Texas ranchland was not Knox's niche, and four percent real estate loans would not keep him in business, so Knox carried the loan personally rather than expose his company to an unjustifiable risk. His explanation to a questioning associate was, "I have tremendous confidence in Dale Rory, both in his character and his abilities. Besides, he was an outstanding basketball player, and his leadership elevated the university's program several notches." Of course, the realtor gave Dale no hint of the personal gamble he was taking.

"Mr. Knox, I can't thank you enough," Dale said.

"Dale, folks down there must've taken to you like a bear to honey," the real estate executive said. "The Wichita Title & Abstract Company and the Cottle County Clerk have certainly rushed this through on your behalf. Of course, I told them that you're a young Hank Iba, and they're lucky to have you coaching their boys. I suspect they want to tie you to that land so you can't leave for quite some time."

"There's nothing like setting high expectations," Dale said, with a laugh. "Why not Adolph Rupp or John Wooden?"

"I'm not sure folks down there have ever heard of Rupp or Wooden, but I bet they know about Iba and the basketball championships he took home to Stillwater."

"No doubt about that," Dale replied. "Now, with your quick approval of my loan, I've got a chance to get the ranch going before school starts. If I'm to live up to Iba's reputation, basketball will have to take priority then."

"You'll be receiving duplicate copies of the paperwork by Federal Express in a couple of days. Sign both sets, keep one, and take the second set to the title company. They'll make their copy, express mail the originals back here, and notify me of the closing date. I'll have a check there for Claude and Hazel Estes, and then the ranch will be officially yours."

"I can't thank you enough," Dale said.

"And," Knox continued, "I just might have a buyer for your forty acres north of Youngstown."

The realtor went on to explain that if Dale would set a price, he thought he could get a contract on the property, and with the horse trainer's lease near expiration, the timing was good.

"Any idea how much the buyer would pay for the land?" Dale asked.

"The going rate in that area is between fourteen and sixteen hundred an acre," the lawyer replied.

Dale hesitated long enough to do the math, using fifteen hundred an acre, and arrived at sixty thousand dollars.

"What do I need to do to finalize the deal?" Dale asked.

"Just send a letter setting your price and authorizing me to sell your land," the realtor said.

"What about the current lease?"

"It'll expire by the time we close the sale."

"What'll your fee be?" Dale asked.

"I'll settle for my expenses, which I estimate will be about five hundred dollars."

"I'm giving my verbal approval to sell for anything over fourteen hundred an acre," Dale said. "I'll stick a letter in the mail tomorrow authorizing you to pursue this deal on my behalf."

"Good," Knox said. "I'll contact the buyer and keep you posted."

Dale slowly placed the handset back on the cradle. All along, this was the deal he had counted on to pay off his ranch and avoid those staggering monthly payments. He felt like pumping his fist in the air in celebration, but it was a little premature for that.

His only knowledge of the forty acres was based on a few childhood trips up there to ride horses. He knew it was considerably improved from when the horse trainer had first leased it. Back then it had been neglected for a decade and was covered with so much brush, trees, vines, and thorns that it was virtually unusable. His parents had been delighted when the man offered to lease it for his horse training facility and a few stables. The trainer had agreed to clear most of the land in lieu of payment for the first two years of the lease, including building a pond on a little stream that flowed through the property. Subsequently, the lease payments had covered the ever-growing property taxes and had accumulated a small reserve, which his parents had annually drawn from to meet Christmas expenses and to cover a few emergencies. What had seemed insignificant property for so long could now pay for his Texas ranch and keep him out of the poor house.

Dale whispered a prayer of thanks, and then headed out to the ranch to update Claude and Hazel Estes. The couple was elated when told they should expect to close the sale of their ranch the following week.

"Honey," the rancher's wife said. "We've got to get packed up and out of here. This young man will want to move in, pronto."

"Don't be in a rush," Dale said. "I've got a place to live, and I don't want to put you in a bind."

"We've made preliminary arrangements for a place in Vernon," Claude said, referring to the nearby town. "I think we'll be cleared out within a week."

"What about your livestock?" Dale asked, wondering if he might purchase them.

"I've sold the entire herd," Claude replied. "A rancher from Guthrie will come and load them up Saturday."

On his way back to town, Dale turned in at the Stone Place Ranch.

"I expect to close the deal on the Estes Ranch next week," he said, beaming as Sybil joined him on the porch.

"Congratulations, Dale," she said. "I know you're thrilled, and I admit that Marilyn and I have warmed up to the idea of having a new neighbor."

"Ma'am, I promise to do my best to not disappoint you. My parents would climb right out of their graves if I ever mistreated a neighbor."

"Tell me about them," Sybil said, motioning to a pair of nearby chairs.

"I'd say the Golden Rule about sums up my dad. He'd go the extra mile every time to make sure no man could accuse him of doing less than his part. He taught me to take responsibility for my own affairs, and to never blame someone else for my failures. At least a hundred times I heard him say, 'Talk is cheap. A man is known by the way he lives every day, every hour. The way to get respect is to earn it.' And he never believed that success was measured in dollars and cents."

"What about your mom?"

"She was a saint. I've never known anyone to do more for unfortunate people. 'But for the sake of God . . .' she would say, meaning that at some point each of us could find ourselves destitute and in need of a helping hand. 'It's not what you have that counts,' she claimed. 'It's what you do with what you have.' The principle that guided my mother's life was, 'To whom much is given, much is required.' Later, I learned that she got that from Luke chapter twelve, verse forty-eight. She was not an overly religious woman, but she applied more Bible truths to life than anyone I ever knew."

"Obviously, you're from good stock, young man," Sybil said. "There's an old adage that we quote out here that says, 'You don't know what you're made of until you've passed through the fire.' With the work you've chewed off for yourself, I expect your mettle will be tested soon enough."

"Ma'am, hard work has never bothered me. Fact is, I look forward to it."

"You'll get your fill, that's a sure bet," Sybil said, rising from the chair. "I'll pass the good news along to Marilyn, but she's gonna be disappointed that she wasn't around to hear it firsthand."

"Is she at school?"

"No. Her courses are all on Tuesday and Thursday, so she drives to Tech on Monday afternoon and comes home on Friday. Right now, she's gone to town for groceries," Sybil explained. "That's another fact of living out here. You don't shop as often, but when you do, you'd better be thorough. You forget something, you're likely to do without for a spell."

"I'm heading back to town now," Dale said. "If I see her, I'll give her the news."

When Dale was about a hundred yards from the house, he saw Marilyn turn onto the drive, so he pulled off to the side and waited.

"Coach," she said, having stopped alongside his car, "I hope you've come to deliver good news."

"I hope you take it that way. I expect to be the new owner of the Estes Ranch by the end of next week."

"That qualifies as headlines around here. I'm really glad for you."

"I'd like to show you something," Dale said, slipping out of his car and pulling a picture from his wallet. "Remind you of someone you know?"

"Where'd you get this?" Marilyn asked, studying the snapshot.

"Before I answer that, tell me who it reminds you of."

"Could be my mother's twin," Marilyn said, still staring at the photograph.

"Not unless your mother was a sister to mine," Dale said, smiling.

"This is your mother?"

"An Italian beauty, wasn't she?"

"I was looking forward to having you as a neighbor," Marilyn said, handing back the picture. "But not as a cousin."

"Well, maybe we'll just keep it a secret."

"I don't know about that," Marilyn said, glancing up at Dale. "Being a close relative of yours might come in handy, once you've made a million or two on your new ranch."

"So far, it's just sunk me into debt. Will you come see me if I end up in debtors prison?"

"I'll swear I never knew you."

"At least I know what kind of neighbor you're going to be."

"You've got a lot to learn, greenhorn. While math is your strong suit, ranching is mine, and if you'll pay attention, I'll keep you outside of those prison bars."

"Paying attention to you is going to be the easy part," he said, and turned toward his car.

"By the way," she called out, "I like your little apartment."

"You've seen my apartment?"

"Just drove by. But if I had known we were cousins, I'm sure Mrs. Everett would have let me in."

They were both laughing when Marilyn headed on up the drive toward the house. Dale watched her for a moment, and then slipped the picture back inside his wallet and stuffed it in his back pocket. As he veered onto the drive, he glanced back at the house where Marilyn had joined her mother on the front porch, and now stood watching him drive away.

"Honey," Sybil said to Marilyn, sliding her arm around her daughter's shoulders, "I've told you a hundred times that there's not a man around here good enough for you. Well, maybe that's just changed."

Closing the deal on the ranch occurred at one o'clock the following Friday.

When all the paperwork was complete and the sellers were paid, Dale followed Claude and Hazel to the parking lot in front of the title company, where the elderly rancher updated him on the progress of their move.

"Should be out by Wednesday," Claude said, folding the two checks totaling fifty-two thousand dollars and stuffing them in his shirt pocket.

"And we left our old washer, dryer, refrigerator, and cook-stove," Hazel added. "They're provided where we're going, and I thought you might need them."

She was right, of course, and Dale thanked them, knowing that they had saved him several hundred dollars. Later he gratefully marked those items off his list of things to be purchased for the ranch house.

While waiting to hear that the bungalow was vacated, Dale busied himself looking for a few necessary furniture items. Trying to conserve his money, he checked with a used furniture store where he selected a refurbished couch, a couple of chairs, a lamp with a stand, a small dining room table with four chairs, a simple bedroom set, and a black-and-white television, asking for delayed delivery of these items. Then he grudgingly invested in a new vacuum cleaner, but limited his expenditure by selecting the most basic model.

It was Wednesday afternoon when Claude Estes notified Dale that he and Hazel had completed their move, prompting Dale to box up the cleaning products and disinfectants he had acquired and head for the ranch. He spent the next two days sweeping, vacuuming, and cleaning the inside of the house, along with trimming the few shrubs along the front porch. Late afternoon of the second day, an hour after he had finished inside the house, Dale was relaxing in the porch swing when Sybil and Marilyn drove up.

"Howdy, neighbors," he said, attempting a Texas welcome. "If you've come to see the house, just step inside, but I warn you, it's as empty as Christ's tomb."

"That's okay. We've come to help you clean the place up," Sybil said.

"I've already made an attempt at that, but you're welcome to inspect my work," he said, pushing the door open.

"How fresh everything smells," Marilyn said, entering the front room. "Mom, I'm not sure he needs our help."

"I'll admit," Sybil said, "I never expected a man could spruce up a place like this."

When the tour reached the first bedroom, Sybil asked Dale about his furniture plans.

"I've found a few things in town," Dale said. "I just haven't had them delivered since I didn't have the house ready."

"A real rancher spends his money on cows, feed, and a good pickup before he invests in house furniture," she said. "Marilyn and I will loan you our spare bedroom suite 'til you get your feet on the ground."

"And we've got more dishes than we'll ever use, Mom," Marilyn said. "Let's bring over some spare plates, glasses, utensils, and cookware."

By the time the tour was over, Sybil and Marilyn had volunteered to lend him just about everything remaining on his list.

"Ladies," Dale said, overwhelmed, "it's not right for you to sacrifice your things when I can manage to buy what I need."

"It's no sacrifice," Sybil said. "However, it'd be the right thing to do, even if it was."

"I can't believe your generosity. I don't know if I can ever repay you for all your kindnesses."

"By the time you've helped us corral them steers we've got," Sybil said, eyebrows raised, "and run them into a chute and vaccinate them, and then haul them to the sale barn, you'll be well on your way to balancing the ledger."

"Yeah," Marilyn added, enjoying teasing the novice rancher, "or when you've sat in a saddle from dark to sunup helping us round up an angry bull that's busted through the fence and had rather fight than come home, you'll see our generosity in a different light."

"Well, what are neighbors for?" Dale said, realizing further resistance was futile. "As long as you'll let me return the favor later, I'll accept your offer."

The next morning, Dale called the furniture store and deleted the bedroom set from his purchase, substituting an old desk and chair he had seen there, and asked for Monday delivery. Then he drove over to the Stone Place Ranch and helped load the bedroom furniture, kitchenware, and various other items into Sybil's pickup for delivery to his new house. With Sybil directing the action, all the items were soon in place. That evening, Dale drove to town, stuffed his apartment items into his car, and finished the move. Now, the little bungalow lacked only those items held at the furniture store to be relatively comfortable.

After church Sunday, Dale stopped by to invite his neighbors over for dinner.

"I'm not much of a cook," he explained, "but to show my appreciation for all your help, I want to invite you two over for hamburgers tomorrow afternoon."

Sybil looked at Marilyn, questioningly.

"It's okay. I'll drive to Tech early Tuesday morning."

"I didn't see a grill at your place," Sybil said. "Why don't you take the one out back? We never use it."

After a mild protest, Dale loaded the grill in the bed of Sybil's pickup and hauled it to his ranch. After returning the truck, Dale headed to the Corner Grocery and picked up the necessary food items.

Monday morning he took delivery of the dining and living room furniture, along with the old desk he had picked out earlier. He proceeded to place the furniture where he thought it best fit. Later that afternoon, as he was preparing the grill about five o'clock, Marilyn drove up.

"Mother's busy with some ladies from church, but I thought I would come on and help," she said, and without further explanation, she began slicing tomatoes.

"How's school?" Dale asked.

"To be honest, I'm struggling a little," she replied. "I drive about a hundred and twenty miles, twice a week, and the room I have at Modine's, Mother's friend in Lubbock, isn't conducive to study. And when I'm home, there's always so much to do. I go to the university library every Wednesday and work on my lessons, and I try to catch up on the weekends."

"What about your math class?"

"It's the worst. I can usually figure out the problems, but it takes so much time."

"Remember, I'm available to help."

"I just might take you up on that, if you have a few minutes after dinner tonight."

Sybil arrived five minutes before six, and the three sat down around the dining table and enjoyed hamburgers and conversation.

After eating, Sybil wandered through the house and then volunteered to improve the arrangement of his furniture. He thought he had done a good job with it, but he quickly learned that she had a different idea. Grudgingly he conceded when she explained how her recommended placements would better utilize room space, while improving overall appearance.

"Dale, have you looked at stocking your ranch?" Sybil asked, when they were seated on the newly arranged couch and chairs.

"Only in general terms," Dale replied. "I'd like to get about fifty cows, if I can afford them."

"When you're ready, I advise you to call Sammy Burns up in Wichita Falls. He's as good a cattleman as I know, and he's as honest as the day is long," Sybil said, writing down a phone number and handing it over to Dale. "He'll locate the cattle for you, buy them, and get them delivered here, all at a reasonable fee."

"First, I'll need to check the fences and gates," Dale said. "It looks like Mr. Estes might have neglected them some lately, and I'll feel better if I take a look before I bring a herd of cows in here. And I'd like to have a horse ready to ride when the cows are delivered. I think the stables and barn are useable just as they are."

"That's good, but there's something else you need to think about," Sybil said. "When winter blows its ice-cold breath down here, you'll have to hay your stock twice a week for four months, longer if it's a bad one. To do that, you'll need a tractor with a hayfork. Tractors, even used ones, are expensive, so I propose that you share ours this winter. You can help feed our cattle and maybe pay for some of the fuel to balance the deal."

"Sybil, I'd hate to break something on your tractor, and it's not right for me to add to its wear and tear. Besides, I've looked at a couple of used ones at the Farm and Ranch Supply in Childress. I think I can manage to buy one."

"Dale, think about how many cows that money would put in your pasture," Sybil replied, wagging a bony finger at him. "Or think about how many bales of hay it would stack in your barn. Always remember, there are things you can do without, and others you can't. If you don't figure out which is which, you'll go broke before the sun sets on your first year."

Sybil Stone was a difficult woman to argue with, Dale was learning, especially when she had the advantage in subject knowledge. And judging by the six-year-old red Firebird Marilyn drove and the rundown F150 pickup Sybil used, this rancher practiced what she preached.

"I concede," he replied, smiling. "No tractor until cattle are grazing my pasture and hay fills my barn."

"Well, I guess I'll head home," Sybil said, rising from her chair. "Marilyn, are you coming along?"

"Not yet. I'll stay and help Dale clean up the kitchen, and maybe get him to check over my math assignment. I should be home in a couple of hours."

"Dale, thank you for a wonderful supper," Sybil said, patting his shoulder. "We'll have to return the favor real soon."

"Mom, I thought you might invite him to attend Wednesday night church with you," Marilyn said. "It would be a chance for him to get to know lots of the school kids and their parents."

"That's a great idea," Sybil said. "Dale, every Wednesday we have a meal prior to a brief service. We'd love to have you attend."

"I'll be glad to do that. Maybe we can swap out driving."

After Sybil left, Dale and Marilyn spent a few minutes clearing the table and taking care of the dishes. Then she stepped out to her car and returned with her math assignment, which she spread out on the table.

The problems dealt with graphing parabolas. Marilyn had solved all except three problems by repeatedly evaluating each equation using varying sets of coordinates, a time-consuming process. Dale showed her how to determine the general shape and graphic location of a curve by examining the elements of the equation, such as the sign and value of the coefficient of the dependent variable, whether the equation included a constant, and which variable is squared. Using Dale's method, Marilyn spent no more than thirty seconds examining each equation before she plotted the curve. In twenty minutes, she had completed the final trio of parabolas.

"If you can make everything that easy," she said, closing her book, "I can quit worrying about my math class."

"Anytime you need help, just let me know. After taking ten college math courses, I should be able to deal with about any problem you'll face."

With the math book and papers put away in the car, Dale and Marilyn swayed back and forth in the porch swing for another thirty minutes, talking about their hopes for the future. Obvious to both was their common goal of running a cattle ranch, but also they shared a love of basketball. As is often the case with a young man and woman experiencing an attraction to each other, they focused on those things they agreed on, rather than any differences.

"Marilyn is a pretty name, a very feminine name," Dale commented.

"Thank you," she replied, "but I have always wanted a nickname. Most of my friends have one, and they just seem more personal. You ever had one?"

"Tex," he said with a laugh. "Not very original, is it?"

"Not down here."

"Well, what nickname would you like?"

"That's the problem. I think a friend or family member has to give a nickname. That's what makes it special."

"Then I'd like to be the one to come up with one for you. What do you think of Merr?"

"I like it, especially because it's just between the two of us."

On that note, Dale walked Marilyn to her car, and then lingered in the front yard until her taillights faded into the night.

It was early July, and Dale had four hundred acres to explore, so the next two mornings he rose early and spent most of the day familiarizing himself with the ranch, stopping to straighten up a post or reattach a loose strand of wire. Then he recalled that when he had driven Sybil to church Wednesday night, she had advised him to check out the windmill and make any necessary repairs while there were no cows to water, so Thursday morning he climbed the tower, locked the rotor blades, and packed fresh grease around the bearings. After inspecting the long shaft, oiling the pump gears, and replacing worn seals, Dale headed to the house for lunch.

After repairing the board fence around a cattle pen that afternoon, he came in and grabbed a glass of ice tea. Just as he headed for the cool of the front porch swing, the phone rang.

"Hello," he said, after rushing back inside.

"Dale Rory?" the caller asked.

"I'm Dale," he replied.

"James Knox," the man said. "I've received a firm offer on your land, and need to know how you want to respond."

"What's the offer?" Dale asked, his throat tightening.

"Sixteen hundred and fifty an acre," the realtor said, "if you accept the offer within three days."

"What's your advice?"

"You can probably get more, if you're willing to hold out."

Meanwhile, Dale had picked up a pencil and notepad and roughly done the math. It totaled sixty-six thousand dollars.

"How much more do you think I could get?"

"Twenty-five to fifty dollars per acre."

Another thousand to two thousand dollars, Dale calculated. However, the more he thought about the anguish of waiting another week or two, the less attractive the additional money became.

"I'll take their offer," he said, anxious to get out of debt. "Go ahead and take out your fee and fifty thousand to pay off my ranch loan, and send a check for the balance."

Hanging up the phone, Dale clapped his hands together and shot his right fist heavenward.

"Hallelujah!" he practically shouted. "This ranch will be mine, and I'll be debt-free!"

For the next couple of days Dale attacked everything with renewed enthusiasm. He had not realized how much the fifty-thousand-dollar debt had been weighing on his mind, as well as a growing concern regarding the additional expenses facing him. It seemed that every day he discovered some new cost or addition to his reliance upon his neighbors, which grated on his preference for independence.

Now, without those loan payments, he felt he had a little financial breathing room.

4 —

On Sunday Dale pulled into the parking lot at the First United Methodist Church, slipped inside, and eased into the pew beside Sybil and Marilyn.

"Hello, neighbor," Sybil whispered.

"What've you been doing?" Marilyn asked, leaning forward to see past her mother.

"Checking fences," he replied quietly, then glanced at Sybil. "And I repacked the bearings on the windmill."

"I'll have time on Saturday to help with the fencing," Marilyn said.

"If you two have got to talk, then swap places with me," Sybil said to her daughter.

Marilyn slipped past her mother and sat next to Dale.

"I've got something to tell you," he whispered, "but it'll have to wait until after the service."

Marilyn nodded, smiling.

Afterwards, the two women introduced Dale to a few couples seated around them. These church members, like most of the others, had already heard that he was the new coach, and they extended him a warm welcome to the community and to their congregation.

"We're always glad to have new members," a man said, "but it's extra special to have the coach around. I expect some of the school kids will follow you to our church."

As the crowd began dispersing, Marilyn led Dale over to a couple of her girlfriends. Along the way she surprised him by looping her arm through his.

"This is Coach Dale Rory, my neighbor," she said, seemingly with a touch of pride. "Coach, this is Charlene Gordon and Wynell Paine."

"Pleased to meet you," Charlene said. "I'm a senior, and Wynell's a junior."

"Which subjects will you teach?" Wynell asked.

"Geometry and both classes of algebra," Dale answered.

"He's a great teacher," Marilyn said. "He helps me with my college math."

"I guess you'll be my algebra teacher," Wynell said, smiling.

"I look forward to having you in my class," Dale said.

"Well, we'd better go," Marilyn said. "We've got to catch up with Mother. She'll be anxious to go to lunch."

As they descended the church steps, Marilyn began easing her arm free of his, but he reached over with his off hand and clasped onto her wrist. When she looked surprised, he smiled and patted her hand.

"You wouldn't want me wandering around like a lost puppy, would you?" he asked.

Without a word, she hooked her arm in the crook of his elbow, smiling as they made their way to the parking lot.

"I've got some news," Dale said when they reached Sybil. "I'd like to take you two to the Steakhouse and tell you about it."

"You'd better save you money and eat lunch at our house, young man," Sybil said. "I've got everything ready except warming up a couple of things."

After eating pot roast, mashed potatoes, and black-eyed peas, the three cleared the table, and settled into the living room.

"Now, what's this news you've been keeping secret?" Marilyn asked.

"I've just sold some land in Ohio that I inherited. It's enough to pay off my loan and still leave enough to buy a small herd of cattle."

"Why, that's wonderful news!" Marilyn said. "Isn't it Mother?"

"About the best a young rancher can hope for. Congratulations, Dale."

"Thank you. Now I can manage to get a tractor and a few other things I need."

"Slow down," Sybil said, shoving an open palm toward Dale. "If I heard you right, once you settle that loan and get a few cows, you're bank account will be right back where it was. You'd better hold on to any cash you have until you get through your first winter. There's still hay to buy, and you'll need a truck and trailer of some sort, a horse, and no rancher goes long without a veterinarian bill or two. We'll share our tractor this winter, just like we planned."

"Ma'am, I hate to burden you when I could get by on my own," he protested.

"Dale, this is a minor burden that I can easily bear, and doing so just might keep you out from under one you can't handle right now. I know you'd like to do it all on your own, but you've got to learn to accept neighborly help. That's how we all get by out here."

"Yes, ma'am," Dale said, resignedly.

A while later as Dale was driving home, he felt mixed emotions. He had been excited about telling Sybil and Marilyn that he would soon be debt-free, but Sybil's response had had a sobering effect. Every time he talked to her, it seemed, he learned a couple more things about operating a ranch, and he had an anxious feeling that there were more surprises lurking in the future. Though his need for his neighbors' help was becoming clearer every day, this creeping erosion of his rather independent lifestyle was frustrating.

After parking in front of his bungalow, Dale made his way over to the porch swing. Swaying slowly back and forth, he let his eyes pan the landscape. Though the terrain was broken with shallow ravines, splotched with mesquite and cedar, and dented with swales and knolls, he guessed the blue horizon was at least four miles distant. A quick calculation told him that the semicircle within his view must cover twenty to twenty-five square miles. Turning westward, he focused on the slowly fading paints the natives' Sun Boy had splashed on the western horizon. The expanse and serenity quickly settled his emotions. With his frustration and worries about future roadblocks dispelled, he welcomed whatever lay ahead. He was where he wanted to be, and nothing was going to drive him away.

Early Monday morning, confident that the sale of his Ohio land would not only pay off his loan but would add a little over fifteen thousand dollars to his bank account, Dale began planning for stocking his ranch. He settled on forty to fifty head of cattle, thinking that was all he could afford. Looking after a herd of cows, even a relatively small one, would necessitate a few other things. Rounding up cattle hidden amid thickets of mesquite bushes, scrub oaks, and dense cedars, and driving them out of rock-strewn ravines required something more maneuverable than even a four-wheeler. He would need a horse and all the trappings that go with a cowpony. And as Sybil had said, a pickup and trailer would be essential for periodically taking a few head of cattle to and from the sale barn, as well as for hauling ranch supplies from town.

Right after lunch James Knox called Dale and explained that he had faxed the paperwork to the title company in Paddock for the sale of the Ohio property. Dale just needed to drop by, sign the papers, and get them express mailed back to his office, which Dale did immediately.

The following morning, the realtor called again and explained that Dale's ranch loan was paid off and the fifteen thousand five hundred dollars left over from the sale had been wired to his bank account in Paddock.

After calling the bank and verifying the deposit, Dale contacted Sammy Burns, the Wichita Falls cattle dealer. When Burns asked for details regarding the type of cattle he wanted, Dale explained that Sybil Stone had recommended him as one who was knowledgeable and trustworthy, so Burns was to purchase the breed and mix of cows, heifers, and calves, along with a bull, as if he were stocking his own ranch.

"I can do that, but first I'd like to get more information about what kind of herd you're looking for. It takes a hearty breed to thrive out here," Burns said. "Can you meet me in Childress Saturday morning?"

Dale agreed to be at the sale barn at nine o'clock.

Considering that he would soon have a pasture full of cattle, Dale decided it was time to get that used pickup and trailer, while he still had money enough to afford them. Who knew how quickly he might have to haul feed, a cow to the vet, or any of a hundred other things that would not fit in his old car.

Dale drove to town for lunch, pulling in at Martha's Café. When he stepped inside, he spotted Charles Kennemer, who motioned him over to share a table. While visiting, Dale mentioned that he was in the market for a used pickup and trailer.

"I know a fellow just out of town who sells used ranch equipment, including pickups. It might be worth your time to check with him before you drive all the way to Childress or Vernon."

"I'll do that," Dale said. "Could you tell me how to locate this fellow?"

"When we've finished lunch, I'll go out there with you. This old dealer's a friend, and I just might be able to persuade him to cut his price a few dollars."

Five minutes later, the principal climbed into the passenger seat of Dale's car and guided him to a farm south of Paddock just off Highway 83. The principal explained to the fellow that Dale was the new basketball coach and a startup rancher, and asked for the best deal available.

"You the newcomer who bought the Estes Ranch?" the dealer asked Dale.

When Dale confirmed that he was, the fellow showed him the pickup and trailer that Claude Estes had left to be sold. Describing the truck as "used" was an understatement, but it was reliable and the trailer was in good shape. Within an hour Dale had written a check for nine thousand dollars and was leading the way out to the ranch with Kennemer following in Claude Estes's old pickup with the trailer hitched behind.

While driving Kennemer back to town, Dale mentioned that he needed a good saddle pony. Again, the principal told Dale where he might get one at a reasonable price.

"If you're interested, I'll call Will and tell him to expect you."

The following morning, Dale purchased the sorrel mare that Kennemer had recommended, loaded her in his trailer, threw an old saddle and bridle in the pickup bed, and headed for Seed & Feed Supply to get a few sacks of corn. He then hauled his loot to the ranch.

Anxious to feel like a real cowboy, that afternoon Dale saddled up the sorrel, climbed aboard, and headed out to ride the fence line. The perimeter of the ranch was over three miles in length, and he soon learned another lesson. Sitting astride a horse for a couple of hours takes a toll, especially on the uninitiated. When Dale finally got back to the ranch house, he could hardly stand up. After tying his horse to a fence post, he hobbled to the front porch and slumped into the swing, releasing a long moan.

From sports, he knew that soreness would get worse with inactivity, so after a short rest, he led the pony to the stables, unsaddled her, and poured two big scoops of corn into a trough. While the mare ate, Dale pulled the pickup over to the storage shed and pitched in a handsaw, an axe, a half spool of barbed wire, a sack of staples, and some fence-mending tools. On his marathon ride, he had found a few posts that needed replacing, so he headed for a thicket of cedar trees where he cut and trimmed about a dozen fence posts which he chunked into the bed of the pickup and headed for the house.

The sun was down when Dale got back to the bungalow, sore, tired, and hungry. This had been his first real taste of cowboy work, and he felt a certain satisfaction amid an ample supply of physical misery. After a shower and a quick dinner, he crawled into bed, hoping that when morning came, he would be able to get up without help.

Up soon after daylight, the first few steps were difficult, but soon Dale was going again. With the cedars and fencing tools in the bed of the pickup, he managed to park close to the damaged places in the fence, where he gathered up his supplies, dug out the old post holes, and planted the new cedars. With the repairs complete, he headed back to the bungalow, arriving in time to shower and dress for Wednesday night church.

Joining Sybil, they headed for the First United Methodist Church where Dale met more of the membership during the seven o'clock dinner, primarily as a result of her taking him around and introducing him to most everyone there.

After the brief church service, they stopped by the Stone Place for coffee and a dessert Sybil had prepared earlier. While relaxing, Dale brought his neighbor up to date on the progress he had made at the ranch.

"I called Sammy Burns," he said. "I'll meet him Saturday morning to work out the details, but I expect to have forty to fifty cows grazing on my place by late next week."

"Congratulations," she said, then paused. "Now, that's when the real work begins."

"Yeah, and that worries me a bit. Not the work, but the heart of winter feeding comes right in the middle of the basketball season."

"We'll help you those times you have to be gone with the team."

"I'm afraid it'll get to be too much. I'm thinking I may need to hire someone to occasionally hay the cattle."

"Every winter we pay Clyde Martin to help feed ours," Sybil said. "We can all pitch in and get you through this first winter, and then after you've sold a crop or two of steers, maybe you can afford your own helper."

"That's agreeable so long as you allow me to pay a proportionate amount of Clyde's salary," Dale said as he stood and headed for the door.

"You'll have about half the herd we run," Sybil said. "Feeding ours takes about two hours a day, and we pay Clyde ten dollars an hour. I expect he can feed yours in an hour. We'll pay him for both of us, and then you can write us a weekly check for your part."

"At most, I'll need help a couple of afternoons a week, and I'll be sure and let you know ahead when I'll be out of town."

The following day, Dale spent most of the morning working on a budget. Recent expenditures and commitments, in addition to fifteen thousand dollars set aside to pay for the cattle, had drained his finances from a little over thirty thousand dollars to less than eight thousand, and hay for winter feed would consume most of that. His first school check would not arrive until late September, so until then he would have to skimp to get by, but he considered that a small price to pay for realizing his life-long dream.

That afternoon Dale worked in the barn and shed, inventorying and arranging the ranch tools that Claude Estes had left. Finding a couple of cracked floorboards in the storage room, he made repairs, along with patching some of the railings on the loading chute and feed troughs in the horse stalls.

From the first day Dale arrived in Cottle County, he recognized that the most precious commodity in the area was water. On the grasslands back East a cattleman could run several head of stock per acre, but in West Texas, the ratio was reversed. Estes had warned Dale that his ranch would support at most a cow for every ten acres. Only with plenty of water, could that ratio be improved. Deep wells provided drinking water and enough for limited irrigation of field crops, but it would take a sizeable lake to change the dynamics of the local cattle industry. With that in mind, Dale saddled the mare on Friday morning and headed for the chasm that the locals called Stone Canyon.

Reining the sorrel mare into one of the shallow ravines, Dale followed it to the dry canyon bed and continued along its descending southward path, watching the red walls grow taller and taller as they angled inward like a funnel. The farther Dale rode, the more signs he saw of debris washed up against bushes by some past rushing water. When he reached the one mile mark, he came to a fence that separated his property from the Thompson Ranch. Anxious to explore the canyon farther, Dale swung down and tied the sorrel to a bush on the shady side of the canyon floor.

After vaulting the fence, Dale continued, wending this way among the brush and large rocks that cluttered the narrowing canyon bed. Periodically, Dale examined the walls of the canyon and found the high-water mark gradually climbing. Having walked a couple of miles, he was satisfied that in the not-too-distant past the canyon had carried a five-foot-deep torrent of water. What if that water could be captured? he thought.

Walking back to his horse, Dale glanced skyward, picturing clear blue water filling the canyon to a depth of forty or fifty feet. That is when he learned another West Texas lesson.

The toe of his boot caught under the edge of a partially embedded, flattop rock, causing him to stumble. As he fell, he lunged forward to clear the three-foot-wide rock, extending his hands in front to cushion the fall. Crashing onto the sandy ground, his head missed another rock by less than a foot. Unhurt but feeling foolish, Dale started to push himself up when he heard a sound unlike anything he had ever experienced. Yet, he immediately knew what it was. He froze while staring down at his feet. The diamondback was coiled, shaking its rattler-ringed tail and repeatedly feinting strikes with its raised head while nervously flicking its tongue.

Trying to control his labored breathing, Dale held still, straining to maintain his awkward position. Gradually the snake lowered its head until it disappeared behind Dale's boots. Glancing slightly to the side, Dale could see the slithering coils slowly unwinding. He could not be sure if the snake was headed toward him or back under the rock, and he did not dare move to find out. Suddenly, he wished the legs of his jeans fit tighter around his boot tops. After what seemed like five minutes, he decided the snake had gone elsewhere, and at glacier speed, he pulled his feet toward his body. When he felt sure the snake was gone, he jumped up, and without taking time to satisfy his curiosity, he sprinted up the canyon toward his horse.

Back in the saddle, Dale gladly reined the mare around and headed home. In spite of the fright still pumping through his veins, Dale was satisfied that the canyon might provide a solution to his need for storing an abundance of water.

Saturday morning Dale kept his nine o'clock appointment with Sammy Burns at the sale barn in Childress. After introductions, Dale followed the buyer out among the stock pens where the cattleman made several suggestions, pointing out specific features of the cows and calves.

"I'll go to a couple of auctions next week," Burns said. "I expect to fill your order from them. I'll get as many Brangus cattle as I can, and you can expect to pay three hundred for a cow, three seventy-five for a mother and calf, and as much as seven hundred for a good bull. To that, you can add three percent for my fee."

"Get the best you can for not more than fifteen thousand dollars," Dale replied. "Have them delivered to the old Estes Ranch seven miles west of Paddock."

Before heading south on Highway 83, Dale stopped at a convenience store to fill up with gas. When he stepped inside to pay, the man in line in front of him purchased a handful of lottery tickets, which got Dale to thinking. A few million dollars would not only solve all his financial woes, it would allow him to quickly expand his ranch and grow his herd of cattle.

"What's the jackpot at right now?" Dale asked as he handed over his gasoline money.

"Seventy-two million," the storekeeper said. "What would you do with it, if you should win?"

"I'm sure I could think of something," Dale replied, picturing a Texas-size ranch with cattle on every hill in sight, along with a new pickup and a fancy tractor. He might even build a real ranch house.

Somewhat impulsively, Dale reached into his pocket and pulled out a five-dollar bill.

"Give me five lottery tickets," he said, feeling foolish for throwing away money when his budget indicated he should be pinching his pennies.

As he drove away with the tickets stuffed in his shirt pocket, he wondered just how much of the jackpot would make it into his bank account, if he should win. Regardless, he concluded, it would be a sizeable fortune, especially to him. Then, he remembered something his dad had said: "A man is more likely to be struck by lightning than win a lottery."

Suddenly, Dale felt terribly foolish. But it was done, and he could not undo it.

5 —

Saturday night, Dale slumped into a chair and flipped on the television to catch the news and the weather report. During an advertisement, he stepped into the kitchen and fixed himself a glass of ice water, and when he returned, the winning lottery numbers were displayed on the television screen. The image of the five tickets he had purchased flashed into his head. But, where were they?

In a panic, Dale grabbed a pencil and flipped over an old sales ticket on the lamp table to his right. Hurriedly he scribbled down the numbers, keeping his eyes glued to the screen. Then, he jumped up and began searching for the tickets, which he found in the pocket of the shirt he had thrown in the clothes hamper earlier.

Feeling a bit ridiculous, he compared the first ticket to the list, but found no match. He got the same result from the second number, but then the third ticket appeared to match the last winning number. Dale blinked his eyes and slid the ticket right under the scribbled numerals. Digit by digit, he checked the ticket number against his writing. Sure enough, if the third figure he had penciled in was a seven, as he believed, the numbers matched.

He let out a panther yell while bouncing around the room as if on a pogo stick, shouting and shoving his hands in the air like an official signaling a touchdown.

"My worries are over!" he yelled. "I can get a real pickup, a tractor, whatever I need. I can have a real Texas ranch."

Then it popped into his mind that the numeral two, without a tail, looked much like a seven. Grabbing the pencil, he made both and compared. But earlier he had copied the numbers in such a hurry. With his heart pounding, he erased the tail on the numeral two. Sure enough, the similarity was scary. How could he be sure?

A quick look at the back of the tickets revealed a toll-free number. He grabbed the phone and punched in the digits. Working his way through a menu of questions, he got a recording of the winning numbers. He listened intently, writing as the voice called out the numerals. There it was; the third digit was a seven. He had won!

Then he recalled that one of the menu options was a description of how a winner could claim the money. He called the number again.

One could receive his winnings, the message explained, over as many as twenty-five years, but the option he had chosen was a one-time, lump-sum payout, which meant he would get about half of the jackpot. That amount would then be further reduced another thirty percent for taxes.

Calculating quickly, he estimated he would pocket twenty-five million dollars. With a deep sigh, he slumped back into the chair, emotionally drained.

Then it struck him that there might be other winners. If so, his share could be considerably less. Regardless, he reasoned, he had won enough to solve his problems.

Though he was afraid to believe his good fortune, he began thinking what he could do with millions of dollars. First, he could buy a new pickup and a tractor. Then he would purchase more land and stock it with more cattle. His four-hundred-acre ranch could grow to tens of thousands of acres. Rather than forty or fifty head of cattle he could have cows, calves, and horses from horizon to horizon. He would build a huge ranch house surrounded by immaculate, matching outbuildings. He would have a long, paved drive up to the house, lined with tall exotic trees. Then a different kind of thought struck him, bringing tears to his eyes.

He thought about his parents and how he wished they were alive and sharing in all of this. His dad had worked hard in that steel mill all his life, just to get by. His mom and dad had never had more than enough for necessities, month by month. They deserved this, not him. For the first time since the funeral, Dale broke down and wept.

Recovered, he thought about the Stones and how they struggled to make ends meet each month, and yet they had given so freely to him. If he should be blessed with an abundance of money, he resolved that he would relieve their burden. He wanted to drive over to Stone Place and tell them, but he knew he must not.

Until he could work through the process and actually receive his winnings, he would tell no one.

He turned the television off and stepped out into the yard. Though it was mid-July, the night air was cool at that hour, under a brilliantly clear sky in arid West Texas. Looking up at a heavenly ceiling dotted with countless blinking stars, his emotions again erupted. Why had God blessed him so? And his mother's favorite saying echoed in his mind: "To whom much is given, much is required." He knew his focus had to change from those things he selfishly wanted, to things more spiritual, to things that would benefit others. He sensed that to do otherwise would somehow bring disappointment and misery into his life, rather than happiness and comfort. It was time to put into action these tenets he had been espousing.

On Sunday morning, sitting in church with Sybil and Marilyn, Dale found it difficult to pay attention to the sermon, though he eagerly took time to offer a prayer of thanks. He found it even more difficult to keep his secret. After the service when he suggested that he take the Stones to the Steakhouse for lunch, Sybil insisted that he save his money and go home with them to have sandwiches. Dale smiled, thinking how differently she might respond if she only knew.

After lunch, Dale visited with his neighbors for a couple of hours, feeling almost giddy. That changed as he began to notice the many evidences of their meager existence, things that had gone unnoticed during past visits. Their furniture was sturdy, but visibly worn. Sybil cooked on a gas range that was probably twenty-five years old. A couple of water fans made the summers bearable, and grated space heaters drove out winter's cold. The wooden floors were clean but bore years of scars and stains. Porcelain pans were chipped and half of their drinking glasses once held peanut butter or jelly. Yet, he knew the Stones were heavyweights when measured in human worth. And it struck him that having millions of dollars would not add one iota to his goodness. "It's not what you have that counts," he had heard his mother say so many times. "It's what you do with what you have." As clearly as if they had been written on the wall before him, the words flashed into his mind: "It's what I do with this blessing that will determine my worth."

But first, he had to claim his winnings. He had decided to use an out-of-town bank to prevent any speculation regarding his winnings by Paddock locals, so on Monday morning, Dale drove to a bank in Plainview and rented a safe-deposit box, in which he stored his winning ticket with an attached note. He got two spare signature cards and stuffed them in his shirt pocket.

Dale then drove to the Stone Place Ranch where he gave the two cards to Sybil and Marilyn, asking them to sign them.

"What's this for?" Sybil asked.

"I need a safe place to store a few important papers," he explained. "I have no family, so in case something should happen to me, I would like for you to take possession of the contents of the box."

They signed and Dale returned to Plainview and filed the cards with his own. He then headed for Lubbock where he pulled into the parking lot at Plains National Bank and asked to speak to the president.

"He's busy," the assistant said. "Could someone else help you?"

"I want to open an account, one that involves several millions of dollars."

"Oh," the assistant said, rising. "Let me check with Mr. Lucas."

Within seconds a graying man of fifty, wearing a shiny charcoal-colored suit, came out and extended his hand.

"Have you handled lottery winnings for a client?" Dale asked Mr. Lucas, once they were inside his glassed-in office.

"Yes," the banker said, his eyes widening. "Did you win the recent jackpot?"

"Yes, sir, and I need advice from someone knowledgeable of the collection process."

"Do you have a lawyer?"

"No, sir."

"I suggest you contact Bob Hamilton, a local attorney. He's worked with us a couple of times on such cases."

The banker ushered Dale into a private office, gave him a phone number, and pulled the door closed as he stepped out.

Dale dialed the number, which connected him with Hamilton's secretary.

"I'm interested in Mr. Hamilton handling a multimillion-dollar financial deal for me," he explained. "Can you give me a list of clients he's helped in similar transactions?"

"Who recommended you to Mr. Hamilton?"

"Harold Lucas, president of Plains National."

After checking with the lawyer, who probably immediately called the banker, the secretary agreed and gave Dale the names and phone numbers of three clients.

Dale called Hamilton's clients and verified his reputation and integrity, and then he called Mr. Hamilton again.

"Bob Hamilton," the lawyer said when his secretary got him on the phone.

Dale explained his need and set up a meeting at Plains National at four o'clock that afternoon, as prearranged with Lucas.

After inspecting Dale's copy of the winning ticket, and verifying it against the official numbers, Hamilton outlined the process Dale needed to follow to claim the jackpot, explaining the various ways of receiving the money.

"When I bought the tickets, I chose a lump-sum payout," Dale said.

"Do you realize that you've given up half your winnings?" the lawyer asked, shaking his head.

"First, that ignores the interest I will earn on the half I will receive immediately, as well as the enormous benefits that can be realized from investing it. Also, only a few years back when Walter Mondale ran for President of the United States, he proposed to repeal the planned ten percent tax reduction, and to replace it with an increased tax burden on the citizens of this country of forty-six billion dollars. One of the keys to this was a special ten percent tax surcharge on income over one hundred thousand dollars. Under such a socialistic law, I would lose well over half of my winnings to income tax."

"But Mondale didn't win."

"Right, but who knows when some other ultra-liberal will push the same type thing through Congress. That would jeopardize all future lottery payments."

The lawyer did not share Dale's concern, but he realized that further discussion was pointless.

Hamilton then advised Dale to rent a Lubbock post office box, which he should give to the lottery officials for any mailings to him and to keep the media off his trail. The lawyer then called the lottery office to set up a meeting the next morning. Before Dale left, Bob Hamilton offered to travel to Austin with him to kick off the process.

Dale rushed back to Plainview, replaced the winning ticket in the safe-deposit box with the copy, and then headed home with the original to prepare for an early morning drive to Lubbock International Airport.

In Austin Dale received his lump-sum payout which was just under twenty-five million dollars, and flew back to Lubbock that afternoon to meet with Mr. Lucas. In the president's office, Dale presented the check and explained how he wanted to place his money.

"I want a hundred thousand dollars placed in ten checking accounts, each in a different area bank," he explained. "Also, I want two million put into a fund I can access to further God's work. I'll call it my Coins for Christ fund. The remainder I want in U. S. Treasury bonds. I'll limit my deposits in each bank to the amount that bank covers with insurance."

The banker drew up the paperwork to implement Dale's instructions, and told him he would be in touch when the money was properly distributed.

Driving home, Dale thought back over the past couple of weeks. He had gone from being over fifty thousand dollars in debt with a dwindling bank account, to being debt-free and having nearly twenty-five million stashed in two dozen banks.

"Thank you, Lord," he said. "Now, I pray for the wisdom to use it wisely."

When Mr. Lucas called two days later to tell Dale his money was in place, he asked if Dale had a will.

"No, sir. I've never needed one before, but I guess I'd better think about that."

Dale had a great deal to think about. He needed a pickup to replace his worn-out Ford and soon would need a tractor to hay his cattle, but he knew the two Stone vehicles were even more unreliable than his. He and Sybil worried every week when Marilyn took off for Lubbock in her old red Firebird. Sybil's pickup was practically wired together and should never be driven off the ranch. A less pressing but larger question dealt with what he would do with his new-found millions, beyond the general concept of buying more land and more cattle. Then there was the banker's question: to whom would he leave everything if he should suddenly die?

With regard to the latter question, it did not take him long to make up his mind. He had no family, and his neighbors meant more to him than anyone else, so Dale scribbled out a will, leaving his land, money, and all his possessions split equally between Sybil and Marilyn Stone. He took the will, along with a few other legal documents, and dropped by the bank where he had them stashed in a safe-deposit box, which only he, Sybil, and Marilyn Stone were authorized to access.

On Friday afternoon Sammy Burns called and explained that he would be delivering Dale's herd of cattle the next morning about nine o'clock.

Like a kid on Christmas morning, Dale was up early that Saturday, anxious to see the essential piece of the puzzle that would change the Roryian to a real ranch, rather than one in name only. He was pacing the front porch when two large trailer trucks pulled up a few minutes before nine, and Sammy Burns supervised the unloading of forty-one head of Brangus cows, along with twenty-one calves and a bull. Once unloaded, the cattle milled around, mooing and investigating their new home. Mother cows pushed their way through the bunched herd, bawling, until they located their calves, while a few heifers on the fringe began grazing. The scene thrilled Dale, reminding him of roundups he had seen in old western movies.

"We penned them last night, so they've been without water for fourteen hours," Burns explained as Dale wrote out a check. "They won't settle down until they've had a drink."

When Dale had paid Burns and the trucks had gone, he saddled the mare and began nudging a few of the more adventurous cows away from the herd and toward the large, circular tub kept filled with fresh water beside the windmill located near the crest of the ridge. Overflow from the tub ran into a nearby pond flanked by willows and a few young cottonwoods. Slowly, the rest of the herd followed, and when the cows smelled the water, they broke into a trot. Thinking he might get trampled in a stampede, Dale quickly heeled his pony into a gallop, surging ahead and away from the moving mass of horns and hooves.

Full of water, the cows slowly drifted away from the tub and pond and began their eager search for grass. By dark, the herd had become a rather loose unit, grazing quietly while gradually moving along to fresh patches of grass.

After church on Sunday, Sybil mentioned to Dale that Marilyn's nineteenth birthday was coming up on Wednesday of the following week, so the next day Dale stopped by to see Sybil while Marilyn was away at school.

"Will Marilyn be here for her birthday?" he asked, since Wednesday was normally her study day at Tech.

"Yes, she'll drive home Wednesday afternoon, and after church we'll have cake and ice cream. Of course, we want you to be there."

"Thanks," he said. "I'll have a little surprise for her. Also, tomorrow I need to take a trip out to Lubbock, and I thought I might take her to lunch while I'm there."

"She'd be thrilled," Sybil said. "If you'd like, I can call her tonight and let her know you'll be there."

That evening Sybil called Dale and explained that Marilyn would meet him at noon at the Denny's Restaurant on the edge of the Tech campus.

Thursday morning Dale arrived in Lubbock a little after eleven o'clock, and drove around the campus until time to meet Marilyn for lunch. He had a late breakfast while she chose a chef salad.

"I need to take care of some business," he explained when they had finished. "Do you have time to go with me?"

Having an hour and a half before her next class, she accepted his invitation, and within minutes Dale pulled into the parking lot at Plains National Bank, where he had both a checking account and a big chunk of his savings.

They stepped inside, and Dale gave his name to the assistant outside the president's large, glassed-in office. Within seconds Harold Lucas rushed out, vigorously shook Dale's hand, and then ushered him into his office. While Dale alerted the banker that he might soon be spending a hundred thousand dollars or more on pickups, tractors, and other items, the secretary showed Marilyn into a plush lounge and offered her a choice of snacks. Having just eaten, she declined and thumbed through a magazine while sipping a cup of orange juice.

A few minutes later, Dale and Lucas entered the lounge where the banker asked Dale if Marilyn was his wife.

"No," Dale said. "Don't you think she's too pretty for me?"

With no safe response coming to mind, Mr. Lucas thanked Dale for his visit and invited him to drop by anytime he was in town.

Heading back toward Tech along the loop, Dale spotted the High Plains Ford dealership ahead, took the exit and pulled up in front of several rows of new vehicles.

"Merr," he said, "if you could pick any vehicle on the lot, which one would it be?"

"Oh, Dale," she said, laughing. "What difference does it make? It'll be a long time before I can afford anything on this lot."

"But if you had a million dollars, which one would you drive home?"

"I guess I'd choose that beige Tempo over there," she finally said, halfheartedly.

"Why?"

"They're economical to drive and easy to park," she replied. "It probably gets half again the gas mileage my old Firebird gets."

"Take a good look, Merr, and be sure that's what you'd pick?"

"The Tempo," she said, somewhat frustrated with the game.

Dale took her back to Denny's for her car, and then returned to the Ford dealership, where he asked to have the Tempo cleaned up and prepared for delivery to Stone Place Ranch the following Wednesday. He wrote a check for the car but asked that the dealer hold it until notified within the next couple of days.

He then looked at pickups for himself, found the one he wanted, and wrote another check, again asking the dealer to hold it for him until the following week. After stopping by a few tractor dealers, Dale headed home.

That night when Sybil knew Marilyn would be in her room, she called her daughter.

"Honey, tell me all about lunch with Coach Rory," Sybil said.

"Mom," Marilyn replied, "lunch was wonderful, but afterward he took me to a big fancy bank."

Marilyn then proceeded to describe the royal treatment they had received there.

"Do you have any idea why?"

"No, but later when the bank president asked Dale if I was his wife, Dale said, 'Don't you think she's too pretty for me?'"

"What did the banker say?"

"He laughed nervously, and then invited Dale to drop in anytime."

"Go on."

"Then Dale stopped off at High Plains Ford and asked me to pick out a car."

"Are you serious?"

"Sure am. I chose a beige Tempo, but I saw a gorgeous blue and white F150 pickup that I'd almost kill to have."

"I wish we could get a new pickup, but we'll have to wait a while for that."

"As we were leaving the bank, I told Dale it must be nice having that banker make such a fuss over him. He said, 'It's nothing to brag about when old men and babies make a fuss over you.' Then I said, 'I'm not an old man or a baby.'"

"How did Dale respond to that?"

"He smiled, squeezed my hand, and said, 'And, I'm glad you're not.'"

"I think our neighbor is becoming quite fond of my daughter," Sybil said.

"Mom, I sure hope so. I think he's wonderful."

The following morning, Sybil telephoned Dale.

"I talked to Marilyn last night. She thoroughly enjoyed lunch and your visit."

"I probably enjoyed it more than she did," he replied.

"She also mentioned a Tempo that she looked at. I sure wish we could afford to get it for her to drive back and forth to school."

"I was surprised that she chose the Tempo."

"Oh, she's just being practical. What she'd love to have is a blue and white, extended-cab F150 pickup that she saw."

"Really?" Dale said, recalling having seen one on the lot.

"Sure, but those things cost over twenty thousand," Sybil said.

Later, Dale called the Ford dealer in Lubbock and asked him to replace his order for a pickup with one for the blue and white F150, explaining that both it and the Tempo were to be delivered the following Wednesday.

Dale found it difficult to get through the weekend without revealing his secret and showing too much excitement. After attending church with Sybil and

Marilyn, he offered to take them to lunch at the Steakhouse, but Sybil insisted that he should save his money and have lunch with them at the ranch. Since Dale was not quite ready to reveal his improved financial status, he had no luck convincing her that he could afford to buy an occasional meal for them.

After church Sunday night, Sybil invited Dale over for coffee and conversation. While Marilyn was out of the room, she suggested that Dale plan to come home with them after church on Wednesday for birthday cake. Half an hour later as Dale was leaving, Marilyn stepped out on the porch with him, and he asked her to stop by his place on her way home Wednesday, so they could share a ride to church. Then on Monday, Dale contacted one of Sybil's lady friends at the church and asked her to invite Sybil over about five o'clock Wednesday afternoon to discuss some church business. "Please keep her there until time for church," Dale said. He went on to explain that it would help him with a surprise he had planned for Sybil and Marilyn.

Right after five o'clock on Wednesday afternoon, Dale drove over to the Stone Place Ranch and took delivery of the new vehicles. He had the Tempo parked in front with a red ribbon draped around it and a big bow on the roof, and a HAPPY BIRTHDAY placard taped to the windshield. He then had the new pickup moved around behind the house before he hurried home, anticipating Marilyn's arrival about six o'clock.

When she drove up, Dale invited her to the porch swing in which they relaxed, talking about school and their ranch plans. Then about six-forty, they drove on to church where they met Sybil.

After dinner and the brief service, they drove out to the Stone Place ranch, Dale riding with Marilyn and Sybil following.

When the Firebird headlights hit the Tempo, Marilyn hit the brakes.

"What's that doing here?" she asked, bewildered.

"Today's your birthday, isn't it?"

"Yes, but . . ."

"You'd better move on before your mother runs over us," he suggested.

Having pulled up past the Tempo, they stepped out of the Firebird, and Marilyn slowly approached the new car, which sat fully illuminated by the headlights of Sybil's pickup.

When Sybil saw the Tempo, she slammed her truck to a stop, swung the door open, and jumped out without killing the engine.

"Dale Rory," she said, "what have you done?"

"I told you I was going to have a birthday surprise for Marilyn."

"Dale, I've told you that you need to put every spare dime you've got into that ranch," she protested. "We can't let you do this."

"But it's done," he said. "And once we're inside, I'll explain why it's okay."

"Do I really get to keep it?" Marilyn asked, afraid to believe it was hers.

"Absolutely," Dale replied, as Marilyn gave him a hug.

Ten minutes later, after Marilyn had driven the Tempo down to the highway and back and Sybil had parked her pickup, the three of them stepped inside where Sybil served ice cream and cake and then gave a couple of birthday gifts to her daughter.

"Now," Sybil said, shifting her eyes to Dale, "I want you to explain how you're gonna pay for that Tempo out there."

Dale nodded his head and then handed a copy of his will to each of them.

"What's this?" Sybil asked, confusion mounting.

"It's my will," he said.

"Dale," Sybil said after scanning the document, "what in the world prompted you to do a thing like this?"

"Finally, I own a little property, and just in case something should happen to me, I want to decide who gets it, rather than have the state choose."

"You don't really think anything is going to happen to you, do you?" Marilyn asked, pleadingly.

"No, of course not, and don't you go plotting anything, cousin."

"Cousin?" Sybil asked, her frustration showing.

"Just a joke," Marilyn said, patting her mother's arm.

"This is no time for jokes," Sybil said, taking a brisk step toward Dale. "Now, I want to know what's going on here."

"Mrs. Stone," Dale said, solemnly, "you're right. You deserve an explanation. You know about the ranch property next door, but also I've just come into quite a bit of money, a little over twenty-four million dollars. So, I . . ."

"I thought you were going to be serious," Sybil said, cutting him off.

"I couldn't be more serious, Mrs. Stone," he replied, and then glanced over at Marilyn who looked as if she had turned to granite with her mouth agape.

"Dale Rory," Sybil said, grabbing the front of his shirt with both hands. "Do you mean to tell me that that poor rancher who I've worried myself sick over and dedicated my bedtime prayers to, that that orphan-of-a-boy that I've tried every way under the sun to help get ahead, that he has twenty-four million American dollars in the bank!"

"I'm afraid so," he replied, smiling.

"Thank you, Lord," she said, rolling her eyes heavenward as she threw her arms around him. "Dale, I've just got to hug your neck."

And she did, along with her daughter, swapping tears all around. It was during those few seconds that Dale realized how right he was to will his possessions to these two women. Obviously, their tears sprung from relief from worry that their new neighbor and young friend might lose everything before he learned how to run a ranch.

"Now," Dale said, when everyone had finally calmed down, "Marilyn, you have a decision to make."

"Like what?" she said, followed by a nervous laugh.

"Like which vehicle do you really want?" Dale said.

"Oh, I love the Tempo," she said, pressing the fingertips of praying hands to her chin.

"But," Dale said, stepping over and flipping on the backyard lights, "would you trade it for this?"

Marilyn screamed when she saw the blue and white, extended-cab pickup, bringing Sybil to the door in a run. Before her mother got there, Marilyn burst through the doorway and into the yard, the beige Tempo suddenly a vague memory.

"Dale Rory," Sybil said, standing beside him and watching her daughter climb into the truck, "what has come over you?"

"Whatever it is," he said, looping his arm around her waist, "it's going to continue until I see you sitting in your own new vehicle."

"Now hold on, Dale," Sybil said. "Willing your stuff to us is one thing, but buying automobiles for us is quite another."

"Ma'am," Dale said, "I yielded when you insisted on loaning me your bedroom furniture, and when you brushed aside my complaints and brought over dishes, silverware, pots, and pans. I agreed to borrow your tractor and put what money I had into cattle and hay. I yielded because you insisted it was the right thing to do. Well, now I'm telling you this is the right thing to do, and I won't budge an inch this time."

"It's a shame when the student turns his lessons against his teacher," Sybil said, and then smiled. "But I warn you, Dale Rory, I'm mighty particular what color vehicle I drive."

They laughed and headed for the pickup where Marilyn was waving them to come along for a ride.

"Be thinking of what kind of vehicle you want," Dale said as Sybil climbed into the seat beside her daughter. "And be as picky as you please about the color."

After riding to town and back, Sybil asked Dale how he would return the Tempo.

"I'm sure the dealer will be glad to take it back when he delivers your present," he replied.

Sybil never told Dale what automobile she preferred, so before he left that evening, he asked Marilyn.

"She'd love to have a red Grand Marquis," she said without hesitation.

"I'll get it delivered late Friday afternoon, allowing time for you to get here before it arrives."

The next day Dale called the Ford dealer and ordered the Marquis, to be delivered as planned. He then called the Plains National Bank in Lubbock and had the money wired to the dealership.

Now that his neighbors knew his secret, he ordered a pickup for himself. Then he made a trip to Childress and purchased a one hundred twenty-five horsepower tractor with an air-conditioned cab and all the necessary implements.

Friday afternoon about five, Marilyn pulled up at the Roryian Ranch in her new pickup, explaining that she managed to get away from school a little earlier than usual.

"I'm so anxious to see Mom when her car arrives," she explained.

After a brief conversation, they drove over to Stone Place, and had hardly stepped inside when the delivery truck showed up.

When Sybil realized what was happening, her hands flew to her face, and she began crying.

"I can't believe it, I just can't believe it," she repeated over and over.

But, soon enough she did, sitting behind the steering wheel and admiring the interior and all the gadgets while the trucker loaded up the Tempo. Soon, Dale and Marilyn climbed in, and they took a ride to town where Dale treated them to dinner at the Steakhouse. Sybil chose a table where she could look out the window and keep an eye on her shiny Marquis.

"With a car that pretty," she said, "they ought to give me a reserved parking spot."

After cake and coffee back at the ranch, Dale headed home, while Sybil and Marilyn stood on their porch watching his taillights slowly disappear.

"Mom," Marilyn said softly, "I love him."

Sybil slipped her arm around her daughter and pulled her close, both momentarily too emotional to speak.

"Does he know?" Sybil finally asked.

"You're the only one I've told," Marilyn explained, still staring ahead.

"Honey, you couldn't find a better man, leastwise not on this earth," her mother said, dabbing at the corners of her eyes. "He couldn't be better, even if his heart was made of pure gold."

6 —

With the start of school only three weeks away, Dale was anxious to get a few time-consuming things done. With his tractor and new pickup delivered, the most pressing need was a supply of winter hay.

Sybil gave him the name of the man who supplied her ranch, and Dale made arrangements for fifty round bales to be delivered on Wednesday. He spent the next day clearing out the open side of the big barn, which was cluttered with the remains of year-old hay. Using his new tractor with its hydraulic hayfork, he scattered the yellow straw throughout the stables and the cattle pens where water tended to collect. Then when the new hay was delivered and unloaded, he turned his tractor to stacking it in the big barn.

With the financial means available, he then concentrated on expanding his ranch. Knowing this process would be time-consuming, especially for him, he decided to first focus on hiring a ranch foreman who would be both a source of expertise and also required to manage the size operation he had in mind.

He began his search by asking for recommendations from Sybil and Marilyn.

"There are lots of big ranches around here," Sybil said. "No doubt, we can locate you a qualified foremen."

"Obviously he's got to have ranching experience," Dale said. "In addition, I want a man I can trust completely. He'll live on the ranch and make decisions even when I'm gone. And I'll set up a bank account for him so he can buy whatever is needed."

Sybil suggested that Dale give her a few days to make some phone calls and talk to a couple of her rancher friends.

"There's a man named Tom Jordan who lives in Clarendon," Sybil reported back to Dale two days later. "I'm told he's the kind of man you're looking for."

Sybil proceeded to share a few details about the candidate, including his past employment, his community involvement, his wife and family, and his church participation.

Convinced, Dale called Jordan and explained that he had moved down from Ohio, bought a ranch, and needed a foreman.

"Mr. Rory," the man said, "I grew up on a ranch and still help out now and then, but I've opened a saddlery and leather-goods shop here, so I'm really not interested in pulling up roots and relocating."

"Mr. Jordan, I'd like to come to Clarendon and meet you," Dale said. "Give me an hour to explain my offer, and if you're still not interested, that'll be the end of it."

Tom Jordan agreed, and Dale drove to Clarendon, arriving at the Dairy Queen near the west side of town at three o'clock the following afternoon.

Stepping inside, Dale soon spotted a wiry, thirty-year-old man approaching from a booth to the right, wearing Wrangler jeans, a western straw hat, and cowboy boots.

"You must be Mr. Rory," the man said. "I'm Tom Jordan."

"How'd you recognize me?" Dale asked, shaking the man's hand.

"I know most of the people who come in here for lunch," Jordan said, and then pointed at Dale's university ring with a diamond set inside a large O. "And, we don't have many visitors from Ohio."

They laughed, ordered hamburgers with soft drinks, and sought out a corner table.

"I'm a coach and teacher, not an experienced rancher," Dale explained. "So, I need a man who knows ranching, and who's willing and capable of taking over the cattle operation. I'm looking more for a partner than a foreman, and I'm prepared to compensate him accordingly."

Dale then gave a brief description of his background and how he grew up with the dream of coaching and owning a ranch in West Texas.

"The Roryian is a small operation right now," Dale said, "but I plan to expand it in several ways."

He went on to explain that within the first year, he hoped to multiply the size of the ranch tenfold. The foreman would be an integral part in making all decisions regarding additional land, cattle, feed and care operations, as well as growth in facilities.

"This area has limited water," Dale said, stating the obvious. "I want to overcome that limitation, not only for my ranch but for the county. And being a coach and teacher, I have a keen interest in kids."

Dale went on to describe his dream of constructing an activities center on the ranch, including a gymnasium, a softball field, and possibly a lake. He would hold summer basketball camps there, and would invite various other area youth groups to use the facility. Jordan's two youngsters could participate in any and all events without charge.

"Mr. Jordan, if you take the job, I'll purchase a double-wide, prefabbed home for you and your family, and I'll let you and your wife pick the one you want."

"What about salary?" Jordan asked.

"Three thousand dollars a month with utilities paid, and I'll provide an old pickup for your use on the ranch."

"Mr. Rory, I'll admit that I'm interested," Jordan said. "But, I need to discuss this with my wife."

"That's understandable," Dale said, handing a fact-sheet to Jordan. "This spells out the details of what I've offered and my phone number. You're the kind of man I want helping me establish what I expect to be a model ranch, and I hope you and your wife find it to be an exciting opportunity."

"Mr. Rory, would you have time to drop by and meet my wife and family?"

Soon Dale was describing his plans to Clara Jordan, watching the redhead's green eyes light up when he mentioned the activities building and youth activities.

"Mr. Rory, would there be anything I could do to help with the youth program you have planned?"

"Yes, ma'am. If you're interested in helping with the campers' meals, laundry, and performing general housekeeping chores around the activities building, I'll pay you fair wages for your time."

Clara looped her arms around their two children and smiled at her husband, indicating her interest as clearly as if she had shouted the words.

"Mr. Rory, you're new to this area and a startup rancher," Jordan said. "How can we be sure you'll make a go of it, and that you'll follow through with your expansion plans?"

"Mr. Jordan, I am new here, but the idea isn't new to me. As I mentioned earlier, I've dreamed of doing this since I was a twelve-year-old. Also, I have the financial means to do the things I've mentioned, whether or not the ranch produces enough income to sustain itself in the next several years. But ultimately you have to decide to accept my offer, or reject it, based on your assessment of me. Our relationship has to be based on trust. I've already made up my mind that I can trust you with hundreds of thousands of dollars. Now, you have to decide if you trust me to do what's fair and right for you and your family."

"We'll talk about it and be in touch in a couple of days," Jordan said, nodding toward his family.

As Dale headed back to Paddock, he felt good about Tom and Clara Jordan, a young, clean-cut couple with an eight-year-old boy and a six-year-old girl. They symbolized the loving family he remembered from his youth, and he hoped they would find his offer agreeable.

The next day when Tom Jordan called to accept the foreman's job, Dale asked what had convinced him.

"I'd say your enthusiasm for what you're doing, your plans for constant growth and improvement, and . . . well, what Clara saw as your passion for helping young people."

"Mr. Jordan, I'm glad that you and Clara share a concern for kids. Now, I hope you'll take your family to see some double-wide homes and pick out the one you like best. When you've done that, call me with the details, and I'll make arrangements to purchase it and get it moved to the ranch. If you and your wife have time to drive down this Saturday, I'll be glad to show you around the property and let you decide where you would like to set your home."

The new foreman accepted Dale's invitation and brought his family to the ranch Saturday morning. After he and Dale had discussed other building plans, Tom and Clara Jordan staked off the site for their home. Three days later Tom called from Plainview. He and his wife had selected a Heritage Homes double-wide. Dale jotted down the specifics and then asked to speak with the salesman. After working out the price and delivery details, including directions to the ranch, Dale agreed to mail a money order.

With only two weeks remaining before the first day of classes, Dale dropped by the school administration offices and got copies of the textbooks he would use. On the way to his assigned classroom, he met some of the other teachers.

"Welcome to Paddock High. I'm Betty Green," a particularly friendly teacher said. "I teach home economics, so if you ever need a snack, I can always scrounge up something."

"And I'm Margie Walker," a tall, lean woman said. "I teach biology and coach the girls' basketball team. I hope we can get together and see how we might help each other prepare for the upcoming season."

Dale had just assured Coach Walker that he would love to work together on their basketball programs, when a six-foot-four, two-hundred-forty-pound man stepped up, and extended his meaty hand.

"I'm Caleb Oaks," the man said, smiling. "You may hear the kids call me 'Scrub' or 'Tiny,' though I can't imagine why. I teach history and shop."

"I hope they're as kind when they refer to me," Dale said with a laugh.

After visiting with a few other teachers, Dale finally made it to his room where he familiarized himself with the layout and checked his desk for chalk and other supplies. Satisfied, he returned to the ranch.

On Friday morning prior to the first day of school, Dale attended a reception for all the high school teachers. Principal Kennemer introduced him, along with two other new teachers, and while they all enjoyed refreshments, Dale met more of his colleagues. They identified a few of his basketball players who were especially good students, along with a couple of marginal ones. Dale encouraged the teachers to let him know if, at any time, they should become concerned about the classroom performance or behavior of any of his players.

"These boys will represent our school, both here in town as well as in our opponents' cities," Dale explained. "I expect them to be ambassadors for the school and role models for our other students."

He realized some might consider the comment to be pompous, but for those he hoped to prove his sincerity in the months ahead.

Dale especially enjoyed seeing Margie Walker again. He knew from conversations with Marilyn that she was a dedicated and enthusiastic coach. After explaining his background, Dale mentioned his plans to have a summer basketball camp.

"That would be wonderful," Margie said. "Do you think the school will allow us to use the gym?"

"I've mentioned it to Superintendent Phillips," Dale replied. "In any case, I plan to build an activities building on my ranch, and it'll include a basketball court. I'm sure we can somehow manage both a camp for boys and one for girls."

Dale promised to keep Margie posted on his progress toward the basketball camps, and she offered to support the project in any way possible.

The weekend passed quickly, and on Monday Dale showed up early in his classroom. After a full day of classes, in which he met his students and supplied them with textbooks and his expectations for the semester, he ended the day with his first meeting with the basketball team.

"The first building block for any successful team is character," he explained. "Character has nothing to do with how good a player you are, or whether we win or lose. Your character is *who* you are."

Dale went on to explain that any player who shows disrespect for his fellow players, for his school, for his family, or for his opponent, will be dismissed from the team.

"Developing a winning basketball program here in Paddock starts with you, but it will also reach down to the lower grades," he said. "Remember that everywhere you go and everything you do, the young eyes of eighth and ninth graders will be on you; they'll emulate your behavior. You'll give one hundred percent effort in every practice and every game because to do less would be cheating your teammates, your school, and yourself."

The coach also explained that he expected the same from them in their classrooms.

"You're grades must be better than those of the average Paddock High student," he said. "If you don't perform up to standard in your classes, you'll be suspended from the team until you correct the deficiency."

Next, he encouraged the players to bring their concerns to him, whether related to basketball or not.

"A small cut, if neglected, festers into a big problem," he told them. "And likewise, ill feelings between people can balloon into grudges and even hate.

"Now, let me tell you what you can expect from me. I'm committed to your success, both on and off the basketball court, as well as now and in the future. I'll be tough on you, demanding of you. You can expect me to put you through the most grueling physical conditioning program you have ever experienced. And for all this, you can expect to see improvement in your basketball skills every week.

"You'll learn how to properly dribble a ball, how to pass, and how to shoot. You'll be drilled in each of these basic facets of the game, developing these skills with both your hands. At times you'll think I expect too much of you. Some of you may not be willing to pay the price. But for those who have the determination to push past what you thought were your limits, you can expect to play the best basketball of your life.

"I'll make mistakes," he said, lowering his voice, "but I make this promise to you. I'll admit my mistakes and take steps to correct them, and I'll never ask more of you than I'm willing to give.

"You've all heard a lot of talk about winners and losers. The scoreboard determines wins and losses. However, contrary to what many think, the scoreboard does not determine winners and losers. Winners always give their best, every practice and every game. Anything less characterizes a loser. Now, don't misunderstand me. The scoreboard is important, just as your classroom report cards are. But when we prepare and compete at our highest possible level, we'll accept the scoreboard results. We won't always win, but we'll never be satisfied with losing. We'll let the fans talk about our wins, while we focus on correcting the reasons for our losses, using them to motivate us to work harder, to improve, and to win the next time.

"Now, I want to make one final point. I'm more interested in your success in life than on the basketball court. Personally, I believe there is a supreme being that watches over and cares for us. We'll receive rewards for being the best that we can be, but also we'll be blessed in ways beyond our control. In all our good fortune, we have a responsibility to use it wisely, and to share it with those who are less fortunate.

"I understand the constitutional law that requires separation of church and state, and I support it one hundred percent. I don't want our lawmakers dictating religion, nor do I want the church to control our laws. However, I don't believe that it means we are to drop our faith or hide our beliefs in any life situation, including in our educational environment. To do so would be as ridiculous as separating eating from your physical nutritional needs. We must allow the free exercise of individual faiths, while not forcing anyone to participate against their will.

"So, I encourage each of you to seek your own source of faith and to be active and faithful in whatever you choose. If it leads you to a specific church or organization, attend regularly, get involved, and practice your beliefs daily. Be no less diligent in spiritual matters than you are in school and in basketball."

When the boys were gone, Dale hoped he had struck a balance between the demands he would make of his players and the rewards they could expect from their dedicated efforts. He had introduced them to the basics of his philosophy of coaching basketball, but in the weeks ahead he would both reinforce those ideas as well as add new ones. The growth and improvement process would require persistence and patience from both him and his players. Being a first-year coach, he anticipated making mistakes, but he had no doubts regarding his approach and ultimate success.

That night he sat at his computer and composed a letter to his players and their parents, hoping to communicate clearly to both. His theme was that to be successful in a team sport, as well as in society, one must expand his vision from self to a larger sphere. The individual traits that he listed as essential in building a winning team were appreciation for others, the desire to see others succeed, willingness to put team goals ahead of individual goals, and to always behave with dignity. "When you enter the Paddock Palominos' dressing room, you've got to check your ego at the door," he explained. In fact, he insisted that an elevated understanding of the value of others is preferable in all aspects of life, and that when a group does so, the resulting whole will exceed the sum of the parts, which is the ultimate team concept.

For the first several weeks of school, Dale did not schedule practice sessions, however, he opened the gymnasium and made basketballs available to players who showed up. He was always there, working on his own ball-handling skills, with the hope that the players would observe and try the same drills.

The third day, Chris Powell, the best player from the prior season, showed up and persuaded the other boys to scrimmage, two-on-two. Chris was taller and skilled, so he dominated the scoring.

Dale took time out to watch and noticed that Chris always handled the ball with his right hand.

"Let me show you how to guard him," the coach said to the boy who was matched up against Chris.

Dale then positioned himself just off Chris's right shoulder, forcing him to dribble to his left. The boy's awkwardness made controlling the ball difficult, so Dale easily stole it from him. The coach repeated this three times, frustrating the talented player while clearly pointing out his weakness.

Dale then took the ball and told Chris to guard him. When Dale made a move to his right, Chris jumped that direction to cut him off, but then Dale used a crossover dribble to shift the ball to his left hand and drove past the defender for an easy left-handed layup. Deciding his coach was left-handed, Chris cheated toward Dale's left shoulder, resulting in his coach slipping past him to the right.

"It's not fair," Chris blurted out. "You're older and played in college."

Dale then stepped aside and let the younger player guard the more talented boy, and of course he mimicked Dale's over-shift technique. Though he did not steal the ball, he stopped Chris cold, allowing his team to win the contest.

Frustrated, Chris headed for the exit, but Dale intercepted him.

"Son," the coach explained, "you've got good basketball talent and instincts, but to be a great player, you need to develop your left side skills."

Dale worked with him for a few minutes, but when Chris kept fumbling the ball away when dribbling with his left hand, he became embarrassed and frustrated and finally stormed out of the gymnasium.

The next day Dale smiled when he saw two of the boys going up and down the court, dribbling with their weaker hand. At first they moved along slowly, frequently glancing at the ball, but soon they were moving faster and becoming more comfortable with handling the ball with either hand. Also, Dale would shoot close-in shots with his left hand, over and over, gradually increasing the complexity of the shots. The boys marveled at his dexterity, and soon they were trying it themselves. Initially, they laughed at their weak efforts, but after a few days their awkwardness began to disappear. Soon six boys were showing up regularly. After doing a few drills, they would scrimmage half court. Immediately the boys who had developed skills with their weaker hand dominated play, inspiring the others to work on their off-hand skills.

When the boys would leave in the late afternoon, Dale would still be practicing goals by shooting one hundred consecutive shots from two different court positions. Each day he would do the same from two new positions. Soon the boys were staying later in the afternoons and similarly practicing their shots.

Eventually, Chris, the talented player, returned to the gymnasium and grudgingly joined his fellow players in working on his ball-handling dexterity.

A month after opening the gymnasium, most every team member would show up in the afternoons to work on basketball skills. The late joiners quickly realized that some of the others had made noticeable improvement over their prior season's ability. In fact, Eddie Krodle, who had been a marginal backup guard the prior season, was the dominant player in their afternoon scrimmages. More and more the newcomers dedicated their afternoons to dexterity drills and repetitious shooting, rather than scrimmaging.

At the end of the first six weeks of school, Dale had each player bring his report card to the gymnasium after their last class. He was delighted to see that most of the players had at least a B+ average, and Donald Winters, a senior forward with limited athletic ability, had made the Honor Roll with an A+ average. However, the coach found two players, Marty and Josh, with less than a seventy average in at least one subject.

"Boys, don't come back to the gym until you have improved your grade by at least ten points," Dale said. "If you haven't elevated it to a passing grade by the time we start official practices, you won't be allowed to participate."

Ten days later, the pair showed up with their most recent test scores, and both had scored ninety or above. Encouraged, Dale commended them and let the boys join in practice that afternoon, with the understanding they would maintain the improvement. After practice, Josh lingered around, shooting jump shots, while the other boys were taking showers. Dale noticed, walked over, and suggested that he vertically align the elbow of his shooting arm with his hand and shoulder.

"Coach," Josh said after trying a few more shots, "Donald Winters spent hours tutoring me and Marty. Without his help, we couldn't have improved our grades so quickly. I thought you should know."

Dale thanked Josh for the tip and sent him to the dressing room.

"Donald," the coach called out when he saw Winters leaving the gymnasium. "I understand that you helped a couple of your teammates with their grades."

"Yes, sir. I tried to."

"I couldn't be prouder of you if you had just made the winning goal for the district championship," the coach said. "I've never seen a better example of unselfishness and teamwork."

"Thanks, Coach," Winters said, pleased but a little embarrassed.

"Donald, obviously you are a good student in the classroom, but I've also noticed how quickly you catch on to basketball concepts. Maybe you should consider coaching someday."

From that day, Donald Winters showed an obvious interest in everything Dale did with the team. And once regular practice sessions began, the coach noticed that after he had introduced a new play or defensive concept, later other players would ask Donald to explain or demonstrate. Off the court, Winters also became the unofficial tutor for the team, and by the time the season began, no player had less than an eighty average in any course.

Throughout these early weeks of school, Dale saw less of Sybil and Marilyn. He attended church with them on Sundays and missed few of the Wednesday night dinners, but otherwise he worked with this basketball players and wrote up lesson plans for algebra I, algebra II, and geometry each night. When he was not preparing for class, he was making out tests or grading papers until eleven o'clock most every night. Though he spent Saturday mornings checking on things at the ranch, he and Marilyn managed to spend time together each Saturday afternoon, and occasionally they took Sybil with them to the Steakhouse on Saturday nights.

Now with regular practices underway, to be followed with two ballgames a week, his schedule was about to get even tighter.

7 ___

While Dale was teaching and working with his basketball team, Tom Jordan moved his family into the double-wide and took over the daily operation of the ranch. He replaced the dilapidated gates with metal ones, and set several new posts supporting the old corral and rebuilt the loading chute.

In addition, based on Dale's specifications, Jordan worked with Ted Jackson, a Lubbock architect, to design the activities building for the ranch, and he had received bids from two different contractors to construct the facility. After reviewing the proposals with Dale, Jordan met with both contractors to scrutinize their bids. After making a few minor adjustments, he then made his recommendation to Dale.

Meanwhile, Marilyn had finished up her second summer semester at Tech and was taking a couple of correspondence courses in the fall, in addition to helping her mother around the ranch. Her decision to continue her education at home rather than driving to Lubbock was predicated on her desire to attend Dale's basketball games and to be available whenever he had time in his busy schedule.

During one of her Saturday afternoon visits with Dale at the Roryian, he suggested that they should surprise her mother by making a few needed repairs to the Stone Ranch house, including repainting the entire house.

"How can we surprise her with it?" Dale asked.

"She's been talking about driving to Vernon to check on Claude and Hazel Estes," Marilyn said. "And I know she'd love to go visit with some friends in Wichita Falls."

"If you could convince her to take three or four days off, that might be long enough," Dale said.

"I don't think she's ever been away from the ranch that long," Marilyn said. "But with her new car, she might drive up to Oklahoma City to visit with her sister."

"When do you think she'd be willing to do that?"

"Her birthday's coming up. Maybe that's the right time."

A few days later, Marilyn reported that it was all arranged. Sybil would be gone four days, returning home the afternoon of her birthday. So, Dale asked Marilyn to make all the arrangements to repair the house, expand the garage to hold two vehicles, and to repaint everything.

While her mother was gone, Marilyn stayed busy with the house improvements, while Dale dropped by each evening to check on progress and to resolve any concerns. Though extraordinarily demanding on their time, these few days were particularly enjoyable for Dale and Marilyn. After inspecting the completed work, he would usually take her to the Steakhouse in town for dinner and then return to the ranch. While she made notes regarding items to discuss with the repairmen the next morning, Dale prepared for another day of school. He would usually leave for home a little before midnight.

After her trip, Sybil returned to find a newly painted house, an expanded garage with a remote-control door opener, and a birthday party. Marilyn had invited a few friends from church, along with Dale, and when Sybil drove up, they all came out on the front porch and stretched a fifteen-foot HAPPY BIRTHDAY banner across the front. Amid tears and laughter, Sybil hugged everyone and then parked the Marquis inside the garage and joined the group inside for birthday cake.

When everyone had gone except Dale and Marilyn, Sybil stood on the front porch between them, her arms looped around each.

"I think this is the best birthday I've ever had," she said. "And I know I have you two to thank."

"You're the best mom in the whole world," Marilyn said, kissing her mother's cheek. "It thrills me to see you so happy."

"And I know you were behind this, Dale," Sybil said, squeezing him against her side. "If I had a son, he couldn't be kinder to me than you have been."

"I'd consider it a privilege to be your son, even an adopted son," he replied, tilting his head down against hers.

Marilyn then walked Dale to his truck while Sybil stepped inside.

"Dale," Marilyn said, catching his arm, "Mother's right. Due to the drought, things have been difficult for us the past few years, but since you've been here, she's been so happy. You can't imagine what you mean to her, to both of us."

"Merr," Dale said, stopping and facing her, "God has blessed me in so many ways, but the best thing He has done for me is bringing you and your mother into my life. I believe that the more God gives you, the more you are to share with others. But, I have to admit there's more involved where you're concerned."

"Please go on," Marilyn said, when Dale hesitated.

Dale dropped his eyes to hers, and then he wrapped both arms around her, pulled her close, and touched his lips to hers.

"I like the way you explain things," she said, leaning her head against his chest.

"And I'll have more to say later," Dale said, kissing her forehead. "But right now I'd better go grade some math papers."

With the architectural drawings of the activities building finalized and a construction bid accepted, Dale approved the start of construction, which would cost three hundred eighty-four thousand dollars with completion planned for mid-December. It was to be one hundred twenty feet long and eighty feet wide, with the central feature being a basketball court surrounded by a three-foot border. The pitched roof would sit atop forty-foot walls. Six-level, riser-style bleachers would occupy eighteen of the twenty-seven feet on the west side of the court, leaving room for coaches and players at courtside. Above the bleachers, five dormitory-style rooms would be constructed, with stairway access. Four of the rooms were designed to accommodate four campers each, while the fifth room would house a couple of camp instructors. The spare twenty feet at the north end of the court would be used for restrooms, dressing rooms, showers, and a small kitchen and dining area. A central air system would cool the facility in the warmer months and heat it in the winter. The synthetic surface of the court would be lined for both basketball and volleyball.

While Tom Jordan watched over the ranch and the construction of the activities building, Dale stayed busy with school and his basketball team. Beyond improving his players' skills through repetitious drills, another and more daunting challenge faced him. Through past years, his players had become accustomed to losing, to the point that winning fifty percent of their games was considered a good season. Dale believed the difference in winning and losing was often explained by attitudes rather than athletic skills. Some teams expect to win, regardless of the opponent. They expect to find a way to win even when it looks impossible. Others expect things to go wrong, even when they are ahead on the scoreboard in the final minute of the last quarter. When one of their players misses a crucial shot, commits an unwise foul, or makes a bad pass, they see the one mistake as the beginning of a downward spiral. Typically, these teams find a way to lose. And he knew that no amount of coaching brilliance could instantly change the mindset of a dozen basketball players. It was more like changing the direction of an ocean liner rather than turning a cutting horse. And winning game after game was necessary to change the boys' expectations.

As the first game approached, the coach was encouraged with the basketball skills his players had developed through the recent weeks. Joe and Chris, two junior starters returning from last year's squad, were the heart of the team, but Eddie, a reserve from the prior season who nobody expected to contribute, was pushing them with his dramatically improved skills and hustle. Added to these three was Chad, a lanky six-foot-four center with poor footwork and little jumping ability, but blessed with long arms, quick hands, and determination. The fifth starter was Jimmy, a mild-mannered kid who was the most accurate shooter on the team but who was inclined to pass up open shots in favor of the more aggressive players.

Dale's practices were grueling, dominated by drills and game-like scrimmages, followed by twenty sprints up and down the court, ten forward and ten backward, in addition to twenty laps around the court, and running up and down the bleachers ten times. The conditioning drills were then followed by practicing fifty consecutive shots from at least two different spots on the floor, and sinking ten consecutive free-throws.

When practices began running smoothly, Dale arranged to have a few eighth-grade basketball players attend the high school practices. A youngster was assigned to each varsity player and would retrieve the ball when his player practiced shots. This saved time for the shooters, gave them a sense of prestige, and taught the youngsters what high school practice was like. Dale not only wanted to instill good practice habits in his varsity players but also in the players in the youth program.

About this time, Dale arranged to have the gymnasium open on Saturday evenings. Soon players were bringing their dates to show them how well they could handle a basketball and how many consecutive shots they could make. When some of Margie's players began showing up, they would scrimmage the boys, or choose up teams with two or three girls on each side. Then parents began coming and setting up a table of snacks and drinks. It became like a family night out. Basketball fever had hit Paddock, and Dale loved it.

The early basketball schedule was relatively easy, and all the hard work paid off when the Palominos captured three wins, all by ten points or more. Then the fourth opponent, a larger school from Vernon, arrived in Paddock on a Friday night, and Dale's squad suffered its first heartbreaker, losing by two points.

Monday afternoon, Dale pointed out that his team had played intense defense for three and a half quarters, but a four-minute letdown at the end of the contest had cost them a win. Thus, he put his starters on defense and kept them there for the duration of practice. Then he added ten trips up and down the court with the players crouched in a defensive position, gradually giving ground to a second stringer dribbling the ball. The players finally headed for the showers at six o'clock.

The following day, Chris and Joe knocked on Dale's office door five minutes before practice time.

"Coach," Chris began, "we love baseball, and we want to get an early start preparing for the spring season. Basketball is just taking too much of our time, so we feel it's best if we quit now rather than later in the season."

"Boys," Dale said, "I would like you to reconsider, but only with the understanding that I will continue to expect one hundred percent effort and a commitment to winning. You're my most talented players, and the team will miss you, but I can't make an exception for you by giving you time off to practice baseball. We are going to build a winning basketball program here, but that can only be done with players who are totally committed and willing to do what's best for the team. I appreciate your candidness and the fact that you're doing this now rather than later, and I wish you the best in whatever you pursue."

And just like that, Dale had lost forty percent of his starting team, and over sixty percent of his teams' scoring. He knew the news would devastate the remainder of the squad. Some would see it as the end of any hope for a winning season.

To no one's surprise, the Palominos lost their next two games, knotting their record at 3 wins and 3 losses. Even so, Dale saw surprising potential in some of his other players. Jimmy, the reluctant shooter, had begun shooting more, making fifty-one percent of his attempts. Chad, the lanky center, had stepped up his game, both offensively and defensively. But the biggest surprise was Eddie, the guard that no one expected to be a factor. With early successes, his confidence skyrocketed, and using his quickness, ball dexterity, and hustle, he was sinking six to eight fast-break points a game, an equal amount off of drives to the goal, and another four or five points on free-throws.

Dale saw the next game as a turning point. If his team dropped to a losing record, he was concerned that his players would see history repeating itself and their confidence would sag; however, if they could defeat Crowell, a team Paddock had not whipped in eight years, his young players' confidence would soar and that might be enough to springboard them to a successful season.

Fortunately, it was a home game, giving his players the advantages of familiarity with the court and the support of their families and fans. Practices leading up to the contest were some of the best of the season, and locker room chatter was about winning rather than drawing parallels to past disappointing seasons.

The Friday night game did not start as Dale would have hoped. Crowell had a tall front line and steady guard play, a combination that shot them to a 12-3 lead. But then Chad grabbed a rebound and hit a streaking Eddie with a long pass. That was followed by Jimmy sinking two jump shots from the corner. Eddie then stole the inbound pass and made a quick layup, and a rattled Crowell team called timeout. In less than a minute of play, the Palominos had pulled to within one point of Crowell, and the crowd was going wild.

Throughout the rest of the first half, Crowell maintained a lead, though it never grew to more than three points, and at intermission the Palominos trailed, 23-22.

Dale's halftime speech praised his boys for their smart play, their hustle, and then he did something totally out of character.

"Boys, during the first half, you matched Crowell's play," he said. "Now, in the second half you're going beat them."

The room erupted with shouts, but Dale quieted them down.

"And I'll tell you why you'll win," he continued, scanning their faces. "You play unselfish basketball. You play hard. You know you can win. But most important, now those guys over there in that other dressing room know you can beat them."

Early in the third quarter, the Palominos grabbed a 28-25 lead, prompting another Crowell timeout.

"Boys," Dale told his huddled players, "after this timeout, they're going to come out and play their best basketball. We've got to fight them off, keep the pressure on, and force them into mistakes."

The two teams fought it out throughout the remainder of the third quarter, with Paddock holding a one-point advantage at its close. The Palomino fans were on their feet most of that period, showing more enthusiasm and excitement than the players could ever remember.

"You've taken their best shot, and you're still on your feet," Dale told his boys. "Now, the fourth quarter will be ours. You're in great physical shape, and with the first sign that they're wearing down, we'll press them and run the court like it's a track meet."

It was as if Dale had scripted the game. Halfway through the final quarter, Crowell began leaving shots short, failing to fight through screens, and were slow getting back on defense. Dale clasped his hands together, signaling his team to go into a full-court press.

When Crowell prepared to inbound the ball, each of Dale's players moved up snug to an opposing player. When Crowell finally put the ball in play, the Palominos made them work for every step down the court. Frustrated, an opposing guard tried a desperate shot which Chad grabbed as it caromed off the backboard. In an instant, he turned and sailed a long pass to Eddie who sank an uncontested layup.

In the next three minutes of play, the Palominos racked up twelve points off two steals of the ball and four fast-breaks, while Crowell added only two, both on free-throws. Paddock was going to win, and everybody in the gymnasium knew it.

"That was the most exciting game I've seen in a long time," Margie said to Dale, having rushed onto the court right after the final buzzer. "I was sitting with my girls, and I guarantee you they're inspired by what they saw tonight. They want me to model our practices after yours."

"You're welcome to drop by anytime," Dale said. "Bring your girls if you like. We might even have a joint practice."

While Dale was talking with Margie, Chris and Joe leaped over the railing and hugged their former teammates. The crowd continued cheering even after the players had disappeared into the dressing room.

Dale did not predict a championship based on that one victory, but he knew his players would expect to win the next game. And if they should win it, then they would expect to win the next, and the next.

They had taken that first step in building a winning program.

8 —

One Sunday afternoon in early December, while visiting with Marilyn and Sybil, Dale expressed a growing concern he had about Donald Winters, a senior forward on the basketball team.

"He's not skilled enough to get a scholarship," Dale said, "but he's a great student and a valued teammate. I hope he can find a way to continue his education after graduation. I think he'd make a great coach someday."

"I know the family," Sybil said, "and I assure you his parents can't afford to send him to college."

"It's a shame," Dale said. "I've talked to other teachers, and they all agree that he has exceptional academic ability. He's always helping one of the boys with their schoolwork, and quickly catches on to every basketball concept I introduce to the players. Though a technique may be difficult for him to perform, he has a knack for explaining everything to his teammates, and they all seek his help when they're having trouble."

"Like Donald, every year too many Paddock kids have to accept some menial job because they can't afford an education," Sybil said. "I wish there was some kind of financial help available to them."

"Why don't we set up a scholarship fund?" Dale asked. "It can't be that expensive to attend Midwestern State, West Texas A&M in Canyon, Clarendon College, or even Texas Tech."

"I think that's a great idea," Marilyn said.

"To do it right," Sybil said, "guidelines will have to be established to determine who qualifies, application forms will be needed, and someone will have to make hard choices if more kids apply than the fund will support."

"Sounds like you're on the right track," Dale said, smiling. "So I suggest that you study the problem and come up with a plan."

"How much money would you be willing to put into the fund?" Sybil asked.

"Two million dollars," Dale replied. "At ten percent interest annually, it should be self-sustaining, and in time maybe we can get local businessmen interested in contributing so we can increase the individual scholarship amount."

Sybil let out a low whistle, expecting no more than a hundred thousand dollars.

"We'll call it the Stone Place Ranch Scholarship Fund," Dale said.

"But it'll be your money," Sybil protested.

"That's the easy part," Dale replied. "You'll be doing all the work."

Sybil knew he was right, and she gladly took on the project, setting up a meeting the next day with the school superintendent to get support and ideas.

After taking his team to a few out-of-town games in a cold, yellow school bus, Dale realized how scattered towns are in West Texas. After back-to-back trips of one hundred miles or more, he noticed that his players became exhausted by the middle of the fourth quarter, and had difficulty paying attention in class the next day.

"The basketball teams need better transportation," he told the principal early Monday morning.

"Dale," Kennemer said, "we just don't have the budget to do anything about it right now."

"What if I purchase a luxury bus and donate it to the school?" Dale asked.

"Son," Kennemer said, flabbergasted, "do you have any idea how much one of those things costs? On your salary, I don't see how you can afford it."

"Sir," Dale said, "if you'll check with the school board and get approval for the bus, I'll provide the funds."

"If it's all paid for . . . I mean, if it's no cost to the school, I'm sure they won't object," the principal said, staring at his coach as if he were an extraterrestrial being.

During the last class period that afternoon, Kennemer showed up at Dale's classroom door, motioning him over.

"I've contacted Superintendent Phillips with your idea of acquiring a luxury bus," he whispered. "He's assured me that the school district will gladly accept it as a gift. However, he's not sure he can provide a qualified driver, and he's concerned about the cost of fuel."

"Please assure the superintendent that I'll furnish those at no expense to the school, as well as insurance and maintenance," Dale said. When Kennemer hesitated, still wide-eyed, Dale asked, "Is there anything else, sir?"

The principal shook his head slowly, and Dale returned to his students.

The next day Marilyn was contacting bus companies in Lubbock and Amarillo, checking on prices, and making appointments to inspect their best passenger carriers. Having traveled on basketball trips the three prior seasons, she understood the need and eagerly took on the assignment. Armed with information, she was waiting for Dale when he left the gymnasium late the next afternoon. They climbed into her pickup to escape the December cold.

"Dale," she said, "we can get a totally refurbished luxury Eagle bus that will accommodate both the girls and boys teams for one hundred and fifty thousand dollars. It'll have lush, reclining seats, restrooms, and a deluxe cooling and heating system. For another six thousand, they'll add a kitchenette with a refrigerator and it'll still seat thirty-five passengers."

"What about storage of our basketball gear?" Dale asked.

"It has more than enough storage space underneath," she replied.

"Why would we need a kitchenette?"

"I've talked to Betty Green, the home economics teacher. If it has a kitchen, she'll get a group of students to make sandwiches and prepare drinks for the players. She'll help me serve snacks on the long trips home."

"Help you serve?"

"That's right," Marilyn replied. "Letting me go along seems fair compensation for my efforts. Besides, I can keep game statistics for you."

"I'm beginning to like the idea of having a kitchen on the bus. I wish I'd thought of it," Dale said, reaching for her hand.

"There can be none of that in front of the players," she said, smugly. "But maybe it'll be allowed while we drive out to the ranch after the games."

"What if we were married?" he asked.

"Well, I guess," she said, too surprised to think clearly. "If we were married."

"All along I've planned for our kids to play in the new activities building," he said, squeezing her hand.

"Our kids? Do you mean your kids and my kids will be the same kids?" she asked.

"That's exactly what I have in mind."

"You haven't even proposed, and yet you're talking about babies."

"There's not much room to kneel here in the truck," he said, "but I love you, and I'm asking you to marry me."

"Dale, are you serious?" she asked, grabbing his hand with both of hers.

"Absolutely. Now, what's your answer?"

"Yes! My answer's yes, a thousand yeses!"

She lunged across the truck and threw her arms around him. They hugged and kissed repeatedly.

"Some of the boys are watching," he whispered softly over her shoulder.

She immediately pushed away and reached both hands to her hair, until she realized it was too dark for anyone to see inside the cab of the pickup.

"I suppose you'll want a bigger house, one with a nursery," he said.

"I'll be perfectly happy living with you right where you live now. I love that little bungalow. Besides, the bedroom furniture is mine, and I'd already made up my mind that I'd take it back if you ever started dating some other girl."

"Well, we won't need a larger place for a while, maybe nine months or so."

"Oh, I can't wait to tell mother," she said, kissing him again. "I hope you can come over for a while tonight. I want us to break the news to her together. She'll be so excited."

Dale agreed, kissed her, and slid out of the pickup.

"By the way," he said, "I want you to get that bus, and make sure it has a kitchenette."

When he got home, his message light was blinking.

"Mom says for you to come over and have dinner with us," the recording said. "Call me as soon as you get this message."

Dale dialed Marilyn and then headed for the Stone Place where they enjoyed a fine steak dinner with salad and baked potatoes. Throughout the meal, Marilyn sat on the front edge of her chair, looking like she might explode with excitement.

When Dale had finished his last bite of steak, Marilyn said, "Mom, Dale has something to tell you."

"Actually, I have something to ask," he said. "Mrs. Stone, I'd like your permission to marry your daughter."

Sybil's mouth dropped open as her hands flew to her face, and she began crying, causing Dale to throw a concerned glance over at Marilyn. Marilyn sprung from her chair, and with tears streaming down her cheeks, rushed to her mother. She threw her arms around Sybil, and for what seemed like five minutes, Dale sat there watching these two women hug and cry.

"Oh, Dale," Sybil finally said between sobs. "I couldn't ask for a better son-in-law. This is so wonderful. It's answered prayer. Come let me hug you."

The three of them embraced for a minute or so, crying and laughing. The celebrating continued until Dale explained that he had papers to grade. Marilyn walked him to his truck, where they lingered, hugging and kissing in the privacy of the night's cold darkness.

The wedding was planned for the Christmas holidays. Since the basketball team had a tournament scheduled for the latter part of the school break, Dale and Marilyn decided to fly to Las Vegas and get married on Saturday after classes let out on Thursday. And they agreed to keep their marriage plans quiet until after school resumed in January.

Sybil arranged a nine o'clock Saturday morning flight for the three of them to leave out of Lubbock International and arrive in Las Vegas at ten-twenty. She then reserved two rooms at the Horseshoe Hotel and a marriage chapel for three o'clock that afternoon. Sybil's return flight was set for Sunday evening, at which time she would spend the night with her friend Modine in Lubbock until Dale and Marilyn returned a day later.

Marilyn met Dale at the school cafeteria for lunch on Thursday. While they ate, she whispered the details of their travel plans to him. Dale noticed several students and a couple of faculty members eyeing them. They had been seen together regularly at church, but this was the first time that many of the students realized they were a pair, and it set them all to speculating about the coach and the former Paddock student.

On Thursday night Marilyn and Sybil met Dale at the Steakhouse after basketball practice to celebrate. Sybil explained that she would follow them to the Lubbock airport in her Marquis, which would provide her transportation to her friend Modine's house on Sunday night while Dale and Marilyn continued their honeymoon until Monday.

"Dale, that'll get you back to Paddock in time to practice your boys on Tuesday and Wednesday afternoons before the tournament in Abilene starts on Thursday," Sybil explained.

"Also," Marilyn added, "I've arranged with David, Betty Green's husband, to pick up the luxury bus on Monday and have it ready to take your team to the tournament. He's a licensed bus driver with three years of experience with Greyhound."

"That's great," Dale said. "I'll drop by the bank tomorrow and arrange payment for the bus. It sounds like you two have taken care of everything else."

"We'll need to leave the ranch by six o'clock Saturday morning," Sybil said. "Allowing two hours to drive to Lubbock and another half hour to park and check our luggage, we'll get to the gate in plenty of time."

"Dale," Marilyn whispered, "if you'll give me a key to your house, I'll get some things moved over there tomorrow. I'd rather have them already there when we return from our honeymoon."

He nodded and handed her a spare key under the table, trying to avoid notice.

As planned, they arrived at their hotel Saturday morning at eleven. Marilyn and her mother took one room and Dale the other, with Marilyn to swap rooms after the wedding.

After lunch, Dale and Marilyn dropped by a boutique for their wedding apparel and then to a jewelry store for rings.

"Dale," she said, "I prefer a simple gold band. I hope that's okay with you."

It was, and soon they returned to their rooms to dress for the ceremony.

Sybil wiped at tears throughout the wedding, declaring her daughter to be the most beautiful bride she had ever seen. After wedding pictures and a small cake with punch, the newlyweds went to their room, and Sybil headed for the slot machines with her allotment of quarters.

After a wonderful time of intimacy and lovemaking, the couple glowed in their discovery of the indescribable splendor of love. Eventually feeling hungry, they ordered room service, which was followed by more intimacy.

The newlyweds met Sybil for breakfast at ten on Sunday morning, feeling an initial flush of embarrassment around her. The mother sensed their awkwardness and quickly dispelled it by telling them all about her adventures and showing them the fist full of quarters she had won.

Later, after taking Sybil to the airport in a limousine, Dale and Marilyn returned to the hotel. They spent a couple of hours sightseeing and then headed back to their room, preferring private time together rather than seeking local entertainment.

Monday morning came all too quickly for the young couple, and a late breakfast was followed with packing, checkout, and a limousine ride to the airport.

With a row of seats to themselves, they enjoyed the flight to Lubbock, spending the time holding hands, kissing, and discussing near-term plans. They then joined Sybil at Modine's, soon followed with the long drive to their ranches.

After putting his team through two days of strenuous practice, Dale had his squad ready for the Abilene tournament. He gathered his boys at the school at nine o'clock Thursday morning for the long trip. They were lounging around the gymnasium entrance with their gear, half asleep, when David Green pulled up in the luxury Eagle bus and pushed open the door. At first the boys were too stunned to move, but when they saw "PADDOCK PALOMINOS" stenciled in large golden letters on the side of the shiny blue bus, they jumped to their feet, grabbed their bags, and while shattering the chilled morning air with shrill whistles and shouts, they rushed to form a loading line.

"Boys, throw you bags in there," Dale called out, pointing to David Green who had opened the storage area doors.

Inside, the boys whistled their delight at seeing the plush interior furnished in sparkling blue and gold, the school's colors. Slowly, they sank into the cushy seats, adjusted their seatbacks, tested the individual lighting, and rattled on and on about the incredible improvement in travel comfort. About the time the boys discovered the restroom in the back, Marilyn and Betty Green showed up with a cooler of drinks and another of sandwiches, which Dale and David lugged to the kitchenette.

An hour into the two-and-a-half-hour trip, the boys finally settled down and got some rest. After stopping for lunch at a Dairy Queen on the edge of Abilene, they drove on to the Abilene Christian University gymnasium.

After defeating Hamlin in their first game, the Palominos faced a stout Aspermont team on Friday morning. After a mediocre first half, the Paddock squad played their best half of basketball of the season, and won by six points. This put the Palominos in the final four teams of the sixteen-team tournament, and matched them against Roscoe on Friday night. In a nip-and-tuck game, Chad Shankle, Dale's lanky center, had his best performance of the season with twenty-four points and led Paddock to a five-point victory. Now, the Palominos would meet Stamford in the finals Saturday night.

The Stamford Bulldogs were state finalists the prior season, and thus they were a prohibitive favorite to win the tournament, but Dale's boys were convinced they had a shot at victory. After the Bulldogs jumped out to an early lead, Paddock fought back, mostly on fast breaks, and had closed the gap to three points by halftime. After faltering in the third period, the Palominos made a furious charge in the final quarter but came up short by three points. Though disappointed in the loss, Dale recognized the tremendous progress his team had made in the past few weeks, especially in their expectations and will to win.

The long ride home proved the value of the luxury bus. After the team captains distributed sandwiches and drinks to their teammates, the boys gradually got comfortable and dozed off to sleep. Meanwhile, Marilyn had slipped in beside Dale and leaned her head against his shoulder.

"Dale, having the captains serve the snacks was a great idea," she whispered. "It reflects a side of their responsibility that the players really appreciate."

"I'm convinced," Dale said, "that the best leaders always serve those they lead, whether they're a coach, a teacher, a pastor, a CEO, or a politician."

"What about a husband?" she asked, looping her arm through his and snuggling closer.

"There are exceptions to every rule," he replied with a chuckle. "Don't you think that your sitting here like this is going to start gossip?"

"No," she replied, lacing her fingers through his. "The players are already saying we act like a married couple."

"What will Betty and David think?" he asked.

"When Betty and I were making the sandwiches, she asked me if I ever get tired of doing so many things for you. Of course I don't, but I was thinking that some things I do for you are more enjoyable than others."

"I don't care what people say about you, kid, I love you," he whispered while squeezing her hand.

Smiling, Marilyn soon dropped off to sleep.

The morning after school resumed, Dale stopped by Principal Kennemer's office at seven-thirty.

"Sir, first I want to notify you of my marriage to Merr, uh, I mean Marilyn Stone."

"Congratulations, Dale!" Kennemer said, jumping to his feet and extending his hand. "There's been lots of speculation around town that you two would tie the knot."

"Thanks," Dale said, a little embarrassed. "Also, I'm asking permission to hire David Green as driver of the athletic bus and as assistant coach for spring sports."

"Dale, I have no objection, but you'll need to discuss this with Superintendent Phillips. Would you like me to make an appointment for you?"

When Dale met with Phillips at noon, he passed along the marriage news and then his request to hire David Green.

"Coaching the high school boys takes all my time, and I just can't do justice to two sports going on simultaneously," Dale explained.

"I just don't have the budget to add Mr. Green to our payroll," the superintendent said.

"I understand, and I'm willing to forego my salary if the school will use it to pay David."

"Son, are you sure?"

"Absolutely."

"Dale, I have no idea where you're getting the money to do all these things, but I'm sure the School Board will approve this. They've jumped at everything else you've offered to do, and you must know they're elated over your early success with the basketball team."

"The money is legal, sir," Dale assured him. "You see, I won the lottery a while back."

"Wow!" the superintendent said. "The jackpot was over seventy million, right?"

"Yes, sir, though I got considerably less than that. Also, I'm asking you to not publicize this."

"I understand, but the way you're spending money, you're doing a pretty good job of announcing it yourself."

"I'm trying to put the money where it'll do the most good. If that draws some attention, I'll deal with it the best I can."

"In my twelve years at this school, this is easily the most exciting one," Phillips said, standing and shaking Dale's hand. "You have taken this town by storm, and I hope you stay another fifty years."

Then a sobering thought struck the superintendent.

"Now, you're not going to retire from coaching and live on your millions, are you?"

"Not a chance. My commitment to coaching has never been stronger. This just means I can do a better job, through things like the bus and summer basketball camps."

The superintendent walked with Dale to the doorway, and then stopped him.

"Dale, we need to tell the community about your providing the athletic bus, and now about David Green," Phillips said. "Also, I'd like to formally announce your marriage. If you and Marilyn will provide me with the details, I'll get with the local newspaper and ask them to run an article."

Dale agreed, then reached in his pocket, pulled out a golden band, and slipped it on his finger. As the coach headed for the cafeteria to wolf down a quick snack, the superintendent marveled at his good fortune. Dale's marriage to a girl deeply rooted in the area, Phillips believed, would tie the coach to the Paddock community for years to come, and based on the past six months, who could guess what bonuses that might bring to the school district and to Cottle County?

While eating lunch, Dale hurriedly scribbled down the details of their wedding, and before returning to his classroom, he dropped the information by the superintendent's office, and then called Marilyn.

"Honey, you can slip on that wedding ring, now," he said. "Superintendent Phillips will announce it to the newspaper next week, so everybody in town will know about our marriage."

"Dale, darling, I'll have a special dinner for you when you get home this evening. We'll celebrate all night!"

Marilyn slipped on her wedding band, stepped into the sunshine beaming through the window, and stared at the gleaming gold while tears formed in the corners of her eyes. Picking up the phone, she called Sybil.

"Mom, it's official. Dale has told the school about our marriage. He say's it'll be in the paper next week."

"My darling daughter, by then it'll be old news," Sybil replied, "because I'm going to spend the rest of the day calling everybody I know. I just might work my way right through the Paddock phone book."

Dale and Marilyn never knew exactly how many friends Sybil called, but when they took a seat in their usual pew Sunday morning, most of the members made their way over and congratulated them.

"It looks like you've told the whole congregation," Marilyn whispered to her mom.

"No," she said. "I forgot one of my quilting queens, and she grabbed me in the foyer, demanding an explanation."

"Quilting queens?" Dale asked.

"Oh, a group of us older ladies meet on Tuesdays to gather things for the needy," she explained. "Every year we make a quilt or two to give to some family."

The pastor, Brother Sammy Burton, walked to the pulpit and began recognizing and welcoming visitors. He then led the congregation through a list of news items.

"Now, one final announcement, though you won't find it in the bulletin," the pastor said. "We have a new family with us today. A couple of our most faithful members, Dale Rory and Marilyn Stone, were recently married. If you haven't congratulated them, please do so after the service, and I know you'll join me in praying that God will bless their marriage in a very special way."

After the service, several more of the congregation did as the pastor had suggested earlier, making their way over to Dale and Marilyn. Sybil, looking as proud as a mother hen with two new chicks, had something to say to each of the congratulators.

"Honey," Marilyn said to Dale on the way home, "Brother Sammy will be retiring soon, and I would like to do something to help him and Margaret. Since we don't have a local hospital, he drives hundreds of miles to visit patients in Wichita Falls, Lubbock, Plainview, and Childress. Do you think we could establish a travel fund for him?"

"That sounds like a good idea," Dale said.

"Also, we'll be getting a new pastor," she continued, "and I'd like to do something to encourage him to reach people who are unable to attend church. We could install a system that records the services, and he could take copies to shut-ins."

"I agree," Dale said. "And since these people can't get out, they must need help with groceries and other items. We could set up a fund for the pastor to use to meet these needs."

"Maybe we could purchase a van to pick up the needed items and deliver them. The van could also provide a ride for people who don't have transportation to church."

"Merr, I think you should find out what's needed, how much should be set aside, and transfer the money from the Coins for Christ fund."

"I think we should expand the fund and make it available to all churches in town. We could pick up and deliver people to whichever church they prefer."

"What if we provide a couple of vans and drivers to meet these needs, as identified by the four pastors in town? Also, I'm sure each church currently has a benevolence fund, and we could offer to contribute five dollars for every one the churches contribute. We could have each church report on how they used these funds, who they helped, and based on a simple audit, we could add to or reduce our funding to each church based on their level of participation."

"You're sure going to become popular with all the widows in town."

"This is going to be your project, and I suspect there are a few widowers who'll be glad of that."

"I don't have time for a widower," she said. "My husband keeps me much too busy."

But beginning the next day, Marilyn found time to contact the various church leaders and get the project started.

9 —

Meanwhile, Sybil began the new year by finalizing the details of the scholarship fund. With a folder containing a list of applicant qualifications, a sample request form, and an approval process, she dropped by the Roryian on Saturday afternoon to discuss it with Dale and Marilyn.

"We'll have fifteen graduating seniors in May," she explained. "Typically, only three or four attend college, but with the aid of a scholarship, maybe that number will double. In the state schools, it'll take about twenty-five hundred dollars per student each semester to cover enrollment, books, dorm, and meal costs. If we have eight applicants that qualify, that's forty-eight thousand dollars for the first year. Each year for four years that amount will double until it reaches about two hundred thousand dollars. Even if we add ten students each year over that time, the fund will sustain itself."

"So are you recommending we lower the funding by half a million dollars?" Dale asked.

"That's right. Some students will drop out of college before they graduate, but I expect that number to be offset by an increase in the number of qualifying seniors."

"Okay, we'll start the fund at a million and a half dollars. If necessary, we'll add to it rather than turn down a single student, even if they just want to go to a trade school."

"Good. I'll get back with Superintendent Phillips and update him, and then I'll set up a meeting and invite every graduating senior."

"Sybil," Dale said, glancing at the form, "I want this named Stone Place Ranch Scholarship Fund, so please get that on all the documentation."

Sybil nodded. "Dale, you can't imagine how much this means to me. When I graduated high school, I couldn't afford to go to college." She hesitated, getting control of her emotions. "This fund provides the greatest hope I have seen in my lifetime for the future of our young people, and ultimately the future of this community. And to have my name associated with it . . . well, I can't thank you enough."

With tears in her eyes, she hugged Dale, and then her speechless daughter. It was a priceless moment for them, one that words could not fathom, one that must be experienced to fully comprehend.

The next day Sybil met with Superintendent Phillips and explained the finalized plan for the scholarship fund.

"This is wonderful," Phillips said. "I think we've got several students who'll be interested in applying."

"I'd like to meet with the seniors," she said. "I want to make sure they understand what the scholarship covers, and how the process works. Can that be arranged for tomorrow?"

Without hesitation the superintendent agreed to notify all the seniors and have them gather in the cafeteria midway of the last class period the following afternoon.

"By the way," Superintendent Phillips said as Sybil rose to leave. "I've had some teachers suggest having a wedding shower for Dale and Marilyn. Do you think they'd agree to that?"

"I'm sure they'd feel honored, Mr. Phillips, but let me talk to them about it."

That evening Sybil told Dale and Marilyn about the teachers' interest in sponsoring a wedding shower.

"I think that's great," Dale said, glancing at his wife, "but I'd rather they donate any gift money to the scholarship fund."

"I agree," Marilyn said. "And I think this presents an excellent opportunity to christen the new activities building by having it out here."

"Of course," Sybil said, jumping to her feet. "We can throw a big party, with barbecue, hotdogs, and all the trimmings. Why, the kids could play basketball after they eat, and we can set up card tables for us old fogies."

"Let's not call it a shower," Marilyn said. "We just want our friends to come and celebrate our marriage."

The next morning Sybil reported the decision to the superintendent and later that day, Betty Green called to discuss a date for the party. They chose Saturday, January 14.

When the marriage announcement came out in the paper, it included plans for the celebration at the Roryian, inviting all the teachers, students and their parents, school administrators, and family friends. No one could remember the last time Paddock had had a area-wide party, but based on phone calls to the ranch, this was shaping up to be just that.

Sybil, Marilyn, and Clara Jordan immediately began preparing the activities building for the event, including bringing in extra tables, chairs, cookware and tableware, decorations, and food. Marilyn bought an extra freezer to store the meat. They were preparing for a feast.

Betty Green and Margie Walker helped with preparations, while Tom Jordan and Dale used the tractor and blade to scrape and level a road to the building and to clear a large parking area.

Cars began turning into the Roryian Ranch driveway at about twenty minutes before four that Saturday afternoon. Within thirty minutes, the parking lot was full, and the locals were packed into the activities building, walking through and inspecting every feature of the new facility.

After an invocation by Brother Sammy Burton, a long serving line formed, starting in the kitchen area and stretching the length of the gymnasium where decorated tables covered the court surface.

After the guests had devoured barbecued meat of every sort, along with potato salad, coleslaw, and gallons of ice tea and coffee, Superintendent Phillips stood at the end of the center row of tables and asked for quiet.

"I'm sure all of you know Dale and Marilyn Rory, whose marriage we're celebrating," he began. "Regardless, I want to introduce them."

He had Dale and Marilyn stand while the crowd applauded and whistled.

Phillips then told how Dale had come to Paddock back in June, looking for a coaching job.

"From the moment I met him, I knew we wanted him here in Paddock, but I had no idea what an enormous impact he would have on our community. Now, he has married our own Marilyn Stone, making him a real West Texan.

"We now sit here in this fine facility, the most recent in a string of projects envisioned and completed by this industrious couple, built for the enjoyment and development of our young people. I'm told basketball camps will be held here this summer, and youth groups will be welcomed, as well as civic functions from time to time.

"Also, I'd like to mention a project that I am particularly excited about, the Stone Ranch Scholarship Fund. Each of our graduating seniors will be offered the opportunity to attend college with the aid of twenty-five hundred dollars per semester. I expect this to double the number of Paddock students who will pursue a college degree."

Phillips then motioned a couple of boys to come forward, carrying a rolled up banner.

"Years ago I heard a story about Captain Burk Burnett, a legendary rancher whose huge herds once roamed these lands. The Comanches revered the Captain," he said and then motioned toward the boys who began unrolling a thirty-foot banner that read, "MASSASUTA, OUR LEADER."

"You see, the Comanches called Captain Burnett, Massasuta, or big leader, because they had such faith in his judgment. Well, I believe we of Paddock and Cottle County have our own big leader. Now, I hope you'll stand and join me in applauding Coach Dale Rory, our Massasuta."

The guests rose to their feet, clapping and whistling, with some of the youngsters chanting, "Massasuta, Massasuta, Massasuta . . ." and followed that with, "speech, speech, speech . . ."

When the chanting continued, Dale slowly rose to his feet, feeling his face flush with embarrassment.

"I'm not a speechmaker, but Marilyn and I want to thank you for coming here today to celebrate our marriage. Also, I owe so much to so many of you, including the school administrators, my fellow teachers, to the boys and girls, and to their parents. None of the projects we have initiated would have been successful without your support. I've been blessed beyond measure, and according to the gospel of Luke, 'to whom much is given, much is required.'

"Now, before you label me a long-winded preacher, I'd like some of you boys to help us clear the court so we can bring out a couple of basketballs and give this place a proper initiation."

Twenty minutes later, the tables and chairs were all put away, and boys and girls were shooting baskets at both goals, while the adults gathered around card tables in the dinning and kitchen area.

About ten o'clock, some of the guests began filing by the table where Dale, Marilyn, and Sybil sat. On their way out, they offered congratulations, and several inquired how they could contribute to the scholarship fund. Sybil told them to mail their check to Superintendent Phillips, designating their contribution. Once the exodus began, it grew until by eleven, only Dale, Marilyn, and Sybil remained.

"What do you think of your new name?" Marilyn asked Dale, pointing to the long banner attached to the far wall.

"I'm honored, but also embarrassed. In any case, I think I'm stuck with it. Everybody in town will have heard that story by Monday morning."

"I kinda like it," Marilyn said, looping her arm through his. "It's got a local flavor to it, and it's unique. What do you think, Mother?"

"I think it fits."

"Maybe you're a bit prejudiced," Dale suggested.

"A few years back, I looked that word up in the dictionary," Sybil replied, a sly smile forming. "It said something about an opinion formed without knowledge or reason. Which do you think I'm lacking?"

Dale just shook his head, recognizing the futility of debating his mother-in-law.

"In any case, it's two against one," Marilyn said, pushing Dale toward the exit. "So, the name sticks."

Upon returning from the next out-of-town basketball game, Dale and

Marilyn arrived at the bungalow about midnight. Upon reaching the front door, Marilyn noticed that it stood slightly ajar.

"Dale," she said, pushing the door open. "I'm sure I locked it when I left this afternoon."

"Honey," Dale said, grabbing her arm, "get in the truck and lock the doors."

"Dale, don't go in there," she said, stepping back. "Let's go to Mother's and call the sheriff."

"Hurry," Dale said sternly. "Get in the truck. At the first sight of trouble, crank it and get out of here."

"I'm not leaving without you," she protested as she headed for the pickup.

Dale slipped through the doorway and quickly stepped to the right, pressing his back against the wall, and waited for his eyes to adjust to the darkness. He took a deep breath to calm himself and listened.

When his eyes had acclimated, he saw papers scattered across the room, seat cushions from the couch piled haphazardly on the floor, and the lamp table drawer pulled out.

What would someone be looking for, and were they still in the house? he wondered.

Slowly, he moved across the room, avoiding the strewn objects and stopped at the doorway to the first bedroom. Again, the floor was covered with papers from the old desk where he had stored college papers, maps, and brochures.

Moving farther down the hall, Dale checked the main bedroom, which had clothes piled in the floor and drawers hanging out of both bureaus.

Dale slipped down to the kitchen doorway and peeked inside. Cabinet doors were swung open, the pantry had been ransacked, and the table was covered with an assortment of kitchen items, but he saw no intruder.

Easing along the wall, Dale made his way to the back door, which stood open. He flipped on the outside light and peeked out, but whoever had been there was gone.

After making his way back to the front door, he ran to the truck and jumped inside.

"Drive up to the Jordans's house," he said. "Flip your lights on high beam."

Everything was dark and quiet at the double-wide, and likewise they found nothing unusual around the other buildings.

"Clearly someone broke into the bungalow," Dale said as Marilyn drove back to the house. "But what could they have been looking for?"

"I'm afraid word is out that you won the lottery," Marilyn said. "We'd better check closely and see if anything is missing."

For the next thirty minutes, they searched through the strewn items, putting the more important things back in place, without discovering any damage or loss. Then Marilyn checked the bathroom.

"Dale!" she shouted. "Come here."

A note was taped to the mirror.

> *Bring a million dollars cash and meet me at the mouth of Stone Canyon at midnight tomorrow. If you don't or if you bring anybody with you, I'll be back to get that pretty little wife of yours.*

"Leave everything as it is," Dale said. "I'm calling the sheriff."

Sheriff Wilhelm drove up fifteen minutes later and inspected every room.

"It's probably a hoax," he said, looking at the note, "but I'm afraid we've got to take it seriously. Maybe you can stay at Sybil's tonight, and I'll post a guard here. Come daylight, we'll look the place over for any evidence. Maybe we'll find fingerprints, or tire tracks that'll help."

As soon as a deputy showed up, Dale and Marilyn drove over to Sybil's. They did not sleep much that night, and at sunrise, Dale headed back to the bungalow. At seven o'clock he called Principal Kennemer and explained he needed to take the day off.

"I'll cover your classes and meet with the basketball team this afternoon," the principal said.

Fortunately, the deputy found a fresh fingerprint on the small glass window inset in the front door.

"I'm guessing that the burglar took his gloves off to search through some of these papers, heard something outside, and pushed back the little curtain to look out. One finger made just enough contact with the pane to leave a pretty good print. Now, if we can just find a match on file."

The sheriff asked Dale to leave everything as it was for the remainder of the day.

"I'm gonna run this print to town, and get it out to every law enforcement office in the area. My deputy will stay here and look after your things. Dale, I'd like you to come with me so we can plan what we'll do tonight, in case we don't nail this character today."

Dale called Marilyn and explained the plan.

"Merr, you stay there with your mother. I'll get back as soon as I can."

While driving to town, Dale realized the burglar must be local. How else would he know about Stone Canyon and how to locate its mouth? And it occurred to him that that fact might improve their chances of matching the fingerprint.

While the sheriff waited for news regarding the print, he and Dale discussed a backup plan.

"I'll take a bag of money to the canyon tonight," Dale said. "I'll carry ten stacks of money, each with a hundred bills inside a wrapper. I'll put a thousand dollar bill on the top and bottom of each stack, while the remainder of the stack will be ones. If he shows up, surely you can get a few men to surround the place and trap this bum."

"I'll arrange to get a few horses, so we can ride out there a couple hours early and get set up without being spotted," the sheriff said. "Today, we'll take a battery-powered light with us and set it on the rim of the canyon. Then we'll select the spot where we want you to meet this character and aim the light there. We might get lucky and blind him with the light long enough to close in without him seeing us."

Dale agreed, and turned to go to the bank.

"Son," the sheriff said, catching Dale's arm, "I've got a bulletproof vest coming from Childress for you to wear tonight, but you realize we're dealing with a criminal, and he'll probably be armed. At the first sign of us, he just might shoot. I can't guarantee that we can protect you."

Dale nodded, and walked out.

When no match of the fingerprint was made by seven o'clock that evening, he and the sheriff took his sack of money and headed for the ranch. Dale saddled up his mare, put on the vest, a loose-fitting shirt, and a big coat.

"Do you want a pistol?" the sheriff asked.

"No," Dale said. "I'm sure he'd spot it and that might panic him."

About ten-thirty, Dale climbed into the saddle.

"I'll ride into the canyon from the upper end," he said. "I'll make my way down through it, but I'll stop well short of the mouth. I'll tie up my horse, and a little before midnight, I'll ease down to the opening, but I won't step out until a minute or two later. I'll hold the sack of money so it's easily seen. If he doesn't show after thirty minutes, I'll head back to my horse. Keep everybody hidden unless he appears. He might just watch tonight to see if it's a trap. If he sees no reason to be suspicious, then he may contact me to meet him again tomorrow night."

Dale made his way through the dark canyon, trusting his horse to avoid the rocks and debris. When he came to the fence, he snipped each strand with wire-cutters and swung back into the saddle. On his way back, he would use the section of wire from the top strand to reattach the other three as a temporary fix.

When he saw the canyon mouth about a hundred feet ahead, he pulled up and slid down, recalling the rattlesnake incident. He tied his horse to a bush, making sure to avoid stumbling over a rock. He checked his watch. Eleven o'clock.

Dale moved ahead about thirty feet and kneeled down behind a cedar bush, hoping to conceal himself. He checked his watch every ten minutes. The glowing hands moved agonizingly slow.

Two minutes after midnight, he stood up and walked slowly toward the opening at the end of the canyon. After a brief pause in the edge of the dark shadows, he took a deep breath and stepped out, the sack of money swinging by his side. He stopped three feet from the large rock designated by the sheriff as the meeting point. He waited, a cold night breeze ruffling his hair and sending chills up and down his spine.

Dale checked his watch. Ten minutes after midnight.

Without moving, he scanned the area, trying to spot any motion, anything that did not fit. There was nothing.

The third time he checked his watch, it was twelve-thirty. He waited another minute, maybe two. He pulled a stack of bills out of the sack and fanned through them, just to tempt his adversary, if he was out there. Still nothing.

Both relieved and frustrated, Dale turned and headed for the darkness of the canyon.

"Wait," a voice called. "Step back out of those shadows."

Slowly, Dale turned and headed toward the rock, his heart pounding.

"Stop right there," the sharp voice said. "Set the sack down on the big rock."

Dale took two more long strides toward the agreed-to spot, and lowered the sack.

"Step back," the shrill voice barked. "Now take off your coat and pitch it onto the rock."

Dale did as he was told.

"Pull your pockets inside out," the voice said.

Dale obeyed again.

"Turn around, put your hands on top of your head, and step away from the sack," the voice said.

Dale took three long strides, hoping to clear the expected target area of the sheriff's spot light.

"Stop," the voice said, sounding edgy.

Dale could hear footsteps on the rocky soil, and then the big light flashed. He took two quick steps and dove into the shadows of the canyon.

"Freeze," a booming voice called out.

A gun roared from behind Dale, and then a second, more distant shot rang out while he scrambled behind a rock.

"You're surrounded," the deep voice shouted. "Throw down your weapon."

As Dale looked back, he saw a man standing beside the sack of money, his empty hands raised. Within thirty seconds, four law officers, including the sheriff, converged on the man with their weapons drawn.

By the time Dale reached the scene, the man was handcuffed. The face was familiar. Then Dale remembered. The captured villain was Carlton Meade, a custodian at the high school. He had been in the same grade with Marilyn, but had dropped out of school in the middle of his junior year.

In the sheriff's office, after confessing to attempted burglary and extortion, Meade explained his actions. He had heard that Coach Rory had come into a considerable amount of money. When he saw the luxury bus and heard that Dale had given it to the school, he was convinced that the coach was rich. While emptying Superintendent Phillips's trash and cleaning his office the night of the superintendent's noon meeting with Dale, the custodian had seen Dale's name penciled on the administrator's calendar and had noticed a handwritten note that said, "Lottery." The custodian put the two together.

When Superintendent Phillips heard, he shook his head.

"After meeting with you," he explained to Dale, "I decided to buy a couple of lottery tickets on my way home, so I penciled a reminder on my calendar, knowing that I always scan back over my calendar and make a few notes before I leave at the end of the day."

With the crisis over, Dale and Marilyn put things back in place in the bungalow, but the uneasiness did not immediately go away.

"Carlton was a good boy," Marilyn said. "His family was dirt poor, his clothes were always ragged, though clean, and he was a good student. When his father died, he quit school, and Superintendent Phillips felt sorry for him and gave him odd jobs around the school."

"What a sad story," Dale said. "I'm afraid a stint in prison will just harden him into a serious criminal."

"Honey, if he'll finish his high school work while in prison, do you think he could qualify for one of our scholarships?"

"That just might be the incentive he needs," Dale said.

After discussing their plan with the sheriff, Marilyn went by the jail and talked to the prisoner.

"Carlton," she said. "I know you've committed a horrible crime, but I still think you're a good person."

"Thank you, ma'am," Meade said, his eyes fixed on the floor. "I promise you, I would never have hurt you, Mrs. Marilyn."

"I know that," she said. "And I want to help you. Carlton, would you be willing to use this time of confinement to finish your high school degree?"

"Yes, ma'am. I hadn't thought about it, but I'd sure like to do that."

"Then I'll make you a promise," she said. "If you'll get your diploma and be a model prisoner, I'll have a college scholarship waiting for you when you're set free."

"Oh, ma'am. I . . ." Meade said, and then hide his face in his hands.

"Carlton, I'll see that you have everything you need to complete your high school education. And I'll set aside your scholarship money. The rest is up to you."

"I can never thank you enough, ma'am," he said, dragging his shirtsleeve across his eyes.

Marilyn wrote a letter to be put in Carlton Meade's prison file. She promised to provide, so long as he stayed out of trouble, whatever the prisoner might need to complete his education, including money, books, supplies, and a tutor. Before leaving, she made sure the sheriff understood her intent and that it would be communicated to the authorities wherever Meade was sent.

"Merr," Dale said that evening when Marilyn told him about her discussion with Carlton Meade and her commitment, "God never made a better woman."

One afternoon during basketball practice, Dale told his players to continue their drills while he made a phone call. When he returned, he found a couple of players standing around talking.

"Boys," he told them, "you can't afford to waste time like this."

"Awe, Coach Mass," one replied. "We've won our last five games, and this next one is against a team we beat by eighteen points just two weeks ago."

"Let me tell you a story," Dale said, as other players gathered around.

"One time a jackrabbit was hopping along, alert and watching for danger. Then he saw a crow sitting on top of a telephone pole. 'What you doin' up there?' the rabbit asked. 'Just sittin' here doin' nothin',' the crow replied. Thinking that crow looked mighty peaceful up there, the jackrabbit sat down in the shade of a mesquite bush and stretched out on his side, exposing his belly. About that time a coyote came along, and snatched up the lazy rabbit.

"Boys, we're the jackrabbit in the story, and our next opponent is the coyote. So, until we are safely atop that championship pole, we can't afford to stop and rest."

Dale's young basketball team did not climb to the top and win its district, but his squad was the only one to defeat Matador, the eventual champion. With a 20-8 record and a district mark of 6-2, the Palominos completed their best season in fifteen years. Since all five starters were underclassmen, fans were predicting the next season would bring a district trophy to Paddock. Likewise, the girls' team had their most successful record in several years.

At some point in every game, the fans would chant, "Massasuta, Massasuta, Massasuta ..." Newspaper articles often used this moniker when referring to Coach Rory, whether a sports article or one regarding one of his many projects. By the end of the basketball season, he had become "Coach Mass" to his players and Paddock fans.

"Honey," Marilyn said, having just returned from the grocery store, "you've got people in town buzzing like mosquitoes in a swamp. Not only are they excited about next season, but also Helen Branch swears that the change in the attitudes of the school kids is even more impressive. She claims that school spirit is at an all-time high."

"Winning is infectious," he said. "But the most important thing is that our kids now expect to win. Never again will they be satisfied with a loss."

"Maybe this is a good time to start promoting our summer basketball camp," Marilyn suggested.

With enthusiasm high and the activities building initiated, Dale and Marilyn designed a flier for the *Paddock Post* to announce the summer basketball camp to be held in July. It would last two weeks, and David Green and Donald Winters had agreed to lead the sessions for the boys. Also, the girls' coach was talking about a camp for her players. Betty and some of her home economics students had volunteered to help with refreshments, along with Clara Jordan.

Three days after the fliers reached the public, Marilyn found responses in the mail almost daily, receiving a dozen applications in the first week. She suggested to Dale that they should consider having two camps rather than turn down applicants.

"I've even received an inquiry from a kid up in Dunlap and another from one over in Roaring Springs," she explained. "Do you want to accept out-of-town boys?"

"I sure do," Dale replied. "We'll accept them even if they play for an opposing school. Be sure and assign the out-of-town boys to a dorm room."

As Dale kicked off the baseball season, Marilyn was implementing the benevolence fund, including the purchase of a couple of vans, hiring drivers, and donating four thousand dollars to Brother Sammy's travel budget. Sybil was busy reviewing applications for college scholarships, including one from Donald Winters, the math student who had inspired the project, and Tom Jordan was bargaining for another four thousand acres of land west of the Roryian.

The coach was not surprised to find that Chris and Joe were outstanding baseball players, Chris a pitcher and Joe a line-drive hitting catcher; however, he was surprised at the number of basketball players who showed up on the diamond.

As he had done in basketball, Dale stressed fundamentals. He drilled infielders on handling ground balls, throwing techniques, turning double plays, and trapping runners between bases.

"Before every pitch," he told his fielders, "decide what you will do with the ball if it's hit to you. To do that, you must know if there are runners on base, what the pitch count is, and the number of outs. Then you must consider your responsibility if the ball is hit elsewhere. Do you need to cover a base for a force out? Should you back up a teammate in case of an errant throw? When do you need to go out to handle a relay from the outfield? What if the hitter should bunt? Should you position yourself at normal depth or move in to cut down a runner at home plate? Do you need to guard the foul line to avoid an extra-base hit? If you wait until the ball is hit to decide, it'll be too late."

While David worked the outfielders, Dale worked with individual hitters, stressing common-sense techniques.

"Keep your hands together on the bat," he said, "and your head steady throughout the swing. Swing the bat on the line determined by the flight of the ball. Getting ahead of the pitcher in the pitch-count gives you tremendous advantage, so don't swing at bad pitches. If the opposing pitcher has walked the batter before you, don't swing until he has thrown at least one strike. Every one of you must be a capable bunter. Moving runners up a base, when we have less than two outs, leads to winning hits."

Then Dale set up game situations, such as a runner on first base with one out. He would quiz each player about what he would do if the ball should be hit to him, on the ground or in the air. Then he would have the pitcher lob an easy pitch and instruct the batter to hit the ball to the infield. He would repeat this drill with fly balls to the outfield. After every practice, he worked with his pitchers and catchers, determining each pitcher's best pitch, developing alternate pitches, and determining when to intentionally throw a pitch inside or outside, high or low.

"On the bench, we'll record the result of every opposing batter," he told them. "Did he strikeout, and if so, was it on a fastball, a curve, or a changeup? If he hit the ball, what pitch did he hit and what was the result? As the game progresses, you'll review these notes every time you come to the dugout so you can adjust your pitches to every batter."

Initially, the players complained that all this thinking was inhibiting their natural abilities in hitting and fielding, but the basketball players assured their teammates that they had gone through the same frustrations, and ultimately it had paid off with wins. Sure enough, as the boys repeatedly followed the coach's instructions to the point of habit, their hitting and fielding began to improve noticeably.

After winning six consecutive non-district games, the Palominos' baseball squad continued undefeated through the first half of their conference schedule. With Chris leading their pitching staff, and the fielders playing almost error-free ball, Paddock typically allowed no more than three runs, while their hitters averaged six walks per game and pounded opposing pitching for seven to ten runs.

With the district trophy captured and graduation completed, the baseball team entered the state playoffs, advancing to the regional tournament where they met teams as drilled in fundamentals as they were, but who proved superior in hitting. After their third game in the tournament, the Palominos were eliminated.

Following the last team meeting, Chris and Joe cornered Dale and explained that they wanted to return to the basketball team in the fall. Dale suggested they begin by attending the upcoming camp at the ranch.

Meanwhile, in early May Marilyn had received a letter from prison authorities confirming that Carlton Meade was earning credits toward his high school diploma, and two weeks later Sybil awarded nine scholarships to graduating seniors. The awards were announced as the students received their diplomas, each accompanied by extended applause by family, friends, and fellow classmates. Donald Winters, the last scholarship winner to cross the stage, drew a standing ovation, initiated by his teammates and the school faculty, sending a surge of emotion through him that blurred his eyes and halted his step. Clearly the enthusiasm displayed by the underclassmen boded well for the future of Stone Place Ranch scholarships.

Arriving home Saturday afternoon after a meeting with the four local pastors regarding the benevolence fund, Marilyn hugged her husband.

"I've got some good news," she said. "While talking to Joe Bob Heath, a deacon at the Baptist church, he told me that he and Susie have a sixteen-year-old nephew from Hays, Kansas, who'll be moving to Paddock this summer. He thinks the boy will complete high school here."

"And what has got you so excited about this kid?"

"Well, his father is a military man and the family will be moving to Germany. As a sophomore the boy was a starter on their championship basketball team, and he wants to stay stateside. Based on what Joe Bob has told his nephew about the basketball program here, the boy asked to come and live with them. They want to get him in the basketball camp."

Later that evening, Marilyn was reading through the latest *Messenger* magazine, a Methodist publication, when she suddenly saw a name that grabbed her attention.

"Honey, didn't you tell me your college roommate was named Thomas Newberry?"

"That's right."

"Here's an article about Thomas Newberry, a seminary student in Saint Louis. Think this fellow could be your friend?"

Dale scanned the article, which explained that Newberry had recently become the pastor of a small congregation in a rundown part of the city. He attended classes through the week, but still held a Wednesday night service and Sunday services. The heart of the story emphasized that the congregation had experienced such rapid growth that the pastor was forced to hold two Sunday morning services to accommodate everyone. The growth was primarily due to Newberry's starting a neighborhood basketball program for boys.

"That's got to be my old roommate," Dale said. "I'd sure like to talk to him."

While Dale was preparing for the basketball camp the next day Marilyn called the Saint Louis seminary named in the article, explained the situation, and got Thomas Newberry's home phone number. That evening Dale called.

"Thomas," Dale said when a man answered the phone, "this is Dale Rory."

"Hey roomy," Thomas said. "Where in the world are you?"

Dale explained how he had found a job in West Texas, teaching and coaching, and told a little about his ranch and his marriage.

"I hear you're a pastor and doing great," Dale said.

"I'm enjoying my work, but it's quite a challenge. There aren't enough hours in the day to get everything done."

"In the *Messenger*, it says you've recruited so many basketball players that your congregation won't fit in the church. You'll work yourself to death, doubling up services like that."

"We just don't have any choice," Thomas said. "I'm delighted to have these young boys filling up the pews, but they don't contribute much financially. And our congregation just can't afford a building program."

"What's the solution?" Dale asked.

"I've asked the Methodist national organization for financial aid. That's how the *Messenger* got the story."

"How much aid do you need?" Dale asked.

"We could expand and repair our building with less than fifty thousand dollars, but I'd like to move to a larger lot right down the street and build a new facility. There's just no way to do that at this time."

"Could you get that lot and build a church for five hundred thousand dollars?"

"Sure," Thomas said, chuckling. "We've been offered the larger lot at no cost, and there's a group of retired men who'll donate their labor to build a church for us. We'd just have to buy the materials and furnish the workers with food and a place to stay. But Dale, the national organization's not going to give our little church that kind of money."

"Thomas, when my parents died, you treated me like a brother, and I've never forgotten that. So, if you'll set up a bank account and send a deposit slip to me, I'll transfer half a million dollars to you to build that church."

For a moment, there was silence on the line.

"I'm serious, Thomas," Dale said.

"Dale," Thomas said, his voice quivering, "I don't know what to say, except God bless you. You must be a saint, a very rich saint."

"God has already blessed me immeasurably, and that's how I'm able to do this," Dale replied.

"With that much money, I think we can build a new church, convert the old one into a gym, and have money left over. After playing basketball in a vacant lot for so long, the boys would be thrilled to have a real gym."

"That's great! And if there's excess money, use it to pay for your schooling and your daily expenses."

After promising to stay in touch, they bid each other goodbye.

Three days later, Dale received a letter from Thomas, thanking him profusely, and it included a bank deposit slip. The next day Dale transferred the money from the million dollars he had set aside in his Coins for Christ fund.

"It's the most satisfying thing I've ever done," he told Marilyn that evening.

"Honey," Marilyn said, easing into his lap and looping her arm around his neck, "I'm so proud of you. If I'm dreaming all of this, please don't wake me up."

10 ——

As the list of applicants for the basketball camp ballooned, Dale and Marilyn quickly scheduled a second camp for the last two weeks in July. Before the ink had dried on the announcement circular, Margie brought by a list of girls who were pleading for their own camp, which was subsequently scheduled for the first two weeks in August.

"Dale," Marilyn said, "I've turned down a dozen camp requests from out-of-town kids because there's just no place for them to stay locally."

"David Green and Donald Winters will take one of the dorm rooms," Dale said. "That means we can't house more than sixteen campers this summer, so we'll have to turn down the others this year. For next summer, we'll build a separate dorm here on the ranch. It can be used for church camps, and youth retreats as well."

The following morning, Dale passed the expanded dorm plans on to Tom Jordan with instructions to get with Ted Jackson, the Lubbock architect, and design a sixteen-room facility.

"Boss," Tom said, after copying down the instructions, "it's time to sell your first crop of steers. They're eight to nine months old and should fetch about twelve thousand dollars."

"Sell them and put the money in the ranch account," Dale said. "I want to reinvest all cattle sales in more cattle and ranch improvements."

"Also, I think we can buy the Colquitt Ranch at a reasonable price. It covers four thousand acres and adjoins us to the west. Would you like to take a look at it?"

Dale did, and at seven o'clock the next morning, they jumped in the old pickup and rattled west across the ranch to a gate that opened onto the adjacent property. It was rugged terrain, covered with cedars and mesquite, dry gullies, and sparse patches of barely edible grass.

"It needs improvement," Tom said. "The fencing is poor, but we can fix it up to the point of running four hundred head of cattle on it."

"All this land, this entire county, could be improved enormously with a good water supply," Dale said, sitting with his chin resting on his hands that gripped the steering wheel. "Tom, we've got to have more water."

Staring straight ahead, Dale drove all the way back to the Roryian without uttering another word, but by the time they reached the ranch house, he had made up his mind.

"Tom," he said, "let's buy the Colquitt Ranch, and also I want you to get some aerial shots of the area and show them to the Army Corps of Engineers. Tell them we want to build a lake with the maximum capacity the watershed will support. Make sure they take a good look at Stone Canyon and all the tributaries that feed into it."

Having made the decision to expand the ranch, Dale returned to the basketball camp the next morning. Joe Bob Heath, the uncle of the Kansas boy, headed his way.

"Coach Rory," Joe Bob said, "I'd like you to meet my nephew, Todd Anderson."

"Welcome to Paddock," Dale said, shaking the boy's large hand.

The smiling youngster stood six-foot-six and weighed an evenly proportioned two hundred fifteen pounds. Having just completed his sophomore year, he appeared likely to grow at least two inches taller, and his frame could easily carry twenty-five more pounds. If he's got good agility, a little quickness, and can handle a basketball, Dale was thinking, he'll be an impact player immediately.

Fifteen players showed up that first day of basketball camp. Donald and David divided them into a high school group and a younger group, one on each end of the court. Donald would work with the older boys, while David handled the younger ones.

Among the high school group were Todd Anderson, the Kansas kid, Chris Powell and Joe Blake from the baseball team, as well as Jimmy, Chad, Marty, Josh, and Eddie, all starters from Dale's previous basketball squad. In addition, two boys from neighboring towns completed the older group.

Donald alternated ball-handling drills with a conditioning regimen, giving the boys a ten-minute break every hour to rest or practice shooting techniques. Other than taking forty-five minutes out for lunch, Donald kept the boys working.

David followed a similar but less strenuous routine on the other end of the court, and at day's end, fifteen boys collapsed onto the nearby bleachers.

"What kind of talent do you have in the younger group?" Dale asked David that evening.

"We've got a couple of good athletes," David said. "But they have a long way to go before they'll be handling the ball the way we want them to."

"I've been pleased with my bunch," Donald said. "The Kansas boy lacks the ball-handling skills of the others, but he's a hard worker, and he's loaded with natural ability. By the time district play starts, I think he'll be the best player in the league."

"What about Chris and Joe?" Dale asked.

"They're a little behind on their skills, but they're better than when they left the team last year. I'm sure they've been in the high school gym working on their own. If they all pan out, you could be looking at a district championship next season."

"It was okay to have that goal last year, but the first day I meet with this team, I'm going to set the expectation of a state championship."

A scrimmage game was scheduled for Friday night at eight. Some parents, mostly mothers, had dropped by and watched the drills through the week, but fans anxious to see the boys' progress filled the activities building for the game.

To form teams, Donald and David combined their groups, trying to balance the talent between two squads. Dale sat in the stands and was pleasantly surprised at the level of play, especially in the fourth quarter when both coaches put their best players on the floor. The two instructors agreed to play all the boys through the first three quarters, and then to play the best performers during the final period.

The coaches matched Chad against Todd in the post position, Chris against Joe at one forward position, Marty against Josh at the other forward spot, Jimmy against Eddie at guard, and split reserves for the remaining position. David coached Chad's team, and Donald took the team led by Todd, the newcomer.

After getting past early jitters, the boys settled down and played tough defense and almost error-free offense. Todd had a twenty-pound and two-inch height advantage on Chad, which gave him the rebounding edge, but Chad had better ball-handling skills, and thus he led in points. Eddie passed the ball better than Jimmy, but Jimmy shot the ball better than his counterpart, while the match-up between Chris and Joe was a close one.

The first half ended with David's team leading by three points, but Eddie erased that advantage within the first minute of the third quarter, giving Donald's team a one point lead. The score seesawed back and forth throughout the third and fourth quarters and stood tied with fifteen seconds left.

"Todd," Donald said during a timeout, "I want you to lineup at the right side of the free-throw circle. Eddie, you're going to drive the ball to the left side of the key, and then pass the ball back to Chris who'll rotate toward the top of the circle. When Chris catches the ball, Todd, spin to your left around Chad and break toward the goal. Chris, lob the ball up to the rim so Todd can jump, grab it, and dunk it, all in one motion."

The play worked to perfection, and when Todd jammed the ball through the goal, the fans jumped to their feet, screaming and clapping.

With the crowd still buzzing over the exciting dunk and with four seconds left on the clock, Chad heaved a long pass to a streaking Jimmy who pulled up six feet from the top of the circle and tried a desperate shot. The crowd roared when the ball swished through the net. The game was tied and the clock showed zeroes.

Both squads were exhausted, so David and Donald decided to settle the contest with a free-throw competition. The ten boys on the floor at the end of the game would compete by rotating between teams, each player shooting one free-throw. The first team to miss a shot would lose, if the opposing player made his. After all ten players made their first two attempts, Joe missed his third shot. If Chris could sink his, David's team would win. It was the kind of game-winning situation Dale wanted to see, and Chris sunk the shot for the victory.

The crowd applauded for five minutes while the players congratulated and consoled each other.

After the players relaxed over the weekend with their families, they returned Monday morning for another week of basketball drills, which included more five-against-five competition, with David and Donald trying different combinations of players. As Dale watched, he saw that he would be facing a challenge in the fall, but one every coach hopes to have. He would have eight players who were capable of starting any game, and two more making rapid improvement in their skills.

The game on Friday night of the second week was as fiercely played as the one a week earlier, but with more skill and polish. Jimmy and Eddie handled the ball error-free, while repeatedly driving the lane and kicking the ball out to Chris and Joe who swished shot after shot. Around the goal, Todd and Chad battled for rebounds and put-back shots like a couple of warhorses. Todd slammed a couple of lob shots that brought the fans to their feet, but Chad countered with unstoppable hook shots. Ultimately, Chad's team pulled out a two-point win when he tipped in a missed last-second shot.

"Coach," Principal Kennemer said, beaming, "I think either of those teams can win the district championship."

"Maybe so," Dale said, "but I plan to put a team on the court that can win in Austin in March."

The second basketball camp did not have players with the talent level of the first one, but Dale saw significant progress by all the players, and in four of the boys he saw potential varsity talent. Overall, the camps were a huge success, and parents of most of the boys immediately signed up their sons to return the next summer.

While Marilyn and David ran the girls' basketball camp, Dale checked on his other projects, including the purchase of the Colquitt Ranch, whose absentee owner lived in Amarillo.

Tom had all the paperwork ready for Dale's review. The contract specified four thousand acres for three hundred sixty thousand dollars, including mineral rights. Dale had an option to buy the Colquitt cattle, but Tom discouraged that. He described the herd as old and inferior. Dale refused the option, and requested that the cattle were to be off the land within two weeks from the date he signed the contract, which he did on August 2. Now, Dale would soon have eleven times the original ranch acreage to manage and make productive. With over four hundred thousand dollars tied up in land, Dale was anxious to build up his herd.

"Tom," Dale said, "call Sammy Burns in Wichita Falls, and let's get the Colquitt Ranch stocked as soon as possible."

"Boss, before we do that, I recommend we clean out the stock ponds, drill a water well, and repair the fences. The extra water will allow us to run fifty more cows."

"How long do you think that'll take?"

"I'm staying awfully busy with the lake project, plans for the dormitory, and searching for winter feed for the cattle. I think we need to hire a couple of hands to get that place ready."

"Hands?"

"Workers."

"Do you have anybody in mind?"

"I know a couple of brothers, Jesus and Jose, who did fence work on a ranch over near Matador, and they just might be available."

"Where'll they stay?"

"There's a little old house on the Colquitt ranch. I'd move it to the western entrance, and fix it up for them. That'll be handy for their work, and it'll also help us keep out unwanted visitors."

Dale agreed and asked Tom to keep him informed of anything he needed in getting the new land ready and stocked.

That night Dale told Marilyn about his decision to hire a couple of new employees, along with the plans for housing them.

"And we need to be planning our new house," Dale said.

"I've been perfectly happy right here," Marilyn replied. "I've always loved this cozy little bungalow. But I admit that it hasn't been quite the same since the break-in."

"I've got Tom laying out plans for a dormitory adjacent to the activities building," Dale said, "and I'd like to build our house a little farther from the collection of buildings down here. Also, after what happened with that burglar, I want our new house to have a first-rate security system that monitors all entrances, including those to the ranch, and we need a vault that'll hold and protect all the legal documents we're collecting. I don't think this bungalow can handle all that."

"I have thought about it," she said, smiling. "I'd like it to have an underground basement as protection from tornadoes, as well as a hideout in case of an intruder. And I'd like to have the best possible view of the ranch."

"Merr, I want to finalize the plans before I get tied up with school in a few weeks."

After dinner they sketched and noted what they wanted, including three bedrooms, a spacious family area, a basement, and a large patio.

"I've already selected the location for the house," Marilyn said, slipping her arm around Dale. "It's right up there at the top of the ridge about half a mile to the east."

"I like that," Dale said. "There're lots of big cedars up there, and when we dam up Stone Canyon, we'll be able to see the water in the distance."

The next day Dale and Marilyn drove to Lubbock and met with Ted Jackson, the architect, who promised to have three house plans ready for them to choose from within ten days.

"What builders do you recommend?" Dale asked.

The man named three, including Caprock Homes, which he seemed to favor, so Dale and Marilyn went there first.

"Once you bring your house plans to me," the builder said, "I can get you a bid within two weeks, unless you want something really exotic."

"We want an underground basement that'll withstand a tornado, and a few other features that might be considered unusual," Dale explained.

"I'll tell you what," the builder said. "When Mr. Jackson completes the drawings, I'll come out to your place with him, just to make sure I know what you want."

Dale and Marilyn thanked the man and headed for their pickup.

"Dale," Marilyn said when he turned east onto Highway 82, "aren't you going to check with the other two home builders?"

"Nope," he said.

"Why not?"

"It's like this," Dale said, smiling. "I heard a story about a man who had outlived two wives. When asked which one he'd be buried beside, he said he had a burial plot right between his two darlings. 'However,' the man explained, 'I've told the funeral director to tilt me a little toward Tillie.' In this case, I felt like that architect was tilted a little toward Caprock Homes."

"Where do you hear such things?" Marilyn asked, shaking her head.

"You'd be surprised what you can learn if you pay attention down at Martha's Café."

When Dale and Marilyn arrived back at the ranch, Tom pulled up beside them in the dusty old pickup.

"Dale," he said hurriedly, "a couple of those Childress engineers from the Army Corps came by today. I showed them Stone Canyon and its tributaries. They even went down into the canyon and checked for watermarks along the walls. They say it's carried six to seven feet of water down near the mouth, probably during a big rain we had during early spring a year ago. They sure sounded optimistic."

"Unfortunately, most of the canyon, at least four miles of it, is on the Thompson ranch. Tom, do you know this Thompson fellow?"

"I know of him," Tom said, shaking his head. "Folks say he's a tough old rascal. I don't think anybody's ever dared to try to buy his place, and I can assure you that the tax people avoid him like the plague. I think they just take whatever he volunteers to pay."

"We could build a private lake using the mile that we own, but if we could put the dam near the south end where it funnels down to less than fifty feet in width, it'd sure be more cost effective, and it'd back up a lot more water."

"Boss, that canyon drains into the South Pease River. Do you think anybody is goin' to howl about us shuttin' that off?"

"I doubt it, since it's not a flowing river, and the canyon is all on private property."

"Yeah, it's on old man Thompson's property, and he's goin' to be the first one to howl."

"Well, I'm going to give him a chance, because that's the only way to build a reservoir large enough to serve this whole area."

"I hope you've got your life insurance paid up," Tom said, smiling.

Through the tax collector's office, Dale got directions to where Jake Thompson lived, including a description of his unmistakable entrance, and headed south on Highway 83, turning west on a country road. Eventually Dale spotted the sign hanging on a rusty gate. Lettered with a branding iron, it said, "HOME TO RATTLESNAKES AND DOGS." Wired to the bottom of that sign was a bullet-riddled one that read, "KEEP OUT." Ignoring the signs and the bullet holes, Dale raised the wire loop, pushed the gate open and drove through. After closing the gate, Dale followed a dusty lane until he pulled up in front of a rustic old ranch house made of weathered cedar.

"Mr. Thompson?" Dale asked when an elderly man responded to his knock.

The six-foot, burly rancher stood staring at his visitor, his gray hair disheveled, a week's growth of matching beard, one strap of his overalls hanging loose, and his rundown work boots unlaced.

"Didn't you see that 'KEEP OUT' sign down yonder on the gate?"

"Yes, sir," Dale said, "but I need to talk to you."

"That ain't the question. Question is, whether I need to talk to you, and I don't."

"Sir, I'd like to build a lake. This whole country needs the water, your place included."

"I've lived here seventy-seven years. Don't you think I know that?"

"I'm sure you do, but to build a lake large enough to do the job, I need to buy your portion of Stone Canyon."

"Ain't for sale. It's dry as a gourd, anyhow."

"It had six feet of water roaring through it spring before last. If we'd had a dam across it then, we'd be well on our way toward a lake."

"Who are you?"

"Coach Dale Rory. I own the Estes . . ."

"I know what you own," the old man said, rubbing his whiskered chin. "You married that Stone gal. I knowed her grandpa, and her grandma. And I know her ma, too."

"I'll pay you a fair price, Mr. Thompson. I just want the canyon and enough right-of-way to manage the lake."

The old man stepped out onto the porch and slipped down in a straw-bottomed rocking chair.

"Fred was a fine man," he said. "Stubborn, but a fine man. He was yore wife's grandpa. Helped me build this house in the fall of thirty-eight."

"I wish I'd known him," Dale said, leaning against a porch post.

"Had no time for foolishness. None of us did back then."

"What about the lake, Mr. Thompson?"

"I ain't sellin' nothin'," the man said, pushing to his feet. "Close the gate on your way out. Let a cow loose, you pay for it."

Dale drove away, discouraged, and yet not convinced that Thompson would not sell. Obviously, the old man had good memories of Marilyn's grandfather, and that might leave the door cracked just enough.

A few days later the architect and homebuilder from Lubbock drove up at the Roryian. After looking at three house plans, Dale and Marilyn prodded them into Dale's pickup and drove up to the planned house site. After making a few adjustments to accommodate the basement and to ease landscaping, they had the building perimeter staked off.

"Dale," Tom Jordan said after the visitors had gone, "I've hired Jesus and Jose, and have a mover coming to relocate the old house. I expect we'll need to spend five thousand fixing it up, about seven thousand for a water well with a windmill, and then we'll need three thousand for fencing supplies."

"I'll adjust the monthly transfer of funds to your account, enough to cover the salaries of the new employees, along with fifteen thousand to cover the other costs."

"Also, I've talked to an aerial photo company in Lubbock. They'll come out and take pictures of the canyon and its tributaries during the next big rain."

"That's great. Now, if I can just convince Mr. Thompson to sell us the rest of Stone Canyon."

"Boss, I think you'd better plan on putting that dam at your fence line. That old fool would sell his dead mother before he'd part with an acre of that ranch."

"I'm not so sure about that," Dale said, laughing. "Maybe his bark is worse than his bite."

"Rattlesnakes don't bark, Boss."

Dale laughed as he headed for the house, recalling his encounter with the diamondback in the canyon. He had avoided a bite then; could he somehow do it again?

Two days later Dale was up looking over the new house site, showing the trenchers the staked corners, when he saw an old International pickup grinding its way up toward the bungalow. Rust colored, the truck's original paint was camouflaged under years of West Texas dirt, but Dale recognized it as Jake Thompson's, and jumped in his pickup and hurried down the hill.

"Mr. Thompson," he called out as the old man swung open the truck door and dropped a badly scuffed boot to the running board.

"You still want to build that lake?" Thompson asked, sitting sideways in his truck.

"I sure do," Dale replied.

"Here's my deal," the old rancher said. "You leave me fifty acres where the house sits and the road to it, along with the barn and cattle pens, and I'll sell you the whole kit and caboodle for eighty-five dollars an acre. That's five sections, or thirty-two hundred acres to you greenhorns, less the home place. But, you gotta name the lake after the Thompson family."

"You've got a deal, Mr. Thompson," Dale said, smiling like a kid at Christmas.

"You get all the paperwork ready and bring it to the ranch, along with cash money, and I'll sign. If anybody gives you trouble, show 'em this paper," Thompson said, pulling a piece of paper torn off a notepad from a top pocket of his overalls.

As Thompson cranked his old truck and drove away, Dale glanced down at the note, which read, "Do what Rory says. He's buying my ranch. J. Thompson." The signature was scrawled across the bottom of the paper.

The next day Dale went to the title company, explained the deal, and showed the note to an attendant.

"Coach, I'd like to help, but that note says nothing about power of attorney."

"I understand," Dale said, taking back the paper.

"Hello, Coach," the manager said, recognizing Dale. "What can we do for you?"

Dale explained as he unfolded the note, prompting the manager to motion Dale into his office.

"That note's not legally binding," the manager said, "but if we don't do what it says, Thompson will be up here threatening the whole lot of us. We're going to do this and hope to goodness no auditor ever challenges it."

Dale then went by the bank and explained that he would need, within the next few days, two hundred sixty-seven thousand, seven hundred fifty dollars in cash. After much consternation, they agreed to have it ready for him.

Two days later, Dale dropped by the title company and picked up the papers and then stopped by the bank for the money. He drove to Thompson's ranch, showed him the papers and the money, and the old man signed without reading a word or counting a single bill.

"All right," the old man said. "Now you get busy and build my lake, young man."

Dale thanked the rancher, jumped in his pickup and left, making sure to close the gate on his way out.

11 ___

"Honey," Dale said to Marilyn, "now that we own the entire canyon, we need to turn this private lake project into a public project. If the watershed will fill the canyon, it could provide water for all of Cottle County, and the people need to take ownership of it. We can provide the land, gather information to justify the lake, and promote it locally, but eventually it needs to be a county-wide endeavor."

"How do we do that?"

"We have to establish a county water district, and I think that means we have to get some politician involved. For that to happen, we've got to put together a presentation to sell the idea to the locals, who are voters to a politician. I think the key to that is proof that a sizeable lake in Stone Canyon is feasible."

"So, we need a big rain," she said. "Then we need that aerial photography company in Lubbock to capture pictures of the runoff."

"That's right, and we need those pictures to show there's adequate water running through the canyon to fill a lake in five to seven years."

"We're just getting into the hurricane season in the Gulf of Mexico," she said. "If we don't get a big rain from that, then it'll probably be springtime before there'll be another chance."

The next morning, Dale headed for the Paddock county clerk's office.

"Ma'am, where can I get aerial photos of Cottle County?" he asked.

"The Soil and Water Conservation office in Childress," she replied. "Are you wanting them for your lake project?"

"You've heard about it?"

"Sure," the woman said. "Everybody's talking about it."

"And what do people think?"

"Some say it's wonderful," she said, and then hesitated. "Others say Coach Mass has become Brother Noah. They say you're building a lake and hoping for a flood."

"I hope we are blessed with a real gully washer," Dale said, laughing. "But, I won't be praying for another flood."

Dale found the photos he needed at the Soil and Water Conservation office, and made copies of those that showed Stone Canyon and the surrounding area. Then he dropped by the office of the Regional Water Planning Group where he described his lake project.

"I hold the deeds to the land and will donate it to the project, if the state will foot the bill for building the lake," Dale explained.

"How many acres do you think the lake will cover?"

"It'll be about five miles long, and allowing access to the shore line, and lakefront property, I'd guess about two thousand acres."

"What do you figure the land's worth?"

"Two hundred thousand dollars as it sits, but well over a million dollars when the lake fills up and folks start buying lake lots."

"Let me get my manager," the representative said.

"Mr. Rory, I'm George Killian, office manager here."

"Pleased to meet you, Mr. Killian."

"Ruth says you want to donate two thousand acres for a lake west of Paddock."

Dale nodded.

"Based on your gift of the land and a recommendation from the Corps of Engineers, I assure you we'll make this project our top priority. If we can help you in any way, just let us know."

"I'll be glad to deed the land to the appropriate entity for the duration of time that the lake is used to provide water to the public. Should public use end at some future date, the land will revert to my ranch."

"That's certainly reasonable."

"Now, what can I do to get this project going?"

"You'll need to gather data relative to the current water supply in Cottle County versus water needs, how your lake will meet those needs, and its impact on the people and economy of the area," the manager told Dale. "Then we'll submit your project to the Texas Water Development Board in Austin."

"Where can I find the kind of data you require?"

"We can give you some socioeconomic data to help you get started. Also, the Association of Texas Soil and Water Conservation Districts can provide help."

After gathering and studying the data, a clear picture began to emerge. Cottle County covered nine hundred square miles and had lost twenty-four percent of its population in the past ten years. Only fifteen percent of its residents had a college degree, and its population density was down to two people per square mile. Its surface water area was zero.

Further study of historical population records showed that nearly ninety-four hundred people had lived in Cottle County back in 1930. The Dust Bowl and the Great Depression of that decade had driven over two thousand residents away and reduced the number of farms from over a thousand to only seven hundred. Then from 1950 to 1960, a prolonged drought period, the population had dropped thirty-one percent and the number of farms plummeted to less than four hundred. Clearly, the county had suffered its greatest losses during drought years. Without stored water to get through these dry periods, the downward spiral would continue.

Armed with this data, combined with his plans for the lake, Dale met with Paddock's Mayor Johnson who enthusiastically agreed to schedule a meeting with the City Council.

"The empty buildings in Paddock," Dale said to the Council members, "are directly attributable to the lack of water. If we don't act soon, we'll lose the critical population mass required to pull off this project."

"Why are you doing this?" Jed Tolbert, the pharmacist councilman asked. "What's in it for you?"

"I'm a part of this community," Dale said. "I'm heavily invested in this area, so whatever is good for the community is good for me. I believe in this project to the point that I'm willing to provide two thousand acres for the lake."

"That represents quite a chunk of money," banker Chet Williams said. "How do you expect to recover your investment?"

"If the lake is a success, it'll bring in boaters, fishermen, and people from Lubbock, Amarillo, Abilene, and Wichita Falls who want a country getaway. I expect to develop a housing addition on adjacent land. Also, all property in the area will increase in value, maybe two or three fold."

"Nobody's going to support this project unless there's enough runoff water to support a lake," the elderly Tolbert said. "And I haven't heard anything that convinces me this is anything more than a boondoggle."

"A Corps of Engineers representative says that about a year ago, following a spring rain, six to seven feet of water ran through the canyon," Dale said. "But I believe it'll take stronger evidence to convince the Regional Water Planning Group up in Childress. That's why I plan to take pictures of the canyon and tributaries right after a big rain."

"Sounds like you need two floods," a doubting councilman said, chuckling, "one to justify your lake and another to fill it up."

"What can we do?" Sylvia Phillips, the school superintendent's wife, asked.

"Contact your state representative and the senator for this district," Dale replied. "We'll need a politician to push this at the state level."

When there were no more questions, Dale thanked the group for their time and promised to return as soon as he had further data.

School started and Dale became immersed in teaching and preparing for the next basketball season. During the first two weeks of September, Dale focused on helping David Green plan for his basketball program for the younger boys, many of whom had attended the summer basketball camps.

When Dale arrived home one afternoon, Marilyn greeted him with a hug and a twinkle in her eyes.

"Honey," she said, "our prayers may be answered this weekend."

"What are you talking about?"

"There's a hurricane in the middle of the gulf, warm air from the southwest, and a cool front pushing down from the northwest. If these get together, we could have that flood."

"Watch it closely, and if it looks like rain, notify that aerial photo place in Lubbock. We've got to have pictures."

The weather systems met over the West Texas plains on Monday of the following week, and indeed produced rain. Dale was at school when Marilyn called the Lubbock photo company. Within an hour, she heard a low-flying plane overhead, and guessed that the Plains Aerial Photography crew was snapping pictures of the canyon and its feeder tributaries.

The next day, with rain still falling, Marilyn called the photography company and asked about pictures.

"We've got some," the man explained, "but we're flying again this afternoon. The weather is not quite as severe, so we can fly lower and get better shots."

On Friday a package of pictures showed up in the Rory post office box, and that evening Dale and Marilyn spread them across the dining table. The pictures covered three days, showing a progression of water flow.

"Look at all that water," Marilyn said, grabbing Dale's arm. "I had no idea all those little gullies and ravines carried so much water."

"The good news is that these feeders maintain a steady, visible flow of water for three days, building into a torrent of water flowing through the canyon. I'm sure the engineers can calculate an approximate volume, and hopefully their numbers will support a lake project."

The following Monday, Marilyn took the pictures to the Corps of Engineers in Childress.

"Ma'am," the chief engineer said, "I believe you've got the evidence we need to give our support to your project, but I'd like to come out and take a look at the drainage patterns and the latest water marks in the canyon."

Two days later the engineers had drawn up a document that estimated the total water flow into the canyon, drained from twenty square miles of watershed, and suggested that it could be filled to capacity within seven years, assuming future weather patterns similar to those of the past five years.

"A positive feature of this lake is that the canyon is narrow and deep, creating a very favorable ratio of water surface to volume. And, being a north-south lake, the canyon rim will shade the water from the sun much of the day.

Large, sprawling lakes in this arid country lose as much as ten feet of water to evaporation in the hot months. That won't happen with this one."

Adding the new information to the old, Dale and Marilyn prepared a presentation to be given to the City Council, including the aerial photos and the Corps of Engineers' report.

"Honey, you may have to make this presentation," Dale explained. "School and preparing for the basketball season is taking all my time."

"Oh no!" she said. "I'd be scared to death. Some of those men have children older than I am."

"Merr, you've gone through all this data, and you understand it as well as I do. I don't care how old those members are, they'll pay attention when you show them that they can have a lake less than ten miles from town."

"Maybe," she said, looping her arm around him, "but you're Mr. Massasuta, the big leader around here. I know they'll listen to you."

"Yeah, like Councilman Tolbert. He listened, but he wasn't convinced. Maybe he'll believe you."

Marilyn continued to worry about it, but she knew she would have to give the presentation. She called Sylvia Phillips, the superintendent's wife, who owned a local gift shop and was a councilwoman.

"Mrs. Phillips, I'll be giving the presentation on the lake project, and I thought you might get me scheduled with the Council."

"Certainly, and I want you to know that we're excited about this undertaking. If there's anything I can do to help, just contact me."

"I'll admit I'm nervous about standing up there in front of the Council, but Dale's tied up at school and this is too important to delay."

"I assure you that we'll support you. Well, Jed Tolbert might be a bit negative, but you can just ignore him."

The City Council set the meeting for the next Wednesday afternoon at five, when Dale would be with his basketball team.

"I'll go with you," Sybil told Marilyn. "Tolbert had better not try to sass my daughter."

For the next few days, Marilyn studied the data, made blowups of pictures, wrote out her speech, and practiced her delivery. She alternated between a short talk that depended almost entirely on the data, the pictures, and the Corps of Engineers' report, and a longer version that emphasized the potential impact to the city and county. Dale encouraged her to make the longer speech.

"They've got to understand that a lack of water accounts for the continual decline in the population and business opportunities," he said. "And you've got to make them see that the lake will reverse that trend."

The morning of the presentation to the City Council, Marilyn took the recent runoff pictures and the Corps of Engineers' report to the Regional Water Planning Group in Childress, along with a document deeding the canyon land, contingent upon the lake being built within a year and the water being used to serve Cottle County. The manager promised to forward the information to the Texas Water Development Board, along with the regional group's plea to give this project top priority.

That afternoon, with enlarged pictures stuck on stiff chart paper supported by four easels, Marilyn and Sybil showed up at the City Council meeting fifteen minutes early. By five o'clock, they had everything ready. Within five minutes, the Council members were seated and an audience of fifteen or twenty people had filed inside.

Marilyn stepped up to the podium and immediately noticed that Jed Tolbert was absent. She suddenly felt a weight lifted from her shoulders and began her presentation.

"Thank you for this opportunity, and I hope you won't mind that I'm here instead of my husband. Because some of you may not know the background of this project, let me briefly explain why we want and need a lake in this area.

"In my lifetime, the population of Cottle County has decreased over thirty percent. Not only has this exodus impacted the county, but it has left its evidence of decay on Paddock as well. Bank deposits are down over twenty-five percent. A dozen businesses have closed their doors in the past twenty years. The local hospital has been shut down. Tax revenues are down comparable to bank deposits, and our streets have been neglected to the point of being beyond repair. Our school system skimps by, leaving our students with inferior lab equipment and without electronic access to remote learning centers. All of this is due to a community drained of its lifeblood, its vitality."

She then covered the data that showed a direct correlation between the drought years and the dramatic reductions in population and the dwindling number of farms in Cottle County, highlighted by the Dust Bowl of the 1930s and the dry years of the 1950s.

"Clearly, our continual decline is tied to a lack of water, and that's why we propose that a reliable water supply for the town and the area will pump new life into vacant buildings, new taxes into the city and county coffers, and new customers through the doors of your businesses.

"What happens if we don't do this?" she asked rhetorically.

"Many of you are reaching retirement age, and you would like to sell your businesses to provide you a retirement nest egg. But who'll buy your dying businesses? What's going to attract a young businessman or businesswoman here? Five out of six of your own adult children leave because there's no job for them here, no future in Paddock.

"Now, how will a lake change all this?

"First, people from surrounding towns will come to the lake for boating, fishing, or recreation. We'll form a water district, and with the lakefront property we're donating, it can sell a million dollars worth of lake lots to fund itself. These vacationers, boaters, fishermen, and campers will spend their weekends locally. That means they'll eat in our restaurants, shop in our stores, and the lake lots will bring in property taxes. They'll bring their boats in for repairs; they'll purchase gasoline, fishing tackle, and a hundred other things. They'll have fishing tournaments and want a room for a couple of nights. Manufacturing companies require water, and we can promise it to them. With an increase in revenue and sales taxes and growth in property-tax dollars, we can build new streets, improve our schools, and you'll find people interested in buying your businesses.

"But how do we get this lake?" she asked.

"In a few minutes, I hope you'll look at the aerial photos my mother has over there, and you'll see that Stone Canyon is the right place to collect water. You'll read a Corps of Engineers' report that says the canyon can be filled with water within seven years. And you'll see a commitment by the Texas Regional Water Planning Group in Childress to prioritize this project.

"So, I believe we have an opportunity to revitalize our trickling business stream with a flow of fresh revenue, if we'll just act now. If, after reviewing the data we have here tonight, you're convinced, then I hope you'll write or otherwise contact our state representative and district senator and urge them to support this project."

At this point she had arranged for Sylvia to hand out copies of the Engineers' report, along with contact information for the referenced politicians.

"Thank you for your time, and after you've taken a look at the pictures and documents, I'll be glad to try to answer any questions."

The Council members and audience scanned the report and then huddled around the information charts and pictures, while Marilyn gathered her notes.

"Young lady," a man said from behind her, "I've never been so impressed by a presentation, or by a presenter."

"Why thank . . ." Marilyn said turning. "Dale, where did you come from?"

Without Marilyn's notice, he had slipped in through a side door midway of the presentation.

By then, several others were congratulating Marilyn on the fine job she had done and thanked her and Dale for sponsoring the project.

After about twenty minutes of looking at the aerial pictures and reading the Engineers' report, the Council reconvened. After no more than ten minutes of discussion, the membership voted to support the lake project and to send a letter to their congressmen requesting help in Austin. Then they passed a resolution commending Marilyn and Dale for their work and contribution to the venture.

Meanwhile, Tom Jordan stayed busy supervising Jesus and Jose's work on the Colquitt Ranch to the west, purchasing and storing winter hay, and selling a crop of eight-month old steers. While doing these things, he also oversaw work on the new house and dormitory.

Melba Kennemer and Sybil sponsored a few events at the activities building, including three church groups and a forty-two tournament. With all the traffic around the main collection of buildings, Marilyn was especially looking forward to moving into the new house and reclaiming some of the privacy she and Dale had lost due to all the commotion at the ranch.

In early October, a team of advisers from the Texas Water Development Board showed up at the Roryian to take a look at the canyon. They seemed favorably impressed with the lake location and local enthusiasm for the project when they met with citizens heading up the new Cottle County Water District.

"You can get all the help you need from the Association of Texas Soil and Water Conservation Districts," the adviser said to the district officers. "And you'll want to join the state-wide organization."

A week later, both congressmen representing Cottle County called the mayor and Dale, committing their vote and full sway of their influence to the project. That was followed by an article in the *Paddock Post* in which the same two issued glowing statements regarding their support of and expectations for funding of the project by the Texas Water Development Board.

Then on Friday of the third week of October, Marilyn got a phone call from the Regional Water Planning Group in Childress.

"We're forwarding a letter to you from the Texas Water Development Board," the manager said. "They've approved the Stone Canyon lake project and set aside twenty million dollars in funding for its construction. I think a contractor will likely show up within a couple of weeks to look at the canyon and plan the dam."

"Officially, it's called Lake Thompson," Marilyn said. "Please make sure that name is on all the documentation, and we'll remind the Cottle County Water District to use that name on all local papers and signs."

Late that afternoon when Dale got home, he noticed his and Marilyn's horses saddled and grazing in a lot beside the barn.

"Let's take a ride," she explained.

Dale followed her lead as they galloped up over the ridge behind the house and down the long slope toward the former Thompson Ranch. It was dusky dark and a brisk, northwest wind blew cold against their backs as they slid out of the saddle along the west rim of Stone Canyon.

"It's beautiful out here," she said, looking first into the shadowed depths of the chasm and then farther into the blue haze hanging over the distant South Pease River.

"And it'll be even more beautiful when it's full of water," Dale said, nodding toward the dark canyon.

"Are you sure? There'll be people everywhere, boat motors buzzing, and car horns blaring. The serenity we see and feel right now will disappear forever."

"There is a degree of sadness in seeing nature rearranged for man's use, but in this case, I think the potential good outweighs the loss."

"Within a couple of weeks they'll be here with dozers, and draglines, and trucks. It'll never be the same again."

"A couple of weeks? Are you sure?"

"I got a call today. Our lake project has been approved."

Dale threw his arms around his wife and lifted her off the ground, swinging her around, and kissing her repeatedly.

"It's going to happen," he said. "It's really going to happen."

"Come over here," she said, leading him toward her grazing pony.

From a saddlebag, she pulled out a blanket, some sandwiches, a couple of can drinks, and a box of matches.

"Build us a little fire while I spread this blanket and set out our dinner," she said.

Within minutes, they were stretched out beside a flickering campfire, finishing their sandwiches, and reviewing their lives together.

"Honey," she said, "a year ago I could not have dreamed of how my life would change so quickly. I'm the happiest woman in all of Texas."

"And you've made me the happiest man in all the world."

"Before we head back to the house, let's just lay close here for a while."

Dale slid closer, pulled her snug against him, and slowly lowered his lips to hers.

12 ___

With the Stone Canyon project approved, Dale and Tom Jordan met with the water district board and asked their approval to build a paved road from Highway 83, south of Paddock, to Lake Thompson and then continue along the east canyon rim overlooking the lake, forming a horseshoe around the upper end. From the road at the shallow end, Dale had penciled in three boat ramps to be cut into the canyon walls and extend to the water's edge, keeping in mind summertime's anticipated low water level. Also, he proposed to construct a camping area and a playground on the east side of the lake and a few picnic spots along the road.

"The district won't have the money to build the needed infrastructure until it can sell or lease lake lots, so I'm offering to do it to attract people to the area now," Dale explained. "Hopefully, by the end of spring the water level will support boaters, but without the ramps, the lake would be inaccessible to them. There's also a somewhat selfish reason. The quicker people flock to the lake, the quicker we can build a housing addition out there."

The water district board was delighted with Dale's proposal, giving its unanimous approval. "The road will accelerate income from the waterfront property," a director predicted, "giving us much-needed working capital."

Meanwhile, Dale and Marilyn's new house was completed just prior to the start of the basketball season. Its prominent features were a spacious and sky-lighted family room with a huge stone fireplace, a large master bedroom with French double doors opening onto a sprawling patio that encircled a three-tiered fountain with water cascading downward into a goldfish pond, and finally a basement beneath the patio that was accessible by a stairway hidden behind a rotating wall inside a master bedroom closet.

The basement housed the satellite-based security system and its monitors, along with a separate central air and ventilation system, furniture, a kitchenette, a bathroom, a stocked cupboard, and a bed, all designed for extended use, if necessary. Electrical power for this underground sanctuary came from a remote generator capable of sustaining the room for sixteen hours before requiring refueling. A battery powered uninterruptible power system monitored input from the public utility power line and automatically kicked in upon its failure. The batteries would provide continuous current until the remote generator powered itself up and was producing the required level of electrical power. Thus, the basement offered protection in case a storm destroyed the house, and a safe haven in case of an intruder. While secure in their underground bunker, they could use the security system as their eyes to the outside.

An escape tunnel connected the basement to a remote pump-station, which provided water to the house from a deep well, and also contained the power generator. This combination facility was hidden in the side of the hill with an inconspicuous vent that released the motor's exhaust fumes through the earthen roof. Dale's determination to protect his wife and eventual family stemmed from fearful accounts he had heard and read about Texas-size killer storms and from the break-in at the bungalow.

"Merr," Dale said, while watching their security monitors, "your mother is as vulnerable as we are to a break-in. We should connect her to this same system."

Marilyn agreed, so Dale instructed the security company to install a remote-controlled gate with a camera at the entrance of Stone Place Ranch. Sybil could watch the entrance on a monitor and open or close the gate from the house, as well as with a hand-held device in her car. The system communicated by satellite dish with the one at the Roryian, so ranch access could be monitored and controlled from either ranch. Additionally, Dale had a pipe fence installed the length of the road-front for both ranches.

While the house construction was proceeding rapidly, Dale was busy with his basketball team. From the first official practice, he knew he had an exceptional team. He spent a few days drilling his squad on fundamentals, but most of his players had a year of experience under his system and a basketball camp under their belts, so they had incorporated his techniques into their play to the point of habit. His top ten players soon ran his offense and defense like they were born to them. Scrimmages were almost like games, with the competition fierce and always competitive. Practicing daily against accomplished players elevated his team's performance to a peak level.

The Palominos won their first five games by twenty points or more, with Dale's second team playing almost as much as his starters. Opponents were often completely demoralized by halftime.

Dale then took his team to Childress for an invitational tournament in which the rest of the invitees were AA and AAA schools. The Palominos fought their way to the championship game against a Wichita Falls squad and won in the last minute of play on a pair of Todd Anderson dunks and a corner three-point shot by Chris Powell. All the area newspapers covered the game and heralded the Palominos as potential state champions of Class A. Most papers carried a picture of the Palominos boarding or exiting their luxury team bus. All the media attention given to Dale's squad essentially stamped a bull's eye on their chest, targeted by every opponent that stepped on the court with them.

Then the Palominos traveled to Abilene for the holiday tournament and won easily. Palomino stories became even more fantastic, and as they breezed through their district schedule, the hype around Dale's undefeated team flourished beyond reason. Yet, the Palominos seemed unaffected as they dominated opponent after opponent all the way to the state tournament in Austin.

Palomino fans packed their bags, while Paddock businesses locked their doors, and followed their amazing team to Austin, where they were not disappointed. The Palominos won the championship game by eighteen points, and three of the starters were named to the Class A, All-State team. A couple of sportswriters claimed that all five Palomino starters should have made the celebrated squad.

"If you didn't get to see the undefeated Paddock Palominos, thoroughbreds from the starter's gate to the finish line," one sportswriter scribbled, "don't fret. They're all underclassmen, so they'll be back next March, taller and better, no doubt."

"Dale," Superintendent Phillips said when the coach handed him the championship trophy, "next year we've got to have our own holiday tournament."

"Mr. Phillips," Dale replied, "our little gym won't seat enough people."

"I've considered that," Phillips said. "I'm going to ask the school board to raise enough money to expand our gym. I'm sure the job can be completed by next fall."

The storybook basketball season infringed on preparations for the baseball schedule, but Dale wasted no time making the transition. In fact, he recognized that he lacked the coaching skills to develop his fine stable of pitchers, so he made a trip to Midwestern State University in Wichita Falls where he met with the baseball coach.

"I've got some pitchers with talent," Dale explained. "With the right guidance, I think they could be outstanding. Do you know a good pitching coach I can hire?"

"There's a retired coach named Willy Collins. He pitched for the Saint Louis Cardinals many years ago, but I don't know if he'd be interested," the man explained. "He's known as Old Leatherarm because he once pitched a seventeen-inning, shutout game."

Dale scribbled down the old pitcher's name and number and gave him a call, explaining his need. Collins gave Dale directions to his little ranch up on the south bank of Red River.

"I've got a six-foot-two pitcher who lost only two games last year," Dale said, sitting on Old Leatherarm's front porch. "I've got another who's six-foot-six and can throw a ball over ninety miles an hour, but he doesn't have good mechanics, and thus he can't throw strikes with consistency."

After half an hour of questions and answers, the retired coach agreed to drive to Paddock and take a look at Dale's pitching staff.

The following afternoon, Willy Collins showed up at the Paddock baseball field. For thirty minutes he sat in the bleachers and watched Chris Powell and Todd Anderson throw pitch after pitch.

"I believe I can help these boys," Old Leatherarm said, as he approached Dale.

"I've checked with the superintendent, and we'll be glad to hire you as a part-time coach," Dale explained.

"I wouldn't do it for the money," Collins explained. "But if these boys want to learn to be real pitchers, I'll work with them two afternoons a week. If they don't listen and work hard, I won't be back."

While Dale and David practiced with the hitters and fielders, Willy Collins restructured the pitching motion of both of Dale's key pitchers, and he came back two days later and continued their lessons.

Old Leatherarm then showed up for the first home game and watched Chris Powell shut down Matador's hitters, allowing only two base-runners through five innings. With the game well in hand, Dale then sent Todd Anderson to the mound, and he battled his way through the last two innings, allowing no hits but walking three batters.

Collins continued to work with the Palomino pitchers through the season, and the team won the district championship handily, Todd pitching the final game with fourteen strikeouts and walking only two batters.

In the regional tournament, Dale's team made it to the finals, with Chris Powell on the mound. Chris struggled with his control, and finally left the game with the Palominos behind, 3-2. Todd came in and shut out the opposing batters, but the Palominos did not score another run, and Paddock was eliminated from the playoffs.

"I can't thank you enough," Dale said to Old Leatherarm. "Our pitching staff improved considerably this season, and clearly all the credit goes to you."

"You've got a couple of dandies," Collins said. "If I can work with them again next season, I expect you'll win the state title."

"With better hitting, we'd have won it this year," Dale said, determining right then that he would find a hitting coach for the next season.

Meanwhile, the first Sunday of the new year had been a special one at the First United Methodist Church. Brother Sammy Burton had retired as of December 31, and Brother Henry Suche was now the new pastor. In a special part of the service, Brother Sammy was honored and presented a check for five thousand dollars from the church, the money coming from Dale's Coins for Christ fund, along with several gifts brought to the altar by various members.

The new pastor was a five-foot-nine, sturdily built man in his mid-fifties, with a quick wit and quicker smile. His abundant energy and ever-ready willingness to help with any community project, when combined with the excitement in town over the possibility of a lake, seemed to revitalize the spirit of the church.

Also, the Stone Canyon dam had been completed six weeks earlier, and with winter and spring rains, it had backed up three miles of water, which stood twenty feet deep near the dam. Sightseers came out every weekend, using the new roads, and the Cottle County Water District had received several inquiries regarding lakefront land, both from individuals and developers.

"I want to wait another year or so and let the lake rise and fish grow before we build our housing section," Dale explained to his wife. "We need an influx of people to justify the project. Also, as the lake fills and people are attracted here, the value of the surrounding property will rise considerably."

Then in June a surprising five-inch rain fell over two days, raising the water level to twenty-four feet and pushing water to the bottom edge of two of the boat ramps.

The water district opened the lake for boaters and skiers, stirring great excitement in town, and the number of people gathering around the lake escalated quickly. The camp ground was full most every weekend, and new customers began showing up in Paddock stores and shops.

"Dale," Mayor Johnson said when he caught the coach and his wife at the grocery store, "some of the shop owners are talking about extending their weekend hours, and we've had contacts from three businessmen interested in locating in Paddock. One is already building a motel on Highway 70 on the western edge of town. He believes that between the lake, our holiday basketball tournament, and your summer camps, he can rent every room through the summer and maintain fifty percent occupancy for ten months of the year."

"The basketball boys and girls will stay in the dorm rooms at the ranch," Dale explained. "However, this year, we'll have a lot more out-of-town campers, and I'm sure their parents will be glad to have a motel room now and then."

"I expected that," the mayor said. "Winning the state championship has got to bring in kids from the surrounding towns."

"It helps, no doubt about that, and I'll have my all-state players leading the camps this summer, so these visiting kids will get to meet them."

"Coach," Mayor Johnson said, "have you heard that Donald Winters, one of your first scholarship winners, made the Dean's List at Midwestern?"

"No, but he's a great kid, and I'll pass the news on to Sybil. She'll make sure he's financially able to stay in school."

"Coach, I need to ask you about something else. There's talk in town about renaming Main Street. They'd like to use your name."

"I appreciate their kind thoughts, but I think that would be premature. I've only been here two years."

"I was afraid you'd feel that way. I'll try to steer them in another direction, but you're a mighty popular man around town. The school kids idolize you; their parents praise you constantly; and our senior citizens who use your van service to go to the doctor, to ride to church, and to get their groceries, swear you must have nail scars in your hands. Now the business people are chiming in. Why, all you'd have to do is put your name on a ballot, and you could have any office in Cottle County, including mine."

"No thanks," Dale said, laughing at the exaggerated praise. "I'll stick with coaching and teaching. You're doing a good job, Mayor, and I hope you'll serve a lot more years."

The addition of a functioning windmill, repairs to fences, cleaning out of five ponds, and the refurbishing of the house on the Colquitt Ranch property were completed during the past winter. Later season rains filled the ponds and as soon as spring grass began sprouting, Tom Jordan bought four hundred fifty head of cattle to stock it. He then put Jesus and Jose to work on the Thompson Ranch, fencing in fifty acres around the old home place. With that done, they began fencing off Stone Canyon, allowing a three-hundred-foot border beyond the road for lakefront property on each side. In early June, Tom explained to Dale that it was ready for cattle, as well.

"A good portion of the Thompson land borders the South Pease, so proportionally it'll graze more cows than the Colquitt Ranch. Allowing two thousand acres for the lake and fifty for the Thompson home-place, that leaves about twelve hundred acres of pasture. I think we can run two hundred head on it."

"Aren't you going to need another worker, another hand?" Dale asked with a chuckle. "Roughly, we'll have seven hundred head of cattle spread over six thousand acres."

"Fact is, Boss, I think we'll need a couple more. Jesus and Jose have a brother, Tomas, who's interested. And there's a cowboy I worked with on the Waggoner Ranch that I'll try to lasso."

"I'm counting on you to do what it takes to run this ranch, so get the help you need."

"Another thing, Boss. With more cowboys and a bigger herd, we need some horses to work the cattle, a *remuda*, as the old-timers used to call a horse herd."

Dale agreed, and while he was busy with the basketball camps, Jordan purchased the cattle and hired Tomas, who moved in with his brothers, and then the foreman signed up the Waggoner cowboy, Luke McCarty.

On Saturday morning a week later, Dale was headed for the activities building when he saw a pickup, pulling a silver trailer camper, stop in front of the bungalow. Knowing the house was empty, he drove on down and introduced himself.

"I'm Luke McCarty," the lean cowboy of about forty replied to Dale's welcome.

"How can I help you?" Dale asked, noticing the man's scraggly beard and long hair hanging from beneath his sweat-stained hat.

"I'm looking for Tom Jordan," the man said. "I'm reporting for work."

"You must be the Waggoner cowboy," Dale said, pointing toward the double-wide. "Just pull on up there."

Later, when Dale saw McCarty's pickup heading across the pasture with the silver-bullet-looking camper bumping along behind, he headed down to see Tom Jordan.

"Tom," Dale said, "is McCarty going to live in that little trailer?"

"Yep, he's a loner. Says he'll park it off out there somewhere and set up house."

"What do you know about his background?"

"Oh, he's a good hand," Jordan said. "He knows cattle ranchin' on a par with any foreman I know. And he's especially good with horses. He'll be buyin' the *remuda* for us."

Dale nodded, hesitated as if he had another question, and then turned back toward his pickup.

"There was one horse thief in the McCarty family," Jordan called out, laughing, "but some cowboys, meaner than he was, hung him from a Kansas cottonwood over a hundred years ago."

Without breaking stride, Dale just wagged his head side to side as he climbed in his pickup.

Dale had little time to worry about McCarty as basketball campers began streaming into the dorm, and the instructors and support workers constantly had questions for him. With twice as many campers as the prior summer, practices required more stringent scheduling, food preparations took more time, and other activities, such as softball games, had to be planned for the kids when they could not be in the gym.

Camp activities filled Dale's summer. A two-week session for girls followed on the heels of three consecutive ones for boys. The dorm rooms were filled with kids, along with David and Melba Green, who moved in as dorm parents. Donald Winters and two of Dale's all-state basketball players moved into one of the gymnasium sky-rooms, as the boys called them, while Margie Walker and an added kitchen worker occupied another. Again, David and Donald would help the all-staters run the boys camp, with Dale making daily appearances. Then Marilyn and David would lead the camp for girls to wind up the summer.

Almost half the campers were from surrounding towns, some as far away as Abilene and Plainview. Camp followers, including parents, grandparents, and friends, along with summer vacationers and boaters, kept the new motel in business, and Martha's Restaurant had more customers than it had chairs. Finding the place full, several of Martha's regulars grumbled all the way to the Paddock Steakhouse where they found little improvement.

Some of the local shops extended their afternoon hours, and to the surprise of many locals, stayed open right through the noon hour. A boat and motor repair business opened in an old abandoned automobile garage, and every issue of the

Paddock Post carried at least one advertisement insert, a happening peculiar to Christmas only for the past ten years.

"I've seen more smiles in town this week," Mayor Johnson said to Dale and Marilyn, "than I've seen in the past year."

"It's great that business is picking up," Dale said. "But with this growth, there's a concern."

"What's that, Dale?"

"Property values are rising," Dale said, "but I'm afraid some of our older families don't realize it. We'll have speculators coming in and taking advantage of them."

"I see what you mean," the mayor said. "What if we have some reputable realtor come in and hold a seminar to alert them?"

"I think that's a great idea."

A week later an article in the newspaper notified Paddock and Cottle County residents of an all-day seminar to be held the coming Saturday in the school cafeteria, sponsored by Newsom Realty from Childress. The article noted that area property, especially in Paddock and west of town, was increasing in value and likely would continue its upward spiral as the lake filled and lots were sold.

Dale did not attend, but the cafeteria was filled with excited locals.

"I'm Jack Wesson from Newsom Realty," the speaker announced, opening the conference. "Our firm has been in business in the Childress area for over fifty years, and some of us have experience with the kind of change you're experiencing."

He went on to detail how property values had escalated forty years earlier when Baylor Creek Reservoir was built on the Prairie Dog Fork of Red River.

"My father owned five hundred acres of land along Baylor Creek in the late 1940s. Its value was about twenty-five dollars an acre. Speculators came in and gobbled up about half of the land in the lake area for forty dollars an acre. The old-timers were glad to sell, thinking they had found a bonanza. But when the lake was completed and began filling up, half-acre lots around it sold for five to eight thousand dollars. Larger acreage was developed into retirement communities and more remote quarter-acre lots sold for two and three thousand dollars.

"As the drought hit in the early 1950s, prices went even higher. And keep in mind, this all happened four decades ago.

"The same thing happened a dozen years later down on White River Reservoir and in 1965 at Lake Meredith, north of Amarillo.

"Now, you have Lake Thompson less than ten miles beyond your city limit sign. The value of your property has already escalated a hundred percent, and as the lake fills and land development gets into high gear, property values will double again. Property closer to the lake will quadruple in value, and in some cases, they'll multiply in value by a factor of ten.

"So, you have to forget what you paid for your property and pay no heed to what land has sold for recently. You've got to start thinking of what its potential value is for someone wanting to plat it and sell it for thousands of dollars an acre, or someone wanting to put in a boat business, or a motel, or a bait and tackle shop.

"Newsom Realty has a trio of representatives here today, one in each of three classrooms just down the hallway. We're available to anyone interested in discussing the specifics of your property.

"Now, are there any questions I can answer for you?"

After several questions by locals about their business property, home values, and property taxes, Councilman Jed Tolbert stood up.

"We've already had a swindler come in and buy up six thousand acres," he said. "He's paid almost nothing for the land, and now he stands to make millions. Is there a precedent for suing these greedy outsiders who come in and steal from us?"

"You'll need to talk to a lawyer to get an answer to that question, sir," the realtor said. "Generally, unless the buyer does something fraudulent, the law is helpless in these cases. It's a case of 'seller beware.' That's why we're here today."

"Jed," Superintendent Phillips said, rising to his feet, "I think you're referring to Coach Dale Rory, and I can't let your accusation go unchallenged.

"It's true that Coach Rory has purchased about six thousand acres of land west of town, but it's also true that it's through his efforts and investments that the value of our property is now escalating. Specifically, it is through his ingenuity and determination that we have a lake, for which he donated two thousand acres. If not for Coach Rory, we wouldn't be having this meeting, and our population and property values would still be on a downward spiral."

Someone stood and started clapping, and soon everyone in the meeting was up applauding the superintendent.

Red-faced, Councilman Tolbert stomped out of the meeting while muttering, "You haven't heard the last from me."

13 ___

Dale's third summer on the Roryian Ranch was his busiest one. Though he had excellent help with the basketball camp, the influx of out-of-town campers meant more parents who wanted to meet the popular coach and mention the unique qualities of their son or daughter. Also, a continuous stream of inquiries regarding the lake and related business opportunities flooded his desk. And most mornings he had breakfast at seven o'clock with Tom Jordan at the activities building to discuss ranch-related issues.

"Boss," Jordan said one August morning, "we've got to cull out some of our older cows and replace them with younger ones. Earlier sales have built up the ranch account, so I have the necessary money, but I don't want you to be surprised when you see cattle trucks driving off with forty or fifty cows."

"How will you select and isolate the cows you want to sell?"

"We'll have a mini-roundup, pasture by pasture. The cowboys will work their horses along the outer edge of the gathered herd, cutting out the keepers. Gradually the gather will dwindle down to the older cows, ones that aren't pregnant and haven't had a calf in a while. Then we'll pen them and eventually consolidate all the culls in the big corral. The following morning, we'll load 'em up and haul them to the sale barn."

"How is Luke McCarty working out?"

"Great. He brought in a fine stable of quarter horses that we'll use for the roundup. In fact, this purging of older cows is Luke's idea, and he's got more thoughts about how we can improve our operation. He's located two hundred acres down along the Pease River that he thinks we should fence off, get some irrigation equipment, and grow most of our own hay. The same land can be used for fattening up our steers on winter grass."

"I like that idea," Dale said. "We're going to have plenty of water, and I'd like us to be the first to use it to improve our land. Get with the water district folks and arrange for us to run a metered line from the lake."

The day the cowboys started the roundup, Dale saddled the sorrel mare and rode out to watch. He was amazed at how instinctively the horses worked the cattle, always alert to a maverick trying to break away from the herd. In a flash, the ponies would gather their weight over their back legs, wheel their front feet around and dash away to head-off the stray and force him back into the bellowing bunched herd. While all this was going on, the cowboy hung on tight with his legs while swinging a rope overhead and calling to the cattle. Slowly, the mass of hooves and horns moved toward the cattle pens, funneled through the entrance by a pair of point riders.

It was hot, dusty work, but the cowboys seemed to thrive on these long-held traditions of their job. Dale learned that they much preferred working from astride a saddle to repairing fences and corrals.

Four days later, sixty-one cows had been loaded and hauled to the sale barn, and had been replaced with fifty Brangus heifers.

After spending an afternoon riding among the herd, checking out the new cows, Dale unsaddled the mare, fed her, and turned her out into the big lot. When he stepped inside the house, Marilyn handed him a drink of tea and a note from Principal Kennemer.

"Have you realized that it's less than a week before school starts?" she asked, thinking the summer could not possibly be over.

Dale just shook his head and dialed the number.

"Coach, some PTA people have asked if you'll speak at their first fall meeting. They're combining the elementary and high school groups, and want to prepare a note for parents, announcing that you'll address the meeting."

"What subject do they want me to talk about, and when do they meet?"

"The theme is, 'How parents need to be involved with their school kids.' They've noticed the parents of your players at all the games, even at practices, and they'd like to see more participation by the parents of the rest of the kids. The meeting will be on Monday evening of the last week of September."

Dale agreed and marked it on his calendar.

An hour or so later, Sybil came over and joined Dale and Marilyn out on the patio.

"I'm considering starting a little business," she said. "What do you think about some riding stables?"

"Located near the lake, I think that just might do well," Dale said.

"While their husbands are fishing," Marilyn said, "I bet lots of wives and kids would love to take a horseback ride."

Soon they had agreed on a location, just off the road on the east rim of the canyon and within walking distance of the park area for overnight campers. Then Marilyn agreed to saddle a couple of horses the next day and go with Sybil to stake out a good riding trail that would start at the back of the stables, wend its way down the rocky slope to the lowland alongside the South Pease River, pass through a grove of cottonwood trees, and climb a switchback path up the slope to the stables.

"I'll see if Clyde would like to help me run it," Sybil said, referring to the cowboy she hires every winter.

Soon, Sybil had Clyde Martin and a couple of other workers constructing stables, while she and Marilyn cleared the riding trail and hired a high school boy and girl as "trail bosses" for weekend cowpokes. Clyde and Sybil believed they could handle the weekday riders. Luke McCarty, considered the best horseman on the ranch, selected and purchased a dozen horses, most of them old and gentle.

Meanwhile, Dale prepared for the new school year, along with putting together his presentation for the PTA meeting. Also, he contacted several area coaches in preparation for selecting the most competitive teams in the area for Paddock's first Christmas holiday tournament.

The first day at school, the coach was pleased to find the expansion of the gymnasium was almost complete. Added bleachers on the east side of the court, under which new, spacious dressing rooms had been built, had doubled seating capacity. The old dressing rooms had been replaced with renovated restrooms, a new office for the coach, and the concession area had been expanded.

The basketball players began volunteer practices in the gymnasium as soon as the expansion was complete. Dale smiled as he dropped by and watched the boys working on drills rather than just shooting hoops.

Dale quickly slipped back into the routine of teaching, grading papers, and watching after his basketball team. With lesson plans available from the prior year, preparation for class was not quite as burdensome.

The weekend before the PTA meeting, he finally organized his thoughts for the presentation and got them on paper. Taking his notes out on the patio with a glass of ice tea, he reviewed the speech a couple of times. He only needed a succinct bullet item for each point he wanted to make. The full text was in his head; it was part of who he was.

"Ladies and gentlemen," the PTA president said, "I'm pleased to welcome Coach Rory, or Coach Mass to some of you, as our speaker tonight."

After sustained applause, Dale thanked the PTA for the opportunity to address its membership and thanked the parents for attending.

"I'm sure we can all agree that the student is first and foremost in everything we do regarding our schools. For every education-related decision we make, whether a teacher, administrator, coach, or a parent, we must assess it based on how it impacts our kids.

"Ultimately, we adults pass or fail based upon how well we have prepared them for life, rather than on their grade point average, their scholastic ranking, or test scores. Now, don't go home and tell your youngsters that I said test scores don't matter, and that GPA doesn't count. But I am saying that these metrics are just data points along the way, from which we can determine if we need to make midcourse adjustments. The final score is determined by how we live life.

"Again, I don't want to leave you with the wrong impression. I don't hold my teachers or my parents responsible for my actions, whether failures or successes. Every one of us must take sole responsibility for our lives. That doesn't mean that my teachers and parents don't deserve credit for the knowledge and wisdom they imparted to me. They do, with interest compounded daily. Our role, our responsibility, is to provide the educational environment, the guidance, the support, and the resources for our kids to have the best opportunity for success. We must give them the best possible starting point in life. But in the final analysis, they must steer their own boat.

"Personally, I add another ingredient: God-given wisdom. Specifically, I point to a portion of Luke chapter twelve, verse forty-eight, which I paraphrase as, 'To whom much is given, much is required.' In fact, I believe that means that we are accountable for how we use whatever blessings we are given, great or small. If you are now having trouble identifying your blessings, let me point you to the one most pertinent to this discussion: your kids. You heard me right, so now let's talk about how we meet that responsibility.

"It starts with how we live our lives. What kind of role models are we? Will our children want to follow in our footsteps, or will they try to avoid them at all costs? I hope it's the former, but if not, then from today forward, I hope we'll dedicate ourselves to setting the example our kids will want to follow. Though I have worded it in terms of we and us, I hope each of you will apply it personally.

"Let's be more specific. How do you spend your time, especially your casual time? Do you expect your kids to get their homework while you watch TV? Or do you ask about their assignments, show an interest in what they're learning at school, or maybe even lend a hand by sharing what you know about whatever subject they are studying? No, I'm not suggesting that you take on the role of a teacher, but rather that you let your child know that you care about their education, that you understand its importance, and that you are ready to do whatever you can to help. Just saying education is all-important doesn't cut it. The old platitude, 'Actions speak louder than words,' is as true today as it was two centuries ago.

"Are classroom studies the only area that we need to focus on? I don't think so.

"As you know, I'm a coach, and I believe my players learn lessons through competition, through teamwork, through dedication and hard work, lessons they are unlikely to learn in the classroom. Additionally, sports also provide an avenue for our youngsters to express and develop themselves physically. But fortunately, there are other avenues for the less sports-minded.

"Kids need to be interactive with their peers, usually based on something they have in common. It can be cheerleading, science experiments, debate teams, drama, church groups, civic or social clubs, as an office assistant, a librarian's helper, to name a few. Ideally, in these pursuits they'll become part of something they deem to be more important than themselves. Life's greatest joys can be realized, I believe, from these cooperative efforts and successes. As a role model, turn off the TV and get involved in the community, your church, or help a friend, mow a sick neighbor's lawn. You might even take a correspondence course or read a classic. We should let our kids see us improving ourselves. Surely, we don't want them thinking that what they see is the best we can be!

"Now, for a moment let's vary from the ideal. Kids, like adults, sometimes need to be disciplined. Done the right way, discipline can be effective. Done the wrong way, it can be detrimental. So, what are some guidelines we should consider for administering discipline?

"First, who should discipline? Ideally, one who, without question, cares for the child, wants what's best for the child, someone the child trusts implicitly. It doesn't mean the kid will be happy when disciplined, but it is imperative that he know that the intent is to help him, not hurt him.

"Next, effective discipline will correct undesirable behavior and protect future victims. This means we want to condition the child to respond differently upon facing whatever circumstances previously triggered his bad behavior. Discipline's purpose must not be to punish an individual, though punishment may be required to meet the ultimate goal. If so, then our first option should be to take away something important, something valued by the one being punished. We all tend to respond to a reward system.

"For every action there tends to be a reaction, sometimes a good result, sometimes a bad one. We try to take those actions that reward our efforts, that satisfy our emotional, spiritual, and physical needs. If an action results in pain, emotional or physical, then we try to avoid that action in the future. We need to apply this principle when disciplining.

"Discipline should reinforce this action-reaction formula. Bad behavior results in the loss of something valued. Good behavior provides something desired.

"Now, I want to talk about character building.

"Character refers to moral and ethical qualities, things that involve our relationship to others. In the case of a single individual isolated on an island, these have little significance, but in a complex society, our interaction with people around us defines who we are.

"The most common character flaw is self-centeredness. Inversely, the greatest ingredient in good character is respect for and a sincere interest in the well-being and happiness of others. In a Biblical sense, it's the Golden Rule: 'Do unto others as you would have them do unto you.'

"We teach good or bad character by the way we interact with our kids. If we don't respect them, if we constantly criticize others, if we break the rules, if we blame others for our failures, if we cheat, lie, and steal, then what should we expect from our children? My dad told me that life is like a mirror. No matter what we say, it will reflect us just as we are. In other words, the mirror of life does not reflect our words, but rather our actions. You can be sure that your kid is watching your mirror.

"We all know that 'Do as I say, not as I do' does not work. Some say, 'Walk the talk' but I prefer 'Let your walking do your talking.'

"Now, regarding attitude, the most important thing I can say is 'approach everything with positive thoughts.' Again my father taught me that if you think positive thoughts, good things tend to come your way. Conversely, if you think negative thoughts, bad things will gravitate to you. Let me point out that there's nothing magical about this. Reverting to sports, let's consider a batter. If he stands at home plate and pictures a level swing and solid bat contact with the ball, his chances of getting a hit are good. On the other hand, if he worries about swinging and missing a pitch, if he's concerned about the pitcher's wicked curve ball, or if he's afraid of being hit, he will most likely make an out. If we expect failure, our expectations will be met.

"So, I believe we should dream big, yet set practical goals and expect to reach them. However, missing a goal is not failure. We fail when we don't try, when we don't make our best effort, when we lose hope and drop out.

"Now, as important as goals and dreams are, I would never tell anyone to bundle all their joy and happiness into a single goal. As I mentioned earlier, life is a series of midcourse corrections, some due to our ignorance, others due to unpredictable events beyond our control. In any case, I maintain that reaching a goal often leaves us less satisfied than we imagined. So how do we attain satisfaction? I believe we must enjoy the journey to the goal. Again, let me put it in sports terms.

"Our goal may be a state championship, but does that mean we are not to enjoy developing our skills in practice, day after day? Does it mean we get no satisfaction from winning that first game? Does a district championship become ho-hum? No, we must savor each of these milestones along the way. Success and winning are infectious precisely because of these baby steps, reaching the next rung on the ladder. It's no different in the business world, in the homemaker's life, or in a retiree's golden years. By example, let's teach our kids to treasure life on a daily basis. Celebrate the little things, such as an improved math grade, making the honor roll, getting a part in a play, winning a spelling contest, finishing a paper on time, or helping a friend solve a problem. Let your kids know that you are watching and pulling for them.

"I've probably talked too long and said too much, so let me try to encapsulate all this into something you can take with you.

"We have a shared goal: the success and happiness of your child. Accept that it's a team effort between you and us teachers and coaches. So, take your parental responsibility seriously and discover the joy that'll be yours when you invest quality time in your children.

"Thank you, and good evening."

The applause was loud and long. The PTA president thanked Dale profusely, as did the superintendent and principal.

While Dale was preparing for the upcoming basketball schedule, the hurricane season in the gulf brought more rain, replacing the four feet of water lost during the hot summer and raising the maximum depth to twenty-eight feet. On October 1 the water district opened the lake to fishing and contracted with a local realtor who had opened an office in town.

"We're ready to sell lakefront property," a board member explained to the real estate agent, while handing over a platted layout of the shoreline on both sides of the lake, with prices marked on each lot.

Also, Sybil and Clyde had their riding stables open and operating, though they and their horses got ample rest except for the weekends. Every weekend campers began dropping by early Friday evening to book rides for the next day. Saturdays and Sundays were busy, so Sybil had a high school boy and girl serve as trail guides and Clyde saw after the horses and stables.

Back in town, two weeks before basketball season was to begin, a few businessmen, led by banker Chet Williams, formed the Basketball Boosters Club.

"What can we do to help?" Williams asked Dale.

"We're planning a Christmas holiday tournament here in Paddock," the coach said. "I think it would add interest if we had programs to hand out at the games. I can provide a list of the teams and coaches, along with phone numbers, if you'll call and request a picture and short bio of each player for the program. I expect you can sell them for a couple of dollars a piece and cover your costs."

The boosters took on the project, first producing a Paddock program. Dale was surprised to see advertisements placed by several of the local businesses on the last three pages. When he asked about it, the banker explained that he had no problem getting twenty dollars from each of the business owners. "We'll have even more in the tournament program, including businesses from several of the surrounding towns," Williams predicted.

At Paddock's first home game, the boosters could have sold fifty more programs. They had not accounted for the doubled seating capacity of the gymnasium. For succeeding games, they increased the number of programs and included a loose flier with the team's won-loss record and the individual statistics of each player, provided by Marilyn.

As the season progressed, with the Palominos winning handily, the crowds grew to standing room only, including fans from nearby towns. The defending state champions were indeed taller and more skilled, so much so that Dale established a routine of replacing his starters with the second team for the last two minutes of each quarter. The first lineup was taller and more accurate shooters than the second, which was faster and anxious to run. Opposing teams found adjusting to the contrasting styles to be extremely difficult. Frequently, the A team sat out the entire final period.

By the time district play began, sportswriters from Childress, Wichita Falls, and Abilene were attending Paddock's games. The Abilene writer, capitalizing on Paddock's gold and blue colors, referred to Dale's team as the Golden Palominos, prompting the cheerleaders to prepare a huge sign for home games, one with a galloping, gold-colored palomino, for the players to burst through.

Dale's team was undefeated heading into the Christmas holiday tournament in Paddock. The boosters club had the programs ready, charging three dollars each, but adding team and individual statistics to it after each contest. The crowds filled the gymnasium to see the best class A, AA, and AAA teams from the area, the brackets arranged to pit teams of the same class against each other until the quarterfinals.

The Palominos played their first game at nine o'clock Monday night, winning easily. They breezed through the class A competition, as everyone expected the defending state champions would do.

Meanwhile, Snyder dominated class AA, and a Wichita Falls team fought their way to the semifinals, along with AAA Plainview.

Paddock matched up against Synder and won by a dozen points. Dale's pressing, running, scrapping second team devastated the opposition in the third quarter. A tall Wichita Falls squad slipped by Plainview in overtime, matching them against Paddock for the championship.

A standing-room-only crowd crammed into the gymnasium to see the big showdown, and they were not disappointed as Dale varied his pattern, switching to his second team three minutes into the game. The taller, slower out-of-town players could not break the Palominos' stifling press, and fell behind eight points by the end of the first quarter. A befuddled opposition then resumed play against Dale's starters who quickly built the lead to fourteen points, prompting a Wichita Falls timeout. Taking advantage of the break in play, Dale reinserted his second team who maintained the lead to halftime.

The Wichita Falls boys redeemed themselves early in the third quarter, dominating inside play and getting four easy baskets. Dale countered by switching his taller first squad to a sagging zone defense, forcing the opposition to take long, outside shots, their obvious weakness. Then the game turned dramatically.

The fourth quarter began with the Palominos second unit, who made the game a track race. After three minutes of wearing the tall Wichita Falls boys down, Dale inserted his starting unit who found easy open shots and built a twenty-two-point lead with a minute to play. The second squad then finished the game by adding four more points to the Palominos' advantage.

While the crowd chanted, "All-state, all-state, all-state . . ." sportswriters were interviewing Dale and his players.

"Coach," a Childress writer asked, "which is your best team?"

"I have only one team," Dale replied.

"Did you expect a blowout like this?"

"I expect every ballgame to be tough, every opponent to be talented," he said. "I think we confused them tonight, but another night on their court and in front of their crowd, the results could be quite different."

"Is this team better than last year's?"

"It's basically the same team, a year older and smarter. I haven't done my job, if they aren't improved."

"So, you're predicting another state championship?"

"We prepare hard for every game, and we plan to win," Dale said. "But, other coaches do the same thing. Winning has put us at the top of the most-wanted list, so every opponent will come after us like a bounty hunter after a king's ransom. But, we plan to make it mighty tough for them to collect."

With the tournament over and Christmas only days away, Dale turned his attention to the ranch, which for the last month he had left totally in Tom Jordan's capable hands. The first free day he had, Dale checked with his foreman.

"Tom, is there anything I need to take care of while I'm out of school?"

"I don't think so, Boss," Jordan replied. "Our hands are keeping the cattle fed, and we've put up some windbreaks to protect the cows from any harsh winter storms."

"You've done a great job, Tom. You and Clara have been stuck on this ranch since the day you showed up. Why don't you two take those kids on a vacation while they're on school break?"

"Boss, I'd feel more comfortable lookin' after things here. After all, that's my job."

"When I hired you and Clara, I promised to be fair with you, and to look out for your best interests. Now, I want you to take a week off and go enjoy your family."

"To be honest, we really don't have a reliable vehicle to travel in. We're saving some money to buy a new truck, but I expect it'll be summer before we'll have enough for that."

"Take my truck," Dale said. "Other than church, I don't plan to leave the ranch until school starts again, but if I do, I can use my wife's pickup."

"Boss, I'd worry about damaging your truck, or the kids spillin' something in it."

"Tom, as of right now, the truck is yours. Also, you're due a three-thousand-dollar Christmas bonus, enough to cover your vacation expenses, I expect."

"What can I say, Boss? You've provided me a home, paid utilities, and the best job of my life. All I can do is thank you from the bottom of my heart, and promise you that I'll do everything in my power to be the best ranch foreman this side of the Mississippi."

"We'll get the truck title switched to your name tomorrow morning," Dale said, handing over the keys. "Meanwhile, you get Clara and those kids packed and ready to hit the road."

"Yes, Boss," Jordan said, watery-eyed.

After a couple days of riding his mare over the ranch, checking the cattle and enjoying being outdoors, Dale and Marilyn dropped by the local Ford dealership and purchased a new pickup. Dale offered to let his wife have the new truck, but she preferred to keep her two-year-old birthday present.

Sooner than it seemed possible, the holidays ended, and the Jordans had returned from a week-long trip to Galveston, telling story after story about their first trip to the Gulf coast.

Dale's boys returned to the court in early January, and after two grueling days of working off their holiday feasts, they demolished one district opponent after another, and then captured the regional crown with relative ease. It was, once again, time for Paddock's faithful to lock their shops and head for Austin.

The Palominos blitzed their first opponent, but found Marlin to be an extremely fast and aggressive opponent in the semifinals match. Marlin's squad was too quick for Dale's starting unit, so he quickly substituted his second lineup that matched up better with the opponent but could not build a lead. Finally, Dale took his two quickest guards and teamed them with his tallest front line, and they built a twelve-point lead midway of the final quarter. With Marlin tired and their key player on the bench with five fouls, Dale went back to his starting unit and pulled away to an eighteen-point victory. The Palominos were one win away from repeating as state champions.

The championship game proved less challenging than the semifinals contest, though the margin of victory was nearly identical.

"The Golden Palominos repeat as undefeated state champions," a sportswriter wrote. "They won by nineteen but could have won by thirty, if young Coach Rory had not reined-in his stable of thoroughbreds."

"I've never seen a team more fundamentally sound than Paddock's," a prominent university coach told a reporter. "It takes a good coach to use ten players as effectively as Coach Rory does. Some big school will steal him within a year."

The foreboding quote made it into the *Paddock Post*, prompting Palomino fans to bombard Superintendent Phillips with phone calls.

"I'm not worried," Phillips told the callers. "What are they going to do? Offer him more money? He won't accept the salary in his contract here. Besides, Coach Rory has deep roots in this area, and he's married to a local girl."

While Dale and his Palominos were storming through a dream season, winter rains added six feet of water to Lake Thompson, and the water district installed a pump station and ran a pipeline to Paddock. With more rain expected in the spring, sure to attract more boaters, vacationers, and campers, the town was bubbly with anticipation.

"If we duplicate last year's growth," a councilman said, "we should look at reopening the hospital. We need a planning group looking at that right now."

"And we're going to need more teachers," councilwoman Sylvia Phillips said. "We've got two retiring, and we have to expect twenty to thirty more high school students, and double that number of elementary kids."

"We don't have adequate housing for that kind of growth," another member said.

"I hear that Coach Rory plans to open a housing addition out near the lake," banker Williams said.

"You can bet that coach has some scheme to line his pockets," pharmacist Tolbert said. "Personally, I think we're being set up for a mighty big tumble."

"Jed," the banker said, with a deep sigh, "you're just worried that some pharmacist will move in here and give you a little competition. Can't you see we're all better off than we were a year ago, and it's just going to keep improving?"

"Mind my words, men," Tolbert said. "Rory is an outsider and as soon as the tide starts receding, and it will, he'll sell out and leave us high and dry."

"What's he gonna do?" Sylvia asked. "Suck all the water out of the lake and take it with him? Can't you see that he's investing in the infrastructure of this community, rather than in some product or business that he can pack up and walk away with?"

Vocalized agreement with the councilwoman was so strong by the other council members that the sullen pharmacist refused to respond.

14 ___

While Dale was preparing for baseball season and lining up Old Leatherarm to work with Todd and Chris, Marilyn found a challenge she could not resist, though she had no idea how to deal with it.

"Marilyn," Betty Green explained one afternoon at the ranch, "we've got a situation at school that I just don't know how to handle. There's a ninth grade girl from a poor family who's being shunned by her classmates, particularly by a clique of four of the most popular girls. The girl's name is Traci Elliot, and she's desperate to be accepted. However, she wears homemade clothes, doesn't bathe regularly, and is a bit overweight."

"Has anyone talked to the girls and asked them to be more considerate?" Marilyn asked.

"I don't think so, but I've thought about suggesting to Traci that she should at least bathe on a regular basis. I just don't want to embarrass her and make her feel that she's even more of an outcast."

"I'm afraid there's no easy answer."

"All the school kids look up to you and Coach Rory. If this clique would listen to anybody, it'd be you two."

"I'll talk to Dale."

Dale agreed to help, and Betty arranged an after-school meeting with the four girls. Marilyn and the coach encouraged the girls to be more considerate, to try to put themselves in the place of this poor girl, and to make an extra effort to be kind to her.

"I just can't stand to be around her," Linda explained. "Sometimes she smells awful, and her hair is always stringy."

"Yeah," Peg said. "It's disgusting how she tries to sit with us in the cafeteria, or tries to force her way into our conversations when we're talking in the hallway. We just don't have anything in common with her."

"Girls," Dale said, "I understand your reluctance, but I can't condone your being mean to her. I firmly believe those of us who are more fortunate, only by the grace of God, have an obligation to go the extra mile, to try harder, to be considerate of those who find themselves in difficult circumstances."

"Maybe one of you could talk privately with Traci and ask her to bathe more regularly," Marilyn said. "I'm sure she'd do almost anything to be accepted and included."

"I could never do that," Jan said. "She's so gross."

"Cindy," Dale said to the quietest of the group, "what do you think?"

"I know it's not right to hurt her feelings," Cindy said, looking down. "And she can't help being poor. I'd offer her some of my clothes, but they wouldn't fit her. I just don't know what to do."

"Girls," Marilyn said, rising to her feet, "I hope you'll think about this and find a way to at least be considerate of Traci. When you lay down at night, just take a minute to think about what she must be feeling."

The girls nodded as Dale and Marilyn headed for their pickup.

"Honey, those girls aren't going to change," Marilyn said. "I could see it in their eyes."

"What would you do?"

"I'd get her on the basketball team, and then she'd have to take a shower every day."

A week later as Dale left the gymnasium with a sack of bats, headed for the baseball field, he heard a commotion at a side exit of the school. He turned just in time to see Linda push the door closed and then brace her shoulder against it. Jan, Peg and Cindy were hurrying toward the parking lot. Then suddenly an arm rammed through the small windowpane in the door, shattering shards of glass on Linda. When Dale saw blood streaking down the protruding arm and heard Linda scream, he dropped the bag and ran.

Linda had backed up against the brick wall and was crying frantically when Dale arrived, and then he saw Traci, pale and weak-kneed, on the other side of the door. Slowly and carefully, he guided Traci's right arm back through the jagged hole in the window, and then used his handkerchief to twist a tourniquet just below her elbow.

By then Jan, Peg, and Cindy had seen the commotion and came racing back to the scene.

"She was chasing us again, Coach," Linda explained tearfully. "I didn't mean to hurt her. She ran up to the door and tried to push it open, but her hand hit the window."

"Cindy," Dale barked, "go tell Principal Kennemer what's happened. Ask him to notify Traci's family, call my wife, and then meet with the baseball team."

With his arm around Traci for support, Dale hurried her toward the nurse's station.

"I can clean up her arm, Coach," Miss Nelson, the school nurse, said, "but we need to get her to a hospital. That deep gash has got to be sewed up."

"While you help her to the main entrance, I'll get my pickup and pull it around front," Dale said, and dashed off down the hallway.

While the nurse and Dale maneuvered Traci into the pickup, the principal came running out.

"Mr. Kennemer," Dale said. "We're taking her to the emergency room in Childress. What about insurance?"

Kennemer just shook his head, indicating Traci's parents had not taken the insurance offered through the school.

"Tell them not to worry. We'll get their daughter taken care of."

With Miss Nelson holding the girl's arm, Dale sped out of the parking lot and headed toward Highway 83 where he turned sharply to the north. Throughout the thirty-two mile drive, the tourniquet kept the bleeding to a minimum, yet Traci remained faint, more from fright than from loss of blood.

The emergency room doctor quickly sterilized the wounds, sedated Traci, and stitched up the worst cut. While the hospital nurse wrapped the patient's arm from elbow to wrist in gauze, Traci opened her eyes, causing the doctor to glance up from his paperwork. With heavy eyelids, she tried to smile, but drifted off again.

"She'll be woozy for an hour or so," the doctor said, "but she's going to be just fine."

Leaving Miss Nelson with Traci, Dale went to the emergency room desk and filled out papers documenting the incident and verifying the treatment. He wrote a check for the bill, leaving his name and address in case additional expenses should be incurred.

As they drove back to Paddock, the sedative wore off enough that Traci raised her head from Miss Nelson's shoulder and looked around.

"Where are we?" she asked, and then glanced at her gauze-bound right arm.

"About fifteen miles from Paddock," Dale said. "The doctor stitched up your arm, and you're going to be okay."

"How does it feel?" Miss Nelson asked.

"It hurts some," the girl responded.

"The doctor warned that once the anesthetic wears off, you'll probably have some discomfort tonight and tomorrow, so he gave you a few pain pills, just in case. As soon as you come back to school, I want you to come see me, first thing."

When they pulled up at the school, Kennemer rushed out the door and met them at the pickup. After asking about Traci's arm, he turned to Dale.

"Marilyn has talked to Traci's mother and arranged for her to stay at your house tonight. If you want to head on out to the ranch, I'll call Marilyn and let her know that Traci's fine and you're on the way."

Dale thanked the principal and Miss Nelson, asked Traci to lie down in the back seat, and turned the pickup toward home.

Marilyn had kept dinner warm, and Traci ate hungrily. Dale and Marilyn mused at how well the girl could feed herself left-handed. Marilyn then guided Traci to the guest bedroom and covered the bandaged arm with a plastic bag before showing the youngster to the shower where towels and a washcloth were laid out.

"I'll check on you in a few minutes," Marilyn said, and headed back to the den.

"Honey," she said to Dale, "Mom drove over to the Elliot home and got a change of clothes for Traci, but they were so pitiful. I asked Mom to go buy her some new ones, matching the size of the old clothes. She should be here soon."

"Did Traci's parents seem concerned about her?" Dale asked.

"Yes, but it's just Traci, her mom, and younger brother," Marilyn said, shaking her head. "Mom said that Mrs. Elliot paced the floor the entire time she was there, alternately worrying that her daughter might be permanently injured and about the cost of treatment. Honey, they're miserably poor. Traci's father left six months ago, and her mother works part-time as a cook at Martha's. She hopes to get on fulltime, but until then, they'll have to skimp along the best they can."

"Where do they live?"

"Out on a country road off Highway 83. After Mr. Elliot deserted them, they had to move into an old rundown farmhouse. Mrs. Elliot pays rent by doing the bachelor owner's washing and ironing, and cleaning his house once a week."

"There's got to be something we can do to help," Dale said, shaking his head.

"We've got basketball camps coming up, and we could use an extra cook for the summer," Marilyn suggested.

"That's a good idea," Dale said, his face brightening. "In fact, let's hire her now and put the three of them in the bungalow. Don't you and Sybil have some events going on in the activities building this spring?"

"We have at least one a week. She can fix snacks for us and clean up afterward. We can keep her pretty busy."

Sybil then drove up, prompting Dale to go out and meet her while Marilyn checked on Traci. Sybil had the back seat of her Marquis loaded down with clothes.

"Dale, that poor girl needs a whole new wardrobe. I couldn't get everything, but I got her three outfits, including underclothes and pajamas."

Dale smiled as he loaded up with packages and followed Sybil inside. While she checked on Marilyn and Traci, Dale brought in a second load.

While Dale checked homework papers, he could hear laughter from the guest bedroom. Traci was trying on the new clothes, while Marilyn and Sybil were raving over how good she looked all dressed up.

An hour later, with Traci settled in for the night and Sybil back at Stone Place, Dale and Marilyn slipped into bed. He was dead tired, and just about to drift off to sleep when Marilyn elbowed him in the ribs.

"Honey, are you awake?"

"Uh, huh," he mumbled.

"I'll keep Traci here tomorrow. Can you pick up her school assignments?"

"Uh, huh."

"Honey, I hope we can keep Traci here with us for a while. She's such a sweet girl, and I really enjoyed dressing her up tonight."

"Talk to her mother tomorrow and see if she'd be willing to move over here and work for us. Tell her we'll pay her a thousand dollars a month, with rent and utilities provided, and she can drive my old car, if she needs it. If she agrees, get Tom and Luke to move her furniture over, pronto."

"Goodnight, Darling."

Elizabeth Elliot broke down the following morning when Sybil explained about the job offer and proposed move to the Roryian.

"Ma'am," she said, between sobs, "I'll do a good job, I promise."

"I know you will. Now, get your personal things packed up, and we'll get you moved to the bungalow tomorrow. By the way, it's pretty well furnished, so it's not necessary that you move this furniture."

"Marilyn," Sybil said to her daughter during lunch, "their furniture is terrible, so I told Mrs. Elliot that they can use the furniture in the bungalow. I hope that's okay."

"Take a look at what's down there," Marilyn said, nodding, "and then pick out anything else you think they'll need and have it delivered. I'm sure that's what Dale would want."

When Sybil asked Tom and Luke to move the Elliots's things, she explained that they were to leave all of the old broken-down furniture, unless Mrs. Elliot insisted that they bring some item.

"Just gather up their clothes, dishes, and anything personal," she explained. "I'll have the bungalow completely furnished by noon tomorrow."

Having completed with the move instructions, Sybil headed for the Corner Grocery store where she loaded up a shopping cart with everything she thought the family might need.

Tom and Luke drove to the Elliot farmhouse the following morning and loaded the few personal things the woman had gathered in the front room. When they arrived at the bungalow, a furniture company had just completed setting up two bedroom suites, along with a couch that made into a bed.

When Elizabeth Elliot stepped through the front door of the bungalow, she stopped dead in her tracks and lifted her hands to her face as she surveyed the room full of neat, though conservative, furniture. She was further surprised when she opened the pantry door and found it fully stocked, as was the refrigerator. Within a couple of hours after noon, the woman had her family's personal items in place.

After three more days with Marilyn and Dale, Traci moved in with her mother and brother. Her arm was improving rapidly, and Elizabeth Elliot proved true to her word. She was an excellent cook, a dependable and thorough worker, and she took great pride in keeping the bungalow clean and tidy.

Late one afternoon as Dale arrived home from baseball practice, he noticed Marilyn's pickup at the activities building, so he stopped and stepped inside. He was shocked at what he saw.

His wife was working with Traci at the far end of the gymnasium. Without being noticed, Dale took a seat in the bleachers.

Traci was large for her age, but her moves on the basketball court were surprisingly quick and athletic. Marilyn was teaching her how to play the post position, and the girl proved to be a quick learner. With her right arm still lightly bandaged, she was predominantly handling the ball with her left hand, yet with no obvious awkwardness. When they noticed Dale, Marilyn walked over while Traci continued to practice.

"How long have you been working with her?" Dale asked.

"A couple of weeks."

"That's amazing. Is she left-handed?" he asked, recalling how well she had handled a knife and fork with her left hand.

"Not exactly. She does most things with her right hand, but she writes left-handed. Also, when she pops the ball up from the floor with her toe, she uses her left foot."

"That kind of dexterity will be an incredible advantage in basketball, and she seems to be enjoying herself."

"Yes, she shows up early every afternoon, and works hard until I tell her we have to leave."

"Honey, I think you've found the key to changing this young lady's life. I hope you'll keep practicing with her."

"I'll have her ready for the basketball camp in August. I've already signed her up, and I waived the fee, of course."

"I can't wait for Margie to see her. She's got quite a surprise coming."

Right after that, Sybil dropped by one afternoon for a visit, and Marilyn invited her to stay for dinner. With Dale and Marilyn's busy schedule and Sybil's scholarship program and horse stables, some weeks they would only see each other at church. So, they used this opportunity to catch up.

"I've taken up a new activity," Sybil announced. "Woodrow and I have played golf with Brother Suche and his wife three times, and I love the game."

"Who's Woodrow?" Marilyn asked.

"Oh, I guess I haven't told you. He's a doctor from Childress whose wife died five years ago, and now he's looking at setting up a limited practice here."

Superintendent Phillips had told Dale about Dr. Chapman who had met with a City Council committee. He guessed this was Sybil's friend, Woodrow. Also, it was common knowledge in the church family that Brother Henry Suche was an avid golfer, but both Dale and Marilyn were totally surprised that Sybil had taken up the sport. Neither Dale nor Marilyn had ever attempted hitting a golf ball.

"Where do you play?" her daughter asked.

"Woodrow likes the course at Childress, so he drives us up there. We have an early lunch and then spend the afternoon on the golf course."

It suddenly occurred to Marilyn how unusual it was for her mother to spend half a day doing anything other than working. Also, Marilyn had noticed the familiarity implied by her mother not referring to the doctor by his title. Was something more than golf involved?

While Dale and Marilyn considered these implications, Sybil continued. "Woodrow and Brother Suche say if we had a course close by, they'd be willing to give golf lessons. The two of them have offered the use of several spare sets of clubs and a tub full of balls."

"Dale, didn't you consider building a golf course over by the lake?" Marilyn asked.

"I think golf lessons are usually taught at a driving range or some kind of practice facility," Dale said. "I don't think Paddock's quite ready for a full golf course."

"Dale," Sybil said, "you've got enough people for a class right out here. The Jordans and their two kids, Elizabeth, Bucky and Traci Elliot, you two and me, and that's not counting Jesus, Jose, Tomas, and Luke."

"Sybil," Dale said, smiling at the idea of his cowboys on a golf course, "why don't you get your golf partners to come take a look around and locate the best place for a minimal course."

"I'm sure they'd be glad to do that."

Nothing else was said on the subject that evening, but Dale was sure Sybil would follow up.

Sure enough, the doctor and Brother Suche showed up two days later. Sybil joined them, and the trio spent three hours driving and walking over the area. Following the survey, they joined Marilyn for lunch on the patio.

"A golf course takes lots of water," the minister explained. "In an arid area like this, it'll have to be watered daily, and it'll require constant care. I think you should consider starting with a private facility, maybe just one large green with three tee boxes approaching it from different directions and from varying distances. That would afford all the necessary elements to teach the basics of the game."

"We just don't know anything about building a golf course," Marilyn said. "Do you know someone who could advise us?"

"I do," Dr. Chapman said. "I have a close friend who runs a country club in Tulsa, and he's built three courses. I'm sure he'd be willing to help us."

Marilyn passed the golfers' recommendation to Dale that evening. He liked the idea of a limited facility and suggested that Sybil ask Dr. Chapman to check into what it would take to get the project going. Marilyn called Sybil and relayed Dale's decision, depending on her to contact her friend.

While Dale led his baseball team to the state playoffs, Marilyn continued working with Traci, along with planning and organizing the upcoming basketball camp. The usual workers helped, with the addition of Elizabeth and Traci Elliot in the kitchen. And Sybil and Dr. Chapman contacted his friend and worked out a plan for the one-hole golf facility.

The recommended location for the single green and trio of tee boxes was on Stone Place property, and Dr. Chapman offered to pay for the construction of the facility if Sybil would donate the land and Brother Suche would give lessons. All agreed.

While the golf pro from Tulsa was designing and planning the construction of the training facility, Dale learned about Jon Satank, a senior baseball player at Midwestern State, who had led the Indians in hitting the past two seasons. When Dale drove to the Wichita Falls campus and asked the baseball coach about Jon, the coach nodded while smiling.

"What's your interest in 'Kiowa'?" the coach asked. "You should be aware of his heritage, something he's quite proud of."

"I'm looking for a part-time hitting instructor," Dale explained. "I hear he's the best you've got."

"He's not only my best hitter; he's the best in the conference."

"I realize he can't receive pay until after he's completed his collegiate career," Dale said, referring to the boy's amateur status. "Is there some other arrangement that might benefit the young man?"

"Yes. He can get credit for a student-teaching course by spending at least six hours a week working in a legitimate baseball program. Obviously, yours would meet that requirement."

The Midwestern coach called Jon and asked him to come over. While waiting, the coach explained to Dale that the boy was from Lawton, Oklahoma, and he was a direct descendent of a Kiowa chief who had signed the Medicine Lodge Treaty in 1867.

"A son of the old chief was killed in a raid on a wagon train in Texas," the coach said. "During Kiowa's three years here, he has murdered opposing pitching with a .406 batting average. I've accused him of coming back to get revenge."

While the two coaches were discussing the young man and his potential future in baseball, Jon knocked on his coach's door.

After hearing Dale's offer, the boy gladly agreed to come to Paddock twice a week and help the Palomino hitters, with the understanding that he would receive credit for the teacher's course. His coach assured Jon that he would take care of the paperwork.

As agreed, Kiowa worked with Dale's hitters on Tuesday and Thursday afternoons, and four weeks later Paddock's team batting average was ten points higher. A highlight of this time occurred late one Thursday afternoon when Todd challenged Kiowa to get a base hit off him. On the third pitch, Kiowa lined a screamer into the left-centerfield gap and raced into second base standing up. To prove it was no accident, the hitting instructor walked back to home plate and did the same thing two pitches later. If the Palomino hitters needed convincing that their batting instructor was qualified, that settled the question.

Again the Palominos won district with Todd and Chris dominating opposing batters. The second year of work with Leatherarm had improved their ratio of strikes to balls by twenty-five percent, while the hitters increased their run support from seven per game to nine.

With strong pitching and hitting, the Palominos won the regional tournament and headed for the state playoffs. By then, Kiowa had graduated and joined a semi-pro team in Oklahoma City and was no longer available. When the Palominos' hitting fizzled, they were eliminated from the state tournament, but Dale's two pitchers and Joe Blake, the catcher, had earned all-state status. The coach felt he had let the team down at a critical time by not having a hitting instructor throughout the playoffs, so he made up his mind to solve that problem for the next season.

While Sybil was awarding eleven college scholarships to Paddock graduating seniors, Dale called Coach Morrison back at his old university in Ohio.

"Coach," he said, after catching up on the past couple of years, "I have three all-state basketball players who you might be interested in."

Dale went on to describe Todd Anderson, Chris Powell, and Joe Blake.

"Do you think these boys would agree to come off up here to play ball?" Coach Morrison asked.

"I'll give you their home phone numbers and let you contact them," Dale responded. "And I'll be glad to recommend both you as a coach and the university as a quality educational institution."

Two weeks after Dale alerted the boys that his old coach might be calling them, he learned that the three players had chosen to stay together and accept Coach Morrison's scholarship offers.

With enormous satisfaction, Dale called his old coach and congratulated him.

"I assure you that these boys will give one hundred percent every day and play sound basketball, Coach."

While the basketball camps overshadowed everything else at the ranch, Dale got with Sybil to talk about platting and developing a housing addition near the lake.

"We need one section of the development to be dedicated to teachers," Dale explained. "With the increased enrollment in school, the district has to hire new teachers and replace a couple of retirees. I want to start construction on a row of houses designed and priced based on a teacher's salary, and then we can focus on custom-made homes."

"What can I do to help?" Sybil asked.

"If you'll manage this project, I'll split the profits with you."

Sybil glanced at the rough layout Dale had on the table and counted over fifty home sites. She guessed that the lots would sell for ten thousand dollars and up, and she knew Dale had paid only eighty-five dollars an acre for the land. Profit on the lots alone would be half a million dollars. Guessing a similar margin on the homes, she knew she was being offered a minimum of five hundred thousand dollars to mange this project.

"You've got yourself a project manager," she said to Dale. "Mrs. Elliot's boy has asked about helping with the riding stables, and I'm going to hire him so I can devote my time to this."

"Working with the horses will be good for Bucky," Dale said, putting his arm across Sybil's shoulders. "And this housing project will move along better because of your involvement."

While getting the housing development started, Sybil kept an eye on the golf project, visiting the selected location daily. She also found time to have dinner with the doctor at the Steakhouse every Friday night.

By summer's end, Teacher's Row was completed and teachers occupied five of the homes. Also, several returning teachers were looking at moving out to the development, and six custom-made homes were under construction, with a couple of them covering double lots and enclosing well over three thousand square feet. Streets for the development were completed along with a park for children located central to the housing area.

The one-hole golf course was completed before school started, including an underground watering system connected to the lake. However, the course would not be playable for another month or six weeks, according to the Tulsa golf pro.

Also, Tom Jordan and Luke McCarty had purchased irrigation equipment, fenced off two hundred acres along the river for hay, and had the metered waterline operational. The herd of cattle numbered over eight hundred, and they were producing over sixty calves a month. One hundred fifty-five steers were taken to market every quarter, adding three hundred thousand dollars a year to the ranch fund.

Six basketball camps had attracted one hundred sixty kids and had generated a revenue in excess of forty thousand dollars, most of which paid for labor and food. However, in the scrimmage games, Dale found three quality players who he hoped would replace Chris, Joe, and Todd, now on their way to play college basketball in Ohio. And Margie was ecstatic over Traci, penciling her in as a starter, though only a sophomore.

With the summer at an end and school about to start, Superintendent Phillips called Dale and proposed changing his title and responsibility to that of athletic director.

"Coach," Phillips said, "we've had some boys move in with football experience, and their parents are clamoring for a team. If you'll accept this new assignment, I'd like you to take a look at starting a football program."

Dale knew that he was facing a rebuilding year, both in basketball and baseball. Adding a new football program would be a struggle. Without an existing feeder system from the lower grades, it might take years to build a winning team. But the town was growing, and adding other sports was inevitable.

"Do we have the funds for uniforms and to build a facility?"

"Dale, your basketball program has brought in enough money to get us started, and we'll get a big boost in tax revenue this year. I think we can afford it."

"I'll do it," Dale said. "But I want to offer the football job to David Green. He played some college football, and I know he loves the sport."

Superintendent Phillips agreed without hesitation.

"Dale, we'll need to reduce your teaching load, don't you think?"

Reluctantly, Dale agreed, and then headed out in search of David Green.

"We'll start with six-man football," Green said when Dale told him about the job. "I think I can get a few games scheduled this fall, and then plan a full slate of contests next year."

"You'll have to play all of this season's games out of town," Dale said. "Even next year, I expect you'll only have minimal facilities."

"If we can develop a winning program, the rest will take care of itself," David said. "You realize this means I won't be as available for helping with basketball."

Dale had already contacted Donald Winters and offered him a part-time job. Donald had agreed to arrange his classes at Midwestern in the morning so he could attend the Palominos' afternoon practices. When Donald had played for Dale that first year in Paddock, he had been a below-average player, but had shown an exceptional understanding of and love for the game.

By mid-October, Brother Suche was teaching golf lessons to Sybil, Marilyn, Traci, Bucky, and both of the Jordan kids. Dale did not have time for golf, but he did stop by one afternoon and watch Sybil and Marilyn hit balls from a par-three tee box, and he was surprised. Either the minister was a miracle worker or these two ladies were naturals at the game, especially Marilyn. Dale began to realize what a good athlete his wife was.

It was about this time that David had his football team suited up and ready for their first contest. They traveled to Roaring Springs and lost badly. That was followed with a better outing at Finney, and then finally the football Palominos won a close contest against Dumont. The short season ended with a 2-3 record, but David was as excited as if his squad had won a championship.

"Coach," he said to Dale, "I've finally found a quarterback who's a natural passer, and we have a couple of good receivers for him to throw to. Next year we'll have a winning record."

Meanwhile, Dale was searching for a winning combination on the hardwood court. Two transfers, Colton Fenner and Zak Thomas, had shown promise in the summer camp, and both were experienced players and hard workers. At six-foot-three, Thomas had quick hands and was an exceptionally bright kid. Fenner was a left-handed slasher and deft passer. In practice, he would dart into the lane, propel himself into the air, and when Thomas's defender slid over to block his shot, Fenner would drop off the ball to Zak who then had a clear path to the goal. When these newcomers were added to Dale's second unit from the previous season, the Palominos suddenly became a contender.

Not only did Paddock win all their preseason contests, but they also captured their holiday tournament in a bitterly fought game against a Plainview team. Game after game, Palomino fans were filling the gymnasium and clamoring for another state title, though Dale knew the odds of that happening were about the same as making a mid-court shot.

The Palominos breezed through their district but ran into trouble at the regional tournament when a seasoned Stamford team sent Paddock home with their only loss of the season.

While Dale was focused on basketball, the old hospital was renovated and reopened, with Dr. Chapman making a permanent move to Paddock and opening his office three days a week. Sybil was adding a couple of houses to her addition every six weeks, and Margie's girls, with a senior-laden team and Traci filling the post position, won district and were headed for the state tournament.

Dale and Marilyn sat in the stands and watched with great satisfaction as Margie's squad dismantled Barnhart in the first round. After a slow start, Traci took over the game and scored a season-high, twenty-eight points.

Next was a strong Elkhart team, but again Margie's squad played flawlessly and won handily. This pitted the lady Palominos against Bremond, the prior year's champions. Bremond was tall and talented, but prone to turnovers. For the first time in the tournament, Margie used a trapping zone press, forcing backcourt passes, which the Palominos either stole or watched sail out of bounds. At the end of the first quarter, Margie's girls led, 15–6.

Continuing the pressure on the taller girls, Paddock's team built their halftime lead to 31–16, and headed to the dressing room while a stunned crowd just shook their heads at seeing the defending champions befuddled and outplayed.

The second half saw a rejuvenated Bremond squad take the court and make a run, closing the gap to 36–28, but then they wore down, and Margie's Lady Palominos pulled away to a 56–41 win and the state championship.

A tearful Elizabeth Elliot hugged Marilyn when the announcer called out Traci's name for the all-state team. Linda, Jan, Peg, and Cindy were among the Paddock students standing and applauding.

What a difference a year had made in that young woman's life and her best year was just ahead.

15 ___

While Paddock celebrated its first-ever girls state championship, Dale was busy searching for a batting coach for his baseball team. Based on a tip from Old Leatherarm, he soon located Vince Hargrove in the small community of Hackberry just southeast of Paddock. While Leatherarm continued to work with the Palomino pitchers, Hargrove set up a batting cage and had the hitters take so many swings they soon had blisters on their hands. "Base hits win games; there's no excuse for a strikeout," he repeated over and over. His philosophy was that anyone who would make the effort to learn a few basics and concentrate could hit a baseball. "Swing for the gaps, not for the fences," he bellowed at the players every afternoon.

The long hours of practice paid off. The team's batting average jumped twenty points from the prior season and propelled the Palominos to a third district championship, but without outstanding talent on the mound, Paddock once again fell short of a state championship.

"Merr," Dale said right after baseball season, "I need a break, and I'd like us to take a week or two for a vacation before the basketball camps start."

"Where do you want to go?"

"You pick. I'll just be glad to get away with my lovely wife for a while."

"I'd like to go see your home town, where you went to school, and maybe meet some of your friends back there."

Instantly, the idea struck a chord with Dale. Images and memories flooded into this mind, creating a longing for his childhood home, a yearning to visit his parents' graves, and a desire to again walk the campus of the university in Ohio and to see his old coach. So, Marilyn made the travel arrangements, and she and Dale headed for Pennsylvania.

After driving by Dale's old home, they stopped by the cemetery where he placed fresh flowers at his parents' headstones and spent half an hour remembering, and desperately wishing to communicate his thanks and love to them. Their sudden and unexpected deaths had left him with a feeling of incompleteness, of something vital left undone. Standing there with a kaleidoscope of childhood images flashing through his mind, that deep ache, so long suppressed by activity, now rushed back into his consciousness. Overcome with emotion, he turned away, looking into the distance beyond the gravestones.

In a grove of nearby trees, birds flitted from limb to limb of a huge elm. The hum of automobiles on the nearby road kept up a dull roar in his head. He had needed this time to be close, to remember, to release deeply held feelings, but now life had to go on. Specifically, his life must go on; through its usefulness, he reasoned, his parents' lives somehow would be extended. Driving away, he renewed his vow to live his life by the legacy of principles so thoroughly instilled by his mother and father.

At the university in Ohio, Dale found his old coach, who thanked him profusely for sending him three outstanding athletes.

"Son," Coach Morrison said, "I've never had a player come in with better basketball skills than Todd, Chris, and Joe. Todd was a starter this season, honorable mention all-conference, and he'll be our best player next year. I expect Chris and Joe will join the starting lineup next season, and I predict we'll win the conference title."

"They dropped by my office when they got home from college," Dale said, proudly. "They enjoyed their first season here and are excited about coming back."

"I hope you'll look after them this summer," Coach Morrison said.

"Yes, sir. They'll be helping with my basketball camps this summer, and I'm sure they'll be working on their game."

Dale then updated the coach on Thomas Newberry and his impoverished, but growing, church in Saint Louis.

"You and Thomas certainly left your marks on our basketball program here," the coach said, laying his hand on Dale's shoulder. "Your boys are just three of many who have benefited by the changes you two helped make in the letterman's association."

Dale had not thought of that. Back when he and Thomas had refused to be physically hazed and had instigated a teammate kind of relationship between new lettermen and old, he could not have guessed its eventual impact. It had just seemed like the right thing to do.

"Before you leave, I want to show you something," Coach Morrison said.

Dale and Marilyn followed the coach over to the gymnasium where he pointed up to a row of three large pictures hanging just below the scoreboard.

"Oh, my goodness," Marilyn said, pointing to the third photo. "It's you, Dale."

"In honor of your outstanding play and leadership, we've hung your picture up there, Dale," the coach said, patting his ex-player on the back. "The athletic council issued a statement that claims that no other single player has equaled your impact on the university's basketball program."

"Sir," Marilyn said, "I love that picture. I've just got to have a copy, and I'd like to get one of the council's statement that you mentioned, also."

Back in his office, Coach Morrison pulled out an eight-by-ten photo and handed it to Marilyn, along with a copy of the athletic council's declaration.

"Coach," Dale said before leaving, "is there a special need that you or the basketball program has that I might help with?"

"You might send me a couple more all-state basketball players," Morrison said, laughing.

"Coach, Chad Shankle and Eddie Krodle were teammates of the three Paddock boys you now have, and their junior college commitments will be up next year. I promise you that their fundamentals are just as sound, and I believe they'd be good additions to your program. Also, in a couple of years, Zak Thomas and Colton Fenner just might be college material. I'll keep you updated on their progress."

"I'll contact Shankle and Krodle," Coach Morrison said, taking a note with phone numbers from Dale.

On their way home, Dale seemed quieter than usual.

"What's on your mind, Honey?" Marilyn asked.

"I'm wondering how to help our graduates make the transition to college," he said. "We're a small town, a small school, and I'd like to make sure our kids are prepared academically for the next level."

"You're saying that helping them get to college isn't enough," Marilyn said, quickly catching on to his thinking. "So, what would improve their chances of success?"

"Maybe entry-level college courses," Dale said. "If they could get a few basic studies under their belts before leaving home, it just might make the adjustment easier."

"Think this is a Sybil project?" she asked.

"I'm afraid the riding stables, housing development project, and the golf facility have her pretty well loaded down. I think I'd better handle this one."

Marilyn leaned her head against Dale's shoulder and said, "Honey, I'm so proud of you. I'm going to have your basketball picture blown up to life-size and hang it in our den."

"Now wait a minute," Dale said. "I'd be embarrassed to have our friends come over and see me staring down at them like a Greek god. I'd much rather have your picture over the mantle to remind me how lucky I am, every time I step foot in that room."

"We'll see," Marilyn said smugly, hugging his arm and closing her eyes.

Back at the ranch, Dale and Marilyn quickly became busy organizing the basketball camps and getting instructors in place, and yet Dale found time to meet with Superintendent Phillips to discuss establishing a college preparatory program for juniors and seniors.

"I'll check with the school board," Phillips said, "but I think we could hold the classes right here on campus, if we can get some college professors to come teach them."

"While you ask permission from the board, I'll check with some people at Midwestern, Texas Tech, and West Texas A&M. I'll pay for the textbooks and the teachers' salaries, along with their travel expenses, if I find a couple of professors who are interested."

"Coach, don't forget those three colleges in Abilene."

Dale laughed at Kennemer's subtle reminder that he was a graduate of Hardin-Simmons University in that city.

The school board gave unanimous approval, including offering classrooms and supplies at the school's expense, while Dale signed up a math teacher from Hardin Simmons, an English teacher from Midwestern State, and a history teacher from Texas Tech. The participating universities also offered to give successful students college credit for the courses.

The *Paddock Post* agreed to run an article announcing the project, along with a class schedule, to alert all juniors and seniors from Paddock High. Immediately, students began calling and signing up for the classes to be offered the last six weeks of the summer. The day that classes began, each session had from ten to twelve students enrolled.

The morning of the first class, Dale set an early alarm to get to the school in time to witness this important event, but then he realized Marilyn was up before him, sick at her stomach.

"Honey, are you going to be okay?" Dale asked, handing her a cool, damp washcloth. "Maybe I should stay here."

"I'll be okay in a few minutes," she said. "I went through this yesterday after you left to meet Tom."

As Marilyn predicted, she recovered within thirty minutes and joined her husband for the trip to town, where Dale declined to make a speech initiating this first semester of college courses in Paddock.

"I don't want to draw attention away from the professors and the students who deserve the credit for getting this off to such a good start," he explained, and then drove his wife home, still concerned that she was sick.

"Honey," Dale said to Marilyn, when she was ill again the next morning, "I think you'd better go see a doctor. You don't seem to be able to get over this stomach virus you've got."

"I'll make an appointment today," she promised.

After a busy day overseeing the basketball camp, Dale rushed to the house late that afternoon when he saw Marilyn return from her medical checkup.

She was smiling when he came through the door.

"Looks like you're feeling better," he said.

"Uh, huh," she replied, sheepishly, and looped her arms around his neck.

"You must be feeling much better," Dale said, kissing her.

"Honey, we forgot something when we designed this house."

"What? I thought you loved our home."

"I do. But now it needs a nursery."

"What do you mean? Oh, you're saying . . . we're going to have a baby?"

"That's what Dr. Dick thinks."

"That's wonderful!" he said. "So you don't have a virus or some incurable disease, after all."

"No, Honey. I'll be perfectly well in about six months."

They hugged, kissed, and cried for five minutes.

Being an only child, Dale knew nothing about pregnancies or babies, and Marilyn's unrecognized morning sickness had worried him. He had to celebrate the news that she was healthy before he could fully rejoice over her pregnancy.

"Which do you prefer, a boy or girl?" she asked.

"Just a healthy wife and baby," he said, pulling her close. "And that reminds me how important the doctor is. What makes you think this fellow is the right one?"

"His name's Dr. David Dick, and his practice is in Plainview. He's about thirty-five to forty years old, a fraction less than six feet tall, has auburn hair, and he smiles constantly."

"Okay, I get the picture, but what does he know about taking care of my pregnant wife?"

"First, mother says that Dr. Chapman recommends him, but also five different women here in Paddock, including Mary Williams, the banker's wife, Helen Branch, and Carol Pierce, the Kennemers's daughter, all swear he's the best. Women are mighty particular when it comes to a gynecologist, and I haven't heard one bad word about Dr. Dick."

"Okay, let's assume he does his job, and we have a child. A baby can be terribly demanding on a mother's time. What about all the projects you have going on?"

"I've thought about that, and I'd like to get a nanny for the baby for a couple of years. We could build a comfortable little satellite house close by for her. Then when mother decides to give up her ranch, she could move into it."

"Honey, we wouldn't want just anybody caring for our baby. Now, I think . . ."

"I've already picked a good one," Marilyn said. "Dr. Dick and his wife hired Billie Ann Guthrie for their two children, and now that they're school age, she's available. Mrs. Guthrie is a retired first grade teacher, and the doctor says she's almost like having a pediatrician around."

"I see that my wife knows what she wants," Dale said, looping his arms around Marilyn. "And, I'm smart enough to know that when you've made up your mind on a subject, I need to spend my time on something else."

The next day, Dale met with Ted Jackson, their house architect, and initiated plans for the satellite house, stressing compatibility in its design and appearance with their existing house.

Meanwhile, the basketball camps drew a record number of players, including two camps for girls, increased interest undoubtedly spurred by the recent state championship. Paddock and the summer camps had become the focal point for basketball in the entire area, including the outskirts of the larger cities. Three state-championship teams in as many years in such a small town, every player having come through Dale's summer camps, were enough to convince most people that Coach Rory must dispense a special basketball magic to the kids in his camps, though Donald Winters and Dale's former players actually ran the practice sessions.

At the end of the summer, Dale was busy getting several ranch projects lined out before he headed back for the classroom, when he got a call from Superintendent Phillips.

"Coach, I've got a few kids here who'd like to come out and see you."

Without asking questions, Dale agreed to meet the youngsters at the activities building at three o'clock that afternoon. He was not prepared for what he met.

"Coach," a recent Paddock graduate said, standing in front of about eighteen students, "we just want to thank you for your support of the summer college courses. With Stone Place scholarships, we seniors are all registered for college, and already have credit for three basic courses. Now, having completed college-level work, we can't adequately express how confident we are that we can be successful and how much we appreciate your help. Also, the incoming Paddock seniors expect to improve their grades in their final high school year, and plan to take more entry-level courses next summer, enough to start college as second-semester freshmen."

Then another student stepped forward, holding a box.

"Every student wanted to thank you personally, Coach, so each of us has written you a letter. Whether or not you have time to read them, we feel better having expressed our gratitude this way."

Dale thanked the group for the letters and wished them success in college and in completing their high school studies.

"I hope each of you recognizes," he said, "that this has been a community endeavor. Citizens of Paddock want you to reach your potential in whatever life pursuit you choose, and we'll be watching each of you and proudly telling everybody that you're one of ours."

Struggling to control his emotions, Dale shook the hand of every student there. Many hugged him, unable to hold back tears of pride and happiness.

That evening, Dale and Marilyn were looking through the letters, commenting on some of the names and what they wrote.

"Oh, my goodness," Marilyn said. "This one's from a girl named Susie."

"Susie?" Dale asked, trying to make a connection.

"She's a senior with a Stone Place scholarship and now has credit for three college courses. Dale, you've got to read this."

I can never repay you for what you've done for me. My family's poor. I'm the first family member to ever complete high school, and I'm determined that I'll be the first to receive a college diploma. Someday, I'll come back to Paddock and teach English. I won't let anything stop me.

I even hope to write a book. It will be about my brother.

When he was a junior in high school, our father died, so he quit school to provide for my mother, me, and my younger sister. Without an education, he took whatever work he could find, which paid very little. Embarrassed at the conditions his family lived in, he became desperate and tried to get money illegally. Now, he's in prison. He doesn't sound like a hero, does he?

He recently completed his G. E. D. and has requested permission to take college-level correspondence courses. I have promised to help him, and now I know I can do it.

You see, the story is not over, but I know it will have a happy ending.

So, I thank you from the bottom of my heart, not only for what you've done for me, but for giving my brother a second chance.

Sincerely,

Susie Meade, sister of Carlton Meade

Dale could not hold back the tears. He slid over to Marilyn and put his arms around her, holding her for several minutes.

Marilyn had stayed in touch with Carlton, had purchased his textbooks and paid all his G. E. D. fees. He had been a model prisoner and had often apologized for trying to extort money from them. But, she did not know about Susie.

When the phone rang, Dale reluctantly pulled away from his wife and reached for the receiver.

"Mr. Rory, this is Grant Clawson of High Plains Ford in Lubbock. I hear you've had considerable growth in Paddock, and I'm thinking about opening an outlet there."

"Mr. Clawson, I think that's great. Paddock desperately needs an automobile dealership. Is there anything I can do to assist the process?"

"Can you recommend a realtor?"

Dale gave the name of a local woman who had opened an office about a year earlier. Based on Sybil's experience with this realtor, selling lots in the housing development, the coach was glad to send business her way.

Two days later, the house architect called and asked to meet with Dale and Marilyn to obtain their approval of the plans for the satellite house, which was accomplished the following day. Dale then took the layout to Tom Jordan and asked him to deliver them to Caprock Homes and initiate construction.

While discussing the satellite house, Dale asked if Marilyn planned to have a sonogram to determine if they would have a boy or a girl.

"Earlier you said it didn't matter, as long as the baby was healthy," she said, smiling

"It doesn't, but I think knowing would make planning a little easier."

"I'll just plan for either."

"What about a name?"

"How about you coming up with a boy's name, and I'll choose one for a girl?"

"Okay, but you choose first."

"I like the name Michelle. Would you be okay with that?"

"Sure. What about Fred for a boy?"

"Fred? Why Fred?"

"That was your grandfather's name."

"That was a long time ago. I don't think our son would want to be called Fred."

"Okay, my dad's name was Horace. How about that?"

"I don't want to be disrespectful to your dad, but . . ."

"What do you suggest?" Dale said, pretending frustration.

"Michael," she said, smiling. "Don't you think that goes well with Michelle?"

"I think this would be a lot easier if we just knew which we are going to have," Dale protested.

"Oh, but I'd rather wait and find out when our baby is born."

"That's okay, but also I think a sonogram might make sure the baby's healthy and forming okay."

"I'll call Dr. Dick and get one scheduled, but I'll ask him not to tell me whether it's a boy or a girl."

Two days after the sonogram, Dale came home and found two baby beds in the nursery, one trimmed in pink and one in blue. The pink one had a sign on it that read, "Michelle" and inside lay a pink blanket and a tiny pink outfit. The blue one was labeled, "Michael" and contained a blue blanket and matching outfit.

"Don't you think those clothes are too small?" Dale asked, holding up the blue outfit.

"Thank goodness that newborns are small, Darling."

Dale laughed, returned the baby clothes, and hugged Marilyn, who obviously was enjoying all the planning and buying for their baby.

Less than a week later, Dale was awakened an hour after midnight by the security system alarm. Hurrying down to the monitors, he saw a cattle truck pulling through a gate on the west side of the Thompson ranch. Dale immediately called the sheriff's office, followed by a similar call to his foreman.

"Tom," Dale said, "we've got rustlers at gate five. Hurry over and get Luke and meet me there. The sheriff is on his way."

Half a mile before reaching gate five, Dale turned off his headlights and eased forward until he was close enough to see if a vehicle should exit the gate, but not close enough to be noticed by the thieves. He cut the engine and waited for help. When two sheriff cars passed him, Dale followed, pulling in just ahead of Tom and Luke.

The rustlers threw up their hands immediately, and Dale was surprised to find two teenagers, along with the truck driver of about thirty-five years. The man's driver's license showed an El Paso address.

The boys were too frightened to speak, so the sheriff focused on the sullen driver who finally said he had worked briefly for "Old Man Thompson" for whom he showed considerable resentment.

"He owes me back wages," the belligerent man said.

"Do you realize these are not his cows?" the sheriff asked.

The man did not answer, other than by the surprise evident on his face.

The next day, with the rustlers in jail, the sheriff explained to Dale that the driver had indeed worked for Jake Thompson, who had fired him for drunkenness and the suspicion of his having stolen several head of Thompson cattle.

A few days later, District Attorney Blackburn called Dale.

"Mack Stanford, the driver, was the ringleader," the attorney explained. "The two boys have been especially cooperative. They've helped us locate forty-four head of Thompson's cattle that were stolen months back and sold to a rancher west of Clovis, New Mexico.

"The driver stole the truck from an outfit in El Paso, so he's got a string of charges against him, but I'm calling to see if you would consider reducing the charges against the boys, based on their doing one hundred and sixty hours of community service and their promise to keep their record clean from here forward."

"Mr. Blackburn, I'm interested in two things. One, make sure these boys are disciplined so they understand the consequences of breaking the law. Second, I'd like to see them take action to get on a positive track with their lives. If those two objectives can be met, I'll drop the charges."

"If you agree that community service satisfies the first, I'll work with the sheriff to establish a probation program where the boys have to check in regularly and report their activities. In fact, I think I can find employment for them that'll help keep them out of trouble."

Dale agreed.

For the second football season, David Green's squad had a real football field to play on, and a schedule of eight games, of which they won half, losing two contests by three points or less. Again, the coach's assessment glowed with positives. His quarterback had won all-conference honors, as had a lineman and a receiver. Also, Dale believed that with a dependable pass defense, the Palominos could have won those two close contests, which would have given them a 6-2 record.

"Next year," Green told Dale, "we'll win the close ones."

Dale had Donald Winters back to help coach the basketball team, and they had watched enough of the informal practices to know their team had the potential to win another title. A lot depended upon the starting five, because he would not have the talented substitutes of some of his prior squads.

Formal practices started two weeks before the football season ended, though the roundballers had not yet played a game. From the first drill, Dale knew that Colton Fenner and Zak Thomas were much improved. Added to these, the coach had five other quality players, one a six-foot-five transfer, Rick Preston, from Abilene. Back during the summer basketball camps, Winters had moved Thomas to forward and worked the taller player at the post position. With six-foot-three Eli Malone at the other forward slot and Fenner and Wade Clark at guards, both steady ball-handlers, Dale's starting unit was set.

After going undefeated through eight preseason games, Dale's boys captured the Paddock holiday tournament with an impressive win over AAA Breckenridge. That was followed with an undefeated district championship, though the Palominos had to come from behind in the final quarter against two opponents.

With basketball playoffs staring him in the face, Marilyn was preparing for the arrival of their baby. The satellite house was completed, so they arranged for Billie Guthrie to move in and help complete the nursery.

The day of the first regional playoff game, Marilyn began contractions at three in the afternoon.

"You go ahead and coach your team," Marilyn told her husband. "Mother and Billie will take care of me."

"I couldn't possibly go off to a ballgame while you're giving birth to our baby," he said. "I'll call Coach Winters and get him to take care of the team. It'll be a good experience for him."

Though Donald Winters almost fainted at the news, he quickly recovered as he and Dale discussed the game plan, which required no significant change for the upcoming opponent.

An hour before tipoff, Marilyn's contractions became long and frequent, so they loaded her into the truck and headed for Plainview, expecting an all-night ordeal.

Dead tired, Dale called Coach Winters a little before midnight, and learned that the Palominos had won easily. They would be playing for the regional championship the next night.

It was four in the morning when Dr. Dick came out and told Dale the mother and babies were fine.

"Babies?" Dale asked, startled.

"Yes," the doctor said. "Didn't Marilyn tell you? She had a sonogram three months ago. You've got a little boy and a girl."

"No, but can I see Marilyn now?"

"Yes. Just follow me."

"I wanted to surprise you," she explained, smiling ever so faintly. "Don't you remember when I told you that we didn't need to be concerned about whether our baby was a boy or a girl?"

"Yes, but . . ."

"And don't you remember that we picked out both names, Michael for a boy and Michelle for a girl?"

"But that was just to have a name ready regardless which we had."

"And didn't you see two baby beds in the nursery, one trimmed in blue and one in pink?"

"Yes, but I thought you would send one back when we knew which our baby was."

"Well, I guess you were just too busy with basketball," she said, trying to smile.

Dale leaned down and hugged Marilyn.

"Now, if you're doing okay, I'll go check on our babies," he said.

She nodded, and Dale headed for the large nursery window.

While Marilyn, Sybil, and Billie took care of little Michael Stone and Sybil Michelle, Dale made his way back to courtside to win the regional championship. Once more, the Paddock Palominos were headed to Austin for the state tournament.

Continuing their hot pace, the Palominos won by twenty-four points in the first game, and breezed to a sixteen-point victory in the semifinals. This matched them against Marlin once again, for the state championship this time.

As before, Marlin was quick and preferred a fast-paced game, but they were prone to turnovers. Their strategy was to win by taking twenty-five percent more shots than their opponent, though they might be successful on less than thirty percent. They counted on creating the shooting imbalance by pressuring their opponents to make excessive turnovers and to outnumber them on fast-breaks. As usual, Dale's team played almost mistake-free ball, and were attuned to capitalize on their opponent's mistakes. In this match-up, something had to give.

With six-foot-five Wade Preston in the middle of the Palominos' zone defense, supported by six-three Zak Thomas and six-four Eli Malone, Marlin did not get rebounds for the second-chance shots they counted on. Likewise, Paddock's boys used overhead passes to break Marlin's pressing defense, resulting in easy fast-break shots for the Palominos. The result was Dale's boys sank fifty-six percent of their field goals, and eighty-seven percent of their free throws. Slowly, but surely, the Palominos justified the sportswriters' faith in them, and won by a dozen points.

While Dale's boys were capturing their third state championship in five years, Margie was leading the lady Palominos to the state finals as well. With Traci a year older, two inches taller, ten pounds leaner, and playoff-savvy, the Paddock girls fought their way to the title game, where they won even more handily than Dale's boys.

With two state-championship trophies added to their collection, Paddock was a basketball-crazy town. Throughout the celebrations, Margie probably did not get the credit she deserved. Most Paddock fans pointed to Dale's arrival and his summer basketball camps as the genesis for all this success.

Throughout the playoffs, Dale had repeatedly checked on Marilyn and the babies. The mother had recovered quickly and had planned to join Dale in Austin for the championship game.

"Honey," she had said when he called to check on her, "I really need to be here with the babies."

"Can't our nanny take care of them for a couple of days?"

"Yes, but I'm just not comfortable leaving them so soon. Besides, they're so cute and cuddly. Did I tell you that they smile all the time now, and they coo at me? I love them so much."

It suddenly occurred to Dale that Marilyn would never again be so readily available to help with all his projects. He knew that she was no less his loving wife, but now she was also a dedicated mother.

A couple of weeks after the championship game, Dale, Marilyn, Sybil and Mrs. Guthrie took the babies to church for the first time. A few days earlier, Marilyn had arranged with Brother Suche to christen the twins at the beginning of the service.

"This sacrament entails your promise to raise the twins in honor of God and Jesus Christ," the pastor explained. "And it signifies your intention of regularly bringing them to church. It is not a conversion experience. That is something they must decide for themselves when they have matured to the point of understanding their earthly nature and need for His salvation through grace."

After the service, Brother Suche laughingly told Dale that he now had two more students to teach golf, nodding toward the twins.

"The way their mother and grandmother have taken to the game, I wouldn't be surprised," Dale said, laughing. "But I plan to have them in the gym by the time they're walking."

On the way home, Dale mentioned his conversation with Brother Suche to Marilyn.

"I plan to take them with me to the golf course as soon as they can swing a club," Marilyn said, teasing her basketball-crazy husband. "It's a game they can learn and play together, and the facility is right here close by."

After pointing out the proximity of the gymnasium in the activities building, Dale turned his thoughts back to the golf facility.

"I've seen lots of customers our there lately," Dale said. "Your mother and Dr. Chapman seem to be there nearly every time I drive by. Now with two more prospective players, they may need to expand the course."

"Don't be surprised if you hear wedding bells from that direction," Marilyn said, referring to Stone Place. "We just might have our own doctor living next door."

Dale thought that might not be a bad deal, especially having a doctor around to keep an eye on the progress of the twins. And the more time Dale spent around the babies, the better he came to understand Marilyn's reluctance to leave them. They changed so quickly in those first few weeks that it seemed that they demonstrated some new ability or trait daily.

Dale had little time to be home, however, as he began preparing for another baseball season. From the first week of practice, he realized that Eli Malone and Zak Thomas were going to be his pitching tandem, and with Leatherarm's help, they just might be the best he had ever had. With Hargrove drilling the hitters, the prospects of a championship looked good.

While Dale was focused on baseball, the town was still reveling in the dual basketball championships, and the Paddock boosters club was planning an athletic banquet. Though labeled an all-sports event, everyone knew it was to celebrate the once-in-a-lifetime accomplishment. For the celebration, the gymnasium floor was covered with long rows of tables, and a platform was moved in at one end of the court, along with a speaker's stand. A table with all the tournament, district, and state trophies was set up near the entrance, and championship banners were hung from the rafters. Even if tickets had been a hundred dollars each, the place would have been filled.

A special edition of the *Paddock Post* came out with pictures and sports stories from the past four years, along with action shots and team photos. The front page was practically covered by a picture of Coach Rory, though the caption read, "Coach Mass." Copies of this special paper were handed out at the door for those who had not already received a copy, along with a Golden Palomino pennant, a stallion on one side and presumably a mare on the other.

After an invocation by Brother Suche and the meal, Superintendent Phillips kicked off the celebration.

"I want to welcome each of you to this first, and most grand, Paddock Palominos athletic banquet. Without the slightest hesitation, or admitted bias, I proclaim that we have the best athletes and the best coaches in the state. And we are here to recognize and applaud their Herculean efforts.

"Also, I want to recognize our booster club president, Chet Williams, and his fellow members for making this event possible."

After a few more glowing comments, the superintendent introduced the coaches, who in turn recognized each of their players.

"Before I ask Coach Rory to come and say a few words, I have a special announcement," Phillips said when the introductions were complete.

"From our representative in Austin I have received a copy of House Concurrent Resolution 162. If you'll bear with me, I'll read an excerpt.

"Whereas, he has exemplified outstanding leadership in his community, sponsoring and leading numerous projects, including Lake Thompson, that have revitalized the once declining economy of Cottle County and inspired its population, and whereas he has shown superior performance as an athlete, soon to be inducted into his university's hall of fame, and as a coach, where he has led his teams to three state championships, it is herein resolved that the seventy-fourth Legislature of the

State of Texas hereby pays tribute to these most remarkable accomplishments of Coach Dale Rory.

"Now, Coach Rory will come and make a few comments."

It took Dale nearly five minutes to get the crowd to hold their applause and take their seats.

"First, I want to thank the athletes for their dedication and hard work. Though our kids do not lack in athletic skills, I firmly believe it is their more uncommon attributes that raise them above the field of contenders. They are great athletes, but of more importance, they are destined to be model citizens.

"Next, I have to applaud my fellow coaches, Donald Winters, David Green, and Margie Walker. Also, I must mention a few other coaches who could not be here tonight. They are Willy Collins, Jon Satank, and Vince Hargrove, without whose help our baseball efforts would have been less successful.

"The student body must be mentioned for their loyalty and support. First and foremost, our athletes are students, something we must never forget.

"And to the parents and fans, we owe a huge 'thank you' for following us to our games, wherever played. Particularly for the fathers and mothers of the athletes, I want to thank you for the privilege of working with your boys and girls.

"When I came here, two of the first people I met were Principal Kennemer and Superintendent Phillips. Every day since then, I have been thankful for these two men. I hope the parents of our students realize how fortunate we are to have them running our school system.

"Lastly, I want to thank God for blessing me in innumerable ways. He has given me much, and to Him much is owed. I promise to you and to Him my utmost effort to be a good steward of all He has entrusted me with.

"Thank you and may God bless you."

Chet Williams then stepped to the podium.

"The array of trophies displayed up here on this table is truly impressive. Each of them represents dedication, teamwork, athletic prowess, and great leadership. However, at this time, I have the privilege of revealing a new and most impressive symbol of excellence in leadership," he said, and motioned toward two boosters.

As the audience whispered guesses as to what mystery was to be disclosed, someone pointed upward toward the far end of the building and yelled, "There it is!"

Slowly dropping down to a position right beneath the scoreboard was a huge copy of Dale's university picture. From the bottom of the photo frame hung a blue banner that read, "COACH RORY, OUR MASSASUTA" emblazoned in gold letters.

While the crowd stood and applauded, Dale, with tears in his eyes, turned and put his arms around Marilyn.

The picture she had loved at first sight, of the man she would adore until her last breath, now occupied a much more distinguished place than the Roryian den.

ABOUT THE AUTHORS

Bud Campbell, a Texan and graduate of Mount Vernon High School, was an all-state member of their 1948 state-championship basketball team, and subsequently played for Texas Christian University. After ten years of leading basketball programs at various Texas schools and inspiring youngsters to develop a winning attitude, Bud spent twenty-seven years as a school principal, the majority at North Mesquite High in the Dallas area.

With humor, wit, and an upbeat personality, Bud has inspired thousands with his motivational speeches at banquets, civic organizations, and staff development programs where he stresses that life's richest blessings are realized through giving freely.

Glen Onley is the author of "Coach Catfish Smith And His Boys," "Beyond Contentment," "Discovery Tree," and "Sunset," all available from Sunstone Press.